Dandelion Dreams
by
Samantha Garman

Other books by Samantha Garman

Charleston Heat
Secrets of a Heart
The Defiant Lady

Contact

garmanpublishing@gmail.com
Twitter: @samgarman
Facebook: Samantha Garman-Author

Acknowledgements

To those of you who helped guide me on this journey,
you have my sincerest thanks.

For winter.

Words call to me, arriving on the wind of sleep.

For now, I sit alone in candlelight.

I hated leaving our bed, leaving you—but my hand aches for a pen. It aches to tell our epic story.

I wish I could paint our legend in the sky, a constellation to be remembered forever—but I am no painter. I am a writer, a weaver of words, and I will inscribe our saga in the book of our lives.

One day, when we are old and gnarled, we will read it—our hearts still young. I will look at you, and see our journey in the smile lines of your eyes. Tears of joy will spill down my cheeks, and you will catch them with your lips like fallen stars.

Let me tell you the tale of our love.

Chapter 1

Kai

I unscrewed the flask and chugged. Liquor was water in a desert of pain.

"Easy there, son," Keith said, putting a large steadying hand on my shoulder.

I wiped my mouth with my fist. "I'm *not* your son." My tone was harsh, wanting to remind Reece's father that I was the one that lived.

As if the cowboy needed the reminder.

"You've always been a real son of a bitch. You know that, right?"

"I do," I stated. "Are we going to get on with this?"

Keith's clear blue eyes were resolute, clear of bourbon, and drowning in grief. He nodded once.

I had all but grown up on Keith's ranch. When we were kids, Tristan, Reece and I had helped muck out the stables countless times, along with other odd jobs. We had learned to ride, worked with heavy, weathered saddles and camped many nights on the open trail. Memories of sweating horses frothy at the saddle and the smell of hot leather beat at my senses. It was the stench of guilt.

I hoped the bourbon would kick in soon.

A few days ago, Keith had dragged me out of some local dive, where I'd holed up and taken refuge. After sleeping off the worst hangover of my life in the guest room of the ranch house, I'd woken up only to have Reece's mother, Alice, slap me across the face. Her handprint left an angry red stain on my cheek.

"That's for your stupidity," she'd said, her tone mild. "And this," she handed me a cup of coffee, "is for your head."

Alice had balls the size of tractors. She always called us on our shit—and boy, did we get in the shit sometimes.

The sound of the cattle iron raking across hot coals dragged my attention back to the matter at hand. I removed my shirt, took a seat on the stool, and placed Tristan's University of Tennessee cap back on my head. I swiped hair out of my eyes, watching Keith approach with the brand, three inches in length.

Keith's hired hand moved behind me to grip my shoulders, and I shoved my t-shirt into my mouth and waited.

When the iron touched my left pectoral I screamed, the muffled sound of a man drowning in shame. Skin sizzled and burned. My head swam, and my vision blurred. I reared like a bucking stallion into the solid legs of the ranch hand. Just as I thought I couldn't stand the pain any longer, Keith flung the offensive rod away in disgust.

Pulling the shirt out of my mouth, I turned my head and vomited. I wiped my lips with faded green cotton, looked at Keith, and grinned.

My smile was ugly. "I'm glad it was the cheap bourbon."

•••

My brand throbbed under its dressing, a reminder that I wasn't hollow. The black tie around my neck felt like a noose. I wanted to strip off my suit and run

11

naked into the woods where I grew up; I was a Southern boy weaned on the land, a mountain child wild and free at heart.

My lungs burned and a small cloud of breath condensed in the winter air. The generic words of the minister were apathetic and uninspiring. Tristan and Reece deserved more than a rudimentary burial. It was a pathetic excuse for a eulogy. I should have been the one to give it, but I had refused.

I wished I was in the mountains and it was summertime.

The woman's hand clutched my arm, and I turned my head, just enough to see the top of her burnished red hair. I couldn't bear to look into her eyes, knowing if I did I would see they were as lost as my own. They were eyes worthy of a love sonnet, Tristan used to say.

The coffins hit the ground with the soft sound of finality.

The minister spoke of a better place. Heaven, he called it. Fuck Heaven. Tristan and Reece were forever wandering in the mountains—there's no place they would rather be.

But this? This was my Hell.

•••

I sat alone on a comfortable black leather couch in the library of my parents' house and took a sip of my drink. My older brother attempted to keep me company, offering silent support. It pissed me off, so I yelled at Wyatt to leave me the hell alone.

He listened, but as he left the room I didn't know if I was grateful or not.

The funeral had been over for hours.

I took another long swallow of bourbon, but there wasn't enough liquor to make me forget the tears trailing down Alice's cheeks, Tristan's father looking somber and haunted. And Lucy…God, Lucy…Lucy's shoulders shaking as she buckled under the weight of her own sobs, the drape of red hair unable to hide her pain.

The door opened, and my father stared at me. "Mind if I join you?"

I shrugged.

Accepting it as an invitation, Dad went to the liquor cart and poured himself a double bourbon. *Like father, like son,* I mused. The resemblance stopped there. Wyatt took after Dad with his light hair coloring, golden eyes, and strong work ethic. But I had dark hair, blue-gray eyes, and a dreamless future.

Loosening his tie, Dad sighed and sat across from me.

"How's Lucy?" I asked.

Dad shook his head. "Laying down. She couldn't be out there anymore."

I understood, wishing I was far away. The winter sun had long since set, and a fire blazed in the hearth. The library would've been almost cheerful if I hadn't just buried my two best friends.

One year later

Chapter 2

Sage

I took a sip of tea and reread the final sentence. I closed the novel, my finger tracing the spine. Late Saturday afternoon sunlight shone through the windows, bathing the book in warm light, like a heavenly beacon.

I sat on an old, cream colored couch, aged and familiar. I had cried many nights on that couch, when the hormones and trials of being a teenager had been too much for me to handle. My mother would put an arm around me, tell me high school girls were bitches, give me a mug of tea, and we'd watch black and white *I Love Lucy* episodes, laughing until we cried.

The Brooklyn apartment in Park Slope had been my home since I was born, and I had no desire to prove anything by moving out. I loved it there.

I heard the key in the lock just before Mom came through the door, setting grocery bags down on the kitchen table. We had the same gray eyes, but she knew more, saw more than me.

"You finished it," Mom said, "didn't you?"

I nodded. "I know I've read it in handwritten pieces, but it doesn't pack the same punch as holding it in my hands and turning the pages." I smiled. "You should be really proud of this one."

"What about the others?" Mom asked with a grin.

I peered at the dark wood shelves lined with Penny Harper's milestone achievements. She was a prolific writer, cranking out stories like a machine.

But when she stalled, it took a seasoned mechanic to grease the wheels of her mind. That job fell to me. "Those are good. This—," I held it up, "no words, Mom. It's…indefinable, unlike anything you have ever written."

She smiled, pleased with my testimonial. "Thank you."

"Make you a cup of tea?" I asked, getting up off the couch.

"Sure, thanks." As I moved around the kitchen and steeped a cup of Earl Grey, Mom said, "You don't have any desire to see your words in print, do you?"

"Not this again…"

She took her mug and sat down in the living room. "Make me understand. Please?"

I wondered what I could say that would make sense to her. "I have a job Mom, what more do you want?"

She snorted in obvious mockery. "How can you enjoy going to that office every day? Working for someone else instead of yourself, surrounded by other people and pickled in fluorescent light? It's unnatural."

"What's it like, seeing your name on a book?" I asked instead, not bothering to defend my job.

"It's one of my greatest accomplishments. Are you going to tell me why you don't want to pursue writing?"

"I don't need to see my words in print. I don't need people to read my stories."

"You mean you don't want *me* to read your stories? Are you afraid you're better than I am?"

16

"No, that's not it," I lied.

I clenched my jaw shut so that hurtful words wouldn't pour out of me. It was one thing to live in another person's shadow; quite another to eclipse it. I was a writer in raw form; words came to me. I didn't need to coax stories; I often dreamed them.

But my mother worried that she'd already committed her best ideas to paper.

If I entered the same pool as Mom, the tidal wave of my success would wash over hers, and I wouldn't—couldn't—do that to her.

Mom laughed and shook her head. "God, I write characters for a living, yet I'm an idiot when it comes to understanding my own daughter. You *are* better than I am, and I couldn't be prouder of that fact. I'm a good writer, Sage, but you—you're a great one."

She said that now, but it would break her, some day in the future. We would stop being mother and daughter and become something else. Something that would make her choke on the bile of jealousy.

Mom got up and went to her bag, pulling out a manuscript and tossing it onto the table almost cavalierly.

I stared at a stack of my neatly typed words. "What did you do?"

"I read it. I want to show it to my agent."

I loved my mother, but sometimes she pushed me into a violent river of anger.

"You won't do anything with it otherwise," Mom said. "You can publish under a pen name. Do whatever you have to do. You're too good *not* to, Sage."

"I don't want to talk about this anymore. Put the manuscript back under the mattress. It's where it belongs. You should never have gone searching for it to begin with."

"And yet, I knew there was something to search for." Mom sighed in defeat. "Sometimes, I wonder if you're really my daughter."

I went to the coffee table, picked up her book, and flipped through the pages. "Sometimes, I wonder that myself."

•••

"Is this good?" a male voice asked.

I continued scanning the paperbacks on the New Fiction table in the Union Square Barnes & Noble as I said, "I don't know."

The store was busy; the escalators were jammed with people, a reading was going on upstairs, and the line to check out was long. It was a good day to be in the book business.

"You have to actually look before you answer."

I sighed in frustration. My day had been shit and I wanted to be at home, curled up on the couch, sharing a bottle of wine with my best friend, who was visiting from upstate. But, it was rush hour, the trains were packed, and I didn't have the energy to stand and bump into other people, fighting for a seat. I'd wait half an hour and then begin the long trek.

This guy was adamant about yanking me out of my own little world—and I wasn't having it. In pure irritation, I glanced up and found myself staring into blue eyes as clear as a Caribbean lagoon. Despite my surliness, I felt my anger melt a little. He held the book in question close to his face. I smiled. "Yes, it's good. I've read it. Many times."

He frowned and lowered the novel. "It just came out."

"My mother wrote it," I explained.

The man with golden blond hair and a tall, slender physique gazed at me in surprise. "Really? What are the odds? I'm Connor Lancaster." He held out his hand, and I shook it.

"Sage. Sage Harper."

"And, your mother is Penny Harper, and she wrote a book."

"She wrote a book," I agreed, the day no longer annoying me.

"Do you want to get a cup of coffee?"

I tilted my head to one side. "Will you excuse me a second? I'll be right back." Not waiting for an answer, I went to the counter and a moment later returned with a pen.

I grabbed the book out of his hands, flipped it open to the first blank page, and wrote down my number before handing it back to him. "I can't right now, but I will go out to dinner with you—when you finish the book. Have to have something to talk about."

Connor smiled. "How's tomorrow night?"

"You'll be done with it in a day?"

"What can I say? You've motivated me."

I laughed. "As it turns out, I'm free tomorrow night. Bring notecards." With a jaunty grin, I hoisted my bag higher on my shoulder and left the bookstore.

•••

The door to the apartment burst open and Jules, my best friend since high school, stood in the doorway. Black curls framed large blue eyes in an expressive pixie face that flickered from thought to thought like pictures on an old film reel.

"About time you got here," Jules said as I stepped inside and stripped off my coat.

I headed to the bathroom and turned on the shower faucet. "Sorry, you know I hate riding the train at rush hour."

"I still can't believe you buy real books." Jules lurked in the doorway while I sat on the edge of the tub and ran hot water on my feet.

"E-readers make books look cheap, and they hurt my eyes. Besides, real men read real books, and I met one today at the store."

Jules raised an eyebrow. "Go on..."

I chuckled. "We're having dinner tomorrow night."

"Let me guess: tall, blond, blue eyes."

"Oh damn, I've become predictable."

"Great, I have to go to a boring seminar, and you get to have dinner with a hot guy who can actually read."

I laughed. "You've been talking about this seminar for six months, and you've never once said it would be boring."

Jules taught theater to middle schoolers in upstate New York. The small town didn't have a lot of culture—not like the city, which was culture on steroids. Jules came down every chance she could get and always stayed with us; she even had a key.

"You talk to Penny today?"

Sighing, I collapsed onto the couch and looked at my friend. Picking up a full wine glass, I downed a healthy swallow. "Briefly."

"How's the book tour going?"

"Fast and furious, as always."

"Was your conversation still riddled with things unsaid?"

"Oh, believe me. Things have been said. Nothing '*un*' about it." My tone was drier than the wine in my glass. "She found my manuscript and wants to show it to her agent."

"What? What manuscript? You've been writing again?"

I sighed heavily. "Yeah, but I wasn't going to show it to anyone."

"You want to tell me about it? Or let me read it?"

"No." I closed my eyes, thinking back to the dialogue with my mother a week ago. We'd existed in uncomfortable silence until she'd left for her book tour. It wasn't the first time we'd had that kind of conversation. In fact, they'd been increasing over the last year, but this one felt different—it was painted with new shades of my mother's disappointment.

Jules turned on the TV, but I didn't see the screen. I thought about my mother and the manuscript under the mattress. So much for thinking I had any secrets.

•••

Connor took me to a candlelit wine bar on the Upper East Side, where we talked about Mom's new book and other things. Connor asked if I was a writer like my mother. I didn't know what to tell him.

Mom had been telling me I was a writer for as long as I could remember. It was hard to accept my fate when someone else was forcing it down my throat. I wrote my thoughts down in notebooks with no intention of letting anyone read them.

I let Connor hold my hand as we walked the streets of Manhattan. Bars were full of people laughing, the thought of finding a distraction for one night clouding their judgment.

We stopped by a bodega. Connor slipped inside and came back with a bouquet of flowers. The blooms were three days old and had lost their fragrance, but I smiled and thanked him for his thoughtfulness.

"So you'll remember me tomorrow," he said.

I laughed.

"When can I see you again?" Connor asked, as we stopped at the subway station that would take me home. Chivalry was a rarity in New York men; most were in too much of a hurry to open doors or hail us cabs. A lot of New York women didn't want it anyway, or so we pretended. It was odd what we'd grown to accept. Maybe Connor was a change from the norm.

"How about a late Sunday afternoon walk through Central Park?" Jules was leaving early that morning.

He smiled and leaned in to kiss me. It was nice, nothing magical, but nice nonetheless.

I didn't need magic; I lived in reality. And the reality was I didn't want to be a writer, I didn't want to dream.

Chapter 3

Sage

When I'd been dating Connor for six months, I introduced him to my mother. We ordered Chinese takeout and sat at the kitchen table of the Park Slope apartment. Connor was urbane, sophisticated, and polite. He had a job where he wore suits. His haircuts cost two hundred dollars, and his shoes were Italian leather. He was out of place among the eclectic, eccentric furniture and decor. His polish made me uncomfortable, but I couldn't say why.

Watching my mother and boyfriend interact was strange. I was the only commonality. They were two people who peered down the kaleidoscope of life and saw different things, wanted different things.

Which way would I lean? Would I be pulled in one direction over the other? Was there even a chance I could find my own way?

After Connor kissed me goodbye, I closed the door after him and turned to look at Mom, who watched me with steady gray eyes. "Just tell me."

"He's very nice." It was her version of saying nothing.

"Why am I not surprised? Can't you say something substantial?"

"What does Jules think of him?" she asked. Answer a question with a question—it was the way of Harpers.

Jules met Connor a while ago, and now that I recalled their encounter, she hadn't said a lot either. Oh, she listed off his *on paper* qualities like they were something to be admired, but I hadn't been able to tell what Jules thought. And Jules was full of thoughts.

Both of them seemed to be thought-*less* when it came to Connor.

I was missing something, I was sure of it.

"He's very driven—very wrapped up in his work."

"So are you," I pointed out.

"It's different."

"I don't want to debate the difference between an artist and an investment banker."

"He's not who I would've picked for you."

I rolled my eyes. "Who would you have picked for me?"

"I don't know. Someone else. Someone who understands you."

"Connor understands me," I protested.

"He understands who he thinks you are."

"What the hell does that mean?"

"It means that life is long, and you're six months in. Soon he'll know the real you, and he won't get it—he won't get you."

"You're the one that doesn't get it." I kept waiting for the wash of my anger, but it never came. Her words infiltrated the walls of my mind, moved in, put up curtains, and did a little dance that wasn't subtle in its mockery. Like illegal squatters, I couldn't evict them.

•••

Connor never asked if my mother liked him. He didn't seem to care if he received her mark of approval or not. I admired him for it; he was secure in who he was and what he wanted. He wasn't a boy. He was a man who knew what he had to offer.

Later that week, I slept at his place, which wasn't unusual. We were spending most of our nights together. I had a few outfits hanging in his closet, and my commute to work was easier from his Midtown apartment. It was convenient.

I woke up, and took a moment to study his sleeping face. He was handsome in that all-American boy-next-door kind of way. He was familiar, comfortable. I wished our relationship didn't feel like sitting in an old lumpy chair that needed to be reupholstered.

That wasn't my thought, I reasoned, but my mother's.

Climbing out of bed, I went into the bathroom to shower. It was large and luxurious, the size of many people's entire apartments. Still, we had never showered together, even though there was plenty of space for two. I'd tried to convince him once, but he'd refused, claiming to like the time to himself. I didn't ask again.

By the time I finished, Connor was awake and drinking coffee at the custom designed kitchen table. I gave him a perfunctory kiss before getting my own cup.

"Do you want to meet for lunch?" I asked, wishing for spontaneity. Maybe I could convince him to have a quick tryst before going back to the banal routines of our day. It was easy to get stuck in a self-made rut.

He shook his head. "I can't. Working through it," he explained. "It will probably be a late night, too."

I nodded, wondering why I wasn't disappointed. Shoving my thoughts aside, I went to the bedroom and got dressed. I grabbed my shoulder bag by the front door and kissed Connor one more time before departing.

I left early, knowing I had some time before work. After getting off the subway, my feet carried me into a bookstore. I wandered the aisles, reaching out to touch the leather bound notebooks. Their beauty taunted me, and my desire for them crescendoed the more I tried to ignore them. I bought one of each.

It was one of those rare, perfect days in New York, sunny but not too hot, and not a cloud in the sky. The idea of being cooped up in a small cubicle in a gigantic building grated on me. Pulling out my cell phone, I called my office, saying I was sick.

Maybe I was sick—I was doing things and having thoughts I'd never had before: Connor might not be the one for me, and I had a need to hold a pen in my hand and write until the ink ran dry.

This was my mother's fault.

•••

I opened the door to the restaurant where I was meeting Connor for dinner. He chose his favorite spot to celebrate our one-year anniversary. It was dimly lit, and complete with white tablecloths and tiny portions. I didn't have the heart to tell him I thought it was pretentious. I would've been happier ordering Thai takeout.

But Connor hated Thai.

I wore my favorite dress, a small black slip that showed my back and hit above the knee. It made me feel elegant and luxurious.

"If you'll follow me, Miss Harper. Mr. Lancaster is already at the table," the maître d' said. I followed him through the restaurant. Connor stood, looking nervous as he leaned over and kissed me.

"Bottle of champagne, please. The best," Connor said after the maître d' pulled out my chair.

"Champagne?"

Connor smiled.

The waiter brought a vintage bottle of Dom Pérignon and opened it, pouring half a flute for each of us before putting it in an ice bucket and leaving us alone.

"A toast," Connor said, raising his flute. I did the same. "To milestones."

"What sort of milestones?"

"To anniversaries, for one. To promotions, for another."

"You got the promotion? I'm so proud of you." My words felt generic, like some actor's line in a mediocre play.

He reached across the table, grabbed my hand, and held it. "Your support means the world to me. I'm so excited about what life will bring."

I had stopped listening. Sometimes Connor would talk and talk, and I had no idea where he was going. But then he pulled out a black velvet jewelry box, and my vision narrowed on it.

His hand tightened on mine. "Sage? Will you marry me?" When he opened it, my breath wedged in my throat. The two-carat solitaire caught the candlelight, reflecting its brilliant perfection. I looked up into Connor's expectant face.

He was everything a woman could hope for. Smart, driven, handsome, and wealthy enough that I'd never have to worry about my future or our life together. But Connor felt like a consolation prize. Had he even spoken of love during his proposal?

I opened my mouth, unsure of what to say, yet what came out made him ecstatic. "Yes, Connor, I'll marry you."

•••

"I'm engaged."

My mother took her time to look up from her computer.

"Say something."

"Does he make you happy?"

"Yes," I stated, though I couldn't be sure.

"Does he make you laugh?"

"Sometimes."

Mom sighed, removed her glasses, and pinched the bridge of her nose as if a headache was coming on.

"Say you're happy for me."

"Okay, I'm happy for you."

"Say it like you mean it," I demanded.

"I won't."

"You don't like Connor."

"I like him fine."

"You're a terrible liar."

"I never claimed to be a good one. Why do you care what I think anyway?"

"You're my mother."

"So what? You're going to do what you want, so what does it matter what I think?"

"Why can't you be happy for me? Why can't you be like other mothers and squeal for joy and start talking about wedding plans?"

"Because that's not who I am. It's not who you are, either. Life with Connor will be like forcing your feet into shoes that are too small. Do you think marriage to an investment banker is going to fulfill you? You'll be jogging down the road toward divorce before you know it."

I wished there was some sort of accusation in my mother's voice, but there was only truth—unyielding, remarkable truth. I didn't want to hear it.

I picked up my bag. "Thanks for the congratulations."

I stormed out of the Park Slope apartment where I'd grown up, wondering if I'd grown up at all.

•••

"Make a wish," I said. "The clock turned 11:11."

"I don't have time." Connor's eyes remained on the legal pad as he scribbled down notes. It was the weekend. We should've been out celebrating our engagement, but instead we were stuck inside because he had to work.

"You don't have time to make a wish?" I demanded. Connor could be such a bore sometimes—

no fun at all. He planned everything meticulously. At first I liked that about him. When did it start to annoy me? He had an organized sock drawer. I didn't need a shrink to tell me what that symbolized. Our sex had become stale and rudimentary long ago.

Nothing about him excited me.

"Do you think I'm beautiful?" I wondered why I had asked such a frivolous question. Shouldn't I have asked if he thought I was intelligent or wise? I didn't feel wise. Not lately, maybe never.

Connor glanced up. "Of course, I think you're beautiful. Do you still want me to make a wish?"

I looked at the clock—it was 11:12. "It's too late now."

•••

"My Aunt Mimi and Uncle Richard make the guest list…two-hundred and eighty-five. What do you think?" Connor asked.

I took a deep breath. "I think I'm getting overwhelmed."

"I told you we should hire a wedding planner."

We had set the date; it was to be June of the following year on Long Island. Connor worked in finance, and it was important to him to have a large wedding; most of our guests would be business associates.

"I don't want—"

"Don't worry about the money. I told you I could afford to give you the wedding of your dreams."

Connor clearly didn't know that this wasn't how I had envisioned my wedding. A small ceremony in

Vermont maybe, or on a remote beach—just family and friends. Not a wedding for show.

Mom had been acting strange, quiet and pensive with somber looks. I assumed it was because she was wrapped up in some new book she was writing, but every time I went to visit, her laptop was closed. Mom was going through something, but she wouldn't share until she was ready. She often withdrew from reality, spending time in make-believe because characters forced her there.

"A wedding planner sounds like a good idea," I conceded.

My mother wasn't convinced Connor was right for me, but she'd still be there to watch me say my vows.

Chapter 4

Sage

"Mom?" I called, letting myself into the Park Slope apartment. I'd moved in with Connor months ago, but I dropped by often. We steered clear of the subject of my fiancé and the wedding. Our relationship was strained, but we'd get past it—we always did. It would just take some time. I set a box of baked goods on the kitchen table and called again, "Mom?"

She made an appearance, coming out of her bedroom, wearing a gray sweater and a turtleneck. It was eighty-five degrees out.

"It's Indian summer. Are you getting a cold or something?" I demanded, heading into the kitchen and filling the teakettle with water.

"Or something," Mom murmured, taking a seat at the table.

I glanced at her as I turned on the burner. "What's wrong?"

"Come here, Sage." My mother's tone was battle weary, exhausted—I didn't like it one bit.

"No."

"Sage," Mom pleaded, "please."

Dropping into another chair, I waited, wondering what she would tell me. She didn't look tired; she looked beaten.

"I have stage four ovarian cancer." Mom had always been blunt; it's what defined her. There was no poetry for real life.

"Say it again."

She did.

"What are your options?"

She stared at me, her eyes stating more than words ever could. We didn't move for a very long time, not even when the teapot began to whistle on the stove, steam angrily escaping from the spout.

As the last of the water evaporated, the kettle sputtered to silence.

•••

The idea that my mother was going to die had never entered my mind. But she would die; that was the brutal truth, a fact that could not be changed.

Her gaunt face peered at me from the bed, a pile of blankets smothering her. The thermostat was up to eighty, but still she shivered.

I caught a glimpse of her meager arm, her body wasting away from disease, and I went to put on a long sleeved shirt, not caring that I would sweat. I wouldn't parade my health.

But Mom never became envious or irate about fate's choice—she was accepting. Too accepting of something she couldn't change.

I was angry enough for both of us.

She deteriorated rapidly in the days following our conversation; cancer was a voracious animal with an insatiable appetite for death.

Though she had round-the-clock care, I temporarily stayed at the Park Slope apartment. I never asked Connor how he felt about it—I went ahead and did it. Nor did I wonder how her sickness affected him or our relationship. My conversations with Connor grew shorter, stilted, as if we'd already spent a lifetime together and there was nothing left to say.

"You shouldn't..." Mom's weak protests went silent on her chapped lips; she didn't have the strength to go on, and she fell asleep as a new dose of morphine journeyed through her veins.

I hoped it gave her comfort—it didn't give me any.

Mom always had the power to make me reevaluate. I fought it most of my life, but now I was aware that soon she wouldn't be there to answer questions with questions. Who would ask me about the things I didn't want to face?

"Shouldn't *what*?" I queried her slumbering form. She slept twenty hours a day now.

She didn't reply.

•••

I stared at my hands fisted in my lap, my eyes vacant and unseeing. It had been hours, but I hadn't been able to bring myself to leave the church, and had missed my mother's burial. The pew was solid beneath me, the quiet room an illusionary comfort.

I had told Connor I needed space, and like a fool, he'd left me.

After pushing him away for weeks, was I surprised he hadn't stayed?

Yes—he was my fiancé. He was supposed to console me, but he was uncomfortable with grief. He didn't contend with emotion; he didn't understand the abstract—and didn't want to.

He was a coward.

"Sage?"

I didn't turn at the sound of his voice.

"Are you ready to go home?"

Home. What a funny word. I hadn't slept beside him in weeks—I found I didn't care.

"I'm not coming home," I heard myself say in a cold, clear voice, like a bell ringing from afar.

"*What?* We're getting married—"

"No, we aren't. I'm sorry." But I wasn't sorry.

He reached out to put a hand on my shoulder and then thought better of it. He looked shocked and a little lost.

Not nearly as lost as me.

I twisted off the beautiful, two-carat prison and held it out to him. He regarded it a long moment before taking it. His quiet footsteps echoed as he walked away.

If only I felt relief. If only I felt sadness. If only I felt something.

•••

"France? You can't move to France!" Jules' eyes widened in shock.

"Like hell I can't." I shoved clothes into my suitcases, not bothering to fold anything; I just wanted to get out of New York as quickly as possible.

"What about Connor?"

"What about him? We broke up."

"When?"

"Right after the funeral."

"Jesus—why?"

I shrugged.

"That's not an answer!"

"What am I supposed to say, Jules?" I demanded. "There's nothing left for me here."

"Come live with me in New Paltz."

"And do what? I don't need a babysitter."

"Don't do this. Don't move across an ocean; this is drastic."

"Yep."

"Who are these people?"

"My mother's oldest friends. I need to start over. I can't do that in New York, and I can't do that with you watching me with those eyes."

"What eyes?"

"You know, those Jules-judgmental eyes. You're worried I've gone off the rails."

"Haven't you? You broke up with your fiancé, and you're leaving the only city you've ever lived in."

"I quit my job, too."

"Obviously."

"Connor was a symptom," I murmured.

"I don't understand."

"When I found out my mother was going to die, I cried in the shower for hours. He pretended he didn't hear me, but I knew he was home."

Jules looked at me, words lost on her tongue.

I closed my eyes. "I just can't do it anymore—I'm tired."

"You'll be so far from—"

"Home? This isn't my home. Not anymore."

Chapter 5

Kai

"What is this?" the blonde asked in stilted English as she stroked a finger across the brand on my chest. It was puckered now, a callused souvenir of all that I'd lost. Sometimes I felt it burning, a phantom pain that was as real as any I'd ever known.

I winced at the memory; two years felt like yesterday. Time hadn't dulled my grief.

"A brand," I evaded, my mind sluggish. I was in Spain, or maybe Portugal. Most of the time I was too drunk to notice where I was, or where I slept—or the women. So many women, and the guilt—it's why I kept moving. Stay still and I'd sink like an old battleship.

"What's it for?" She pouted her sultry lips.

I found her irritating, and there were only two things to do at this point; get up and leave, or bury myself in her and lose my thoughts all together.

"You want to waste our time talking?" I asked, bringing her face close to mine for a kiss.

She purred in the back of her throat. Thankful for the brief respite, I grasped her hips and hauled her on top of me.

My memories disappeared like a wisp of smoke.

•••

I left the blonde and headed to London without purpose.

It was raining. There was nothing unusual about the weather—it always rained in England; it didn't matter what time of year it was or what season.

The pub was dark, and I pushed back my University of Tennessee baseball cap in an attempt to see. I perched on a stool and grinned at an attractive woman that approached the wooden, scarred slab of a bar.

"Buy you a drink?" I drawled.

The brunette smiled, dimpling. A flush stole up her cheeks as I perused her with bold eyes. It was almost too easy—they never put up a fight, but I was glad because I didn't want the challenge. I wanted to forget.

"Sure."

"What will it be?"

"Surprise me," she said, her posh London accent rolling over me. She attempted to tease, yet I didn't get the tingling rush of the hunt.

It had been a long time since I'd felt much of anything—I doubted I'd recognize it when I did.

Dipping my hat, I ordered a bourbon and ginger ale and squeezed the lime into the glass. "There ya go. It's a good old fashioned Southern drink."

She raised an eyebrow, took a sip, and then smiled. "This is good!"

I chuckled. "Don't sound so surprised. What's your name?"

"Erin."

I didn't care; I wouldn't remember it in the morning. It was always the same. Every night, wherever I was I'd go to a bar, single out a pretty girl and go home with her, hoping it would be enough to see me through the next day.

Some nights I didn't even bother; it was too much effort, the guilt of being alive too much. Whenever that feeling stewed near the surface, I knew it was time to move on. Sometimes I had a few weeks in a place before that happened; sometimes it wasn't even a day.

I never knew peace.

Two years ago with only Tristan's baseball cap and my grandfather's mandolin, I picked up, headed for Asia, and hadn't talked to my family since. I walked dirt roads, ate unusual foods, and wondered why old men with craggy, brown faces and very few teeth were so happy—content even.

"Want to sit with me a minute?" I asked.

Erin looked over her shoulder at her three friends, who were seated at a battered table.

I leaned my five-ten frame toward her, appearing taller than most men over six feet. It was the confidence, Tristan used to say.

"Just a minute?" I coerced.

"Okay," she said, sliding onto the stool next to me. "What's your name?"

"Kai."

"Where are you from, Kai?"

"Wherever." Out of the corner of my eye, I glimpsed two blurry shadows. I swiveled my head, expecting my best friends to be sitting at the other end of the bar. Instead, I saw two middle-aged men, who looked nothing like Reece and Tristan, and they peered back at me in curiosity. I sighed. "Wanna get out of here?"

"Let me tell my friends—in case you're a crazy person." She smiled.

Already, I felt the drive to move on. After I said goodbye to what's-her-name in the morning, I'd hop a train or a plane bound for somewhere else.

Maybe Amsterdam. Tristan always wanted to visit the Red Light District. I'd go there.

What else did I have to do?

•••

"I bet chicks are digging that brand of yours," Tristan says, pointing at my shirtless chest.

I grin and shrug. We're both dressed in ratty jeans rolled up to the ankles and wading into the silvery water. I can almost feel the sun beating down on me, almost remember the smell of Monteagle in summer.

"What country are you in now?" Reece asks from the bank.

"Not sure."

"Have you become an alcoholic?" Tristan teases.

"I can still remember my name, so what do you think?" I quip.

"I think you're boozing hard," Reece says with concern.

"You always were the mother hen, weren't you?" Tristan laughs, but Reece doesn't smile.

"It's going to catch up to you, you know," Reece says, as if Tristan hadn't spoken.

"Don't listen to him, Kai. If you need to drink to get through this, then do it."

"It's been two years," Reece says, his anger evident. He rarely gets irate, so when he does, it means I have to listen. "You going to drink yourself to death? Is that what you want?"

"I want you guys back."

"We're dead. No amount of drinking will change that fact. Don't these dreams make you crazy?" Reece wonders aloud.

"These dreams feel more real than the life I've been living."

"You call this a life? Traveling from place to place, but not actually doing anything. Losing yourself in the arms of women you can't recall?"

"You guys are so melancholy. You're worse than a Nirvana album. Here." Tristan tosses me a fishing pole. "Morning's coming, and then Kai will have to leave. Might as well get in some good fishing. What do you say?"

I grip the rod, cast it into the lake, and get an immediate bite.

"How the hell do you do that?" Tristan asks.

"I'm a regular Huck Finn."

"Kai was always a better fisherman than you, Tristan. Always has been, always will be. Doesn't matter where we are."

"At least I still have my luck with women."

"Yep, you found El Dorado when you got Lucy," I say.

Tristan grins. "I did, didn't I?"

"We should all be so lucky," I mutter.

"Luck? You call this luck?" Tristan fumes, and looks like he wants to throw a punch. He chucks his *pole instead, and it splashes into the water, shattering the dream lake's serenity. "We're the ones that died."*

I grimace. "Like I could ever forget."

Reece shakes his head. "You have one life, and you're wasting it."

"I wonder what you'd do in my shoes," I say, my own voice rising. "Would you be any different?" My gaze slides to Tristan. "You would've had Lucy. You would've had a woman to love you back to life. I don't have that. I've got a bottle of bourbon, a mandolin, and the need to keep moving."

Tristan looks at me. "That's what you think. Your life can change in a heartbeat."

"I know that," I state.

"You ready for it?" Reece asks.

"Won't matter if I am or not. What do you guys know that I don't?"

"Not a damn thing," Tristan answers.

Chapter 6

Sage

I pressed my forehead against the cold window of the airplane. Sighing in exhaustion, I pulled the seat belt tight against my stomach and attempted to tune out the flight attendant's chirpy voice filtering through the intercom.

I took out the *Sky Mall* magazine, flipped through it, and marveled at the things people could be coerced into buying. Who wanted a *Lord of the Rings* chess set, a washroom for their cat, or a hideous frog fountain?

People are deranged.

I put the *Sky Mall* catalog back and took out the airline's safety brochure. The first page I turned to had an illustration of an airplane floating in the middle of the ocean with no land in sight, complete with smiling passengers hopping into life rafts as though they had reached their destination.

Right.

I shut the brochure and closed my eyes, anxiety curling in my belly at the thought that I was about to cross the Atlantic Ocean in an aluminum death trap.

"Nervous?"

I looked over to see a middle-aged, matronly woman who reminded me very much of my mother. It suddenly hurt to breathe. I didn't respond.

"Is this your first time going to France?"

"Yes," I replied, answering both questions simultaneously. I turned my head back to the window and gazed out at the runway. In the darkening light, men in orange jumpsuits sprayed down the plane, trying to scrape off ice and snow in preparation for takeoff.

I tugged at the collar on my thick, black sweater as a cold chill trailed down my neck.

"Vacation?" the woman asked, attempting to pull me into a dialogue.

"Sure." I closed my eyes again, hoping my obvious desire to be left alone would stop the woman's attempt at chitchat.

It didn't.

"Are you going to Paris? Paris is so romantic, even in this kind of weather. French winters are more rainy than snowy, but it's still a wonderful city."

I made a vague sound in the back of my throat. The flight attendant finished her safety demonstration, and the pilot announced it would be a few more minutes until takeoff.

The woman droned on, "You look like you're in college. Is this your Christmas break?"

I should have been flattered that I still appeared young after all I had been through. I swore I looked like a haggard old woman at the end of my life, a crone that had seen everything. "I'm not in college."

"Are you from New York? I don't know how people live there. The huge buildings, the subway— the homeless."

What would it take to shut her up? Her enthusiastic prattle grated on my last nerve. I thought about recounting my most horrific subway story that featured a homeless man exposing himself, wondering if it would stun her into silence. All I had hoped for after weeks of emotional upheaval was a long, quiet flight without having to engage with anyone.

"Excuse me," I uttered, unbuckling my seat belt. "I need to use the restroom."

The woman's eyes widened. "But you can't go now, we're about to—"

"When you gotta go, you gotta go."

A perky blonde flight attendant, perhaps the one who had spoken over the intercom, appeared in the aisle almost instantly. She must have had a sensor for recalcitrant passengers. "Excuse me, ma'am, you have to sit down."

"I need to use the bathroom for one second," I whispered, my voice beginning to tremble. Emotion flooded my veins as I tried to remain collected. It was everything I could to do to keep from screaming.

"Ma'am, we will be in the air in a moment. The captain will turn off the seat belt sign when it's safe, and then you'll be able to use the restroom." The attendant's voice was firm, her stance pugnacious.

I could only imagine how I appeared—gray eyes stained red from non-stop crying, my face white with pain and anger. Matted, dull chestnut hair I couldn't be bothered to brush because it didn't matter. Nothing mattered; especially not appearances.

It was all bullshit.

The flight attendant's tone turned combative. "Please sit down."

For one long moment, I didn't move, didn't breathe. With reluctance, I took my seat and buckled myself in. The flight attendant nodded and then continued moving down the aisle, closing compartments in rapid succession.

The woman next to me remained blessedly silent.

As the plane began to pull away from the gate, I shut my eyes. I didn't watch as I flew away from the city I had once called home.

•••

"Would you like something to drink?" It was the flight attendant whose pleasant mask was back in place. How did she do it? I wore my emotions like a sweater, and I didn't have any acting talent to conceal my grief.

"Coke, please," the woman next to me answered.

"And for you, ma'am?"

"What scotch do you have?" I inquired. It was an evening flight, but if it had been eight o'clock in the morning, I might have asked for it anyway.

"Canadian Club, Dewar's, and Glenlivet."

"Glenlivet, please," I replied, handing the attendant my credit card and ID.

"Want anything in it?" She glanced at the ID and swiped the credit card before returning them.

"No, thanks." I opened the mini bottle of scotch, pouring it into cup I'd been given. She rolled her cart along, serving other passengers.

"You don't look old enough to drink." There was a dose of protective concern in my companion's voice.

It made me hesitate ever so briefly. "Well, I am. Would you like to see my ID, too?" Inhaling a shaky breath, I took a liberal sip, feeling warmth blast through me. "Consider it a sedative," I said, trying for levity and failing.

"You're afraid to fly, right?"

I didn't answer as I gazed out the window into a bank of clouds. I wanted to forget the horror of the last couple of weeks, the endless days and nights of my mother's pain, and then what came after.

The tears fell unchecked down my face, and I sniffed.

A tissue appeared, and then my compatriot put a hand on mine and squeezed in sympathy. It only made it worse, and I wondered if I would ever be able to take a deep breath without feeling like I was dying.

•••

Eight hours later, the plane landed at Charles de Gaulle Airport. Tired passengers unhooked their seat belts and stood, wanting to stretch their legs and disembark.

I didn't move, waiting until it cleared. When half the plane was empty, the woman next to me rose and pulled a bag from the overhead compartment. With one final look at me, she inclined her head and left.

We had come to an understanding somewhere over the ocean.

I trudged through the airport, looking for baggage claim signs through bleary eyes. I wondered how tourists ever found their way through the labyrinth of French confusion. Even I, who spoke and read French, had trouble.

Only a few pieces of luggage remained when I arrived at the carousel. Celia, with her sleek brown bob and willowy form, waited for me. Had it really been a week since I'd seen my mother's oldest friend at the funeral? Grief moved differently through time—it wasn't linear; it was everywhere, relentless and constant.

"Hello, Sage."

"Hello."

"Want me to wheel those for you?" Celia didn't wait for an answer. Reaching out, she began to drag my suitcases behind her, walking in silence to the car park. Though it was only ten in the morning, it was dark, and drizzling winter storm clouds hovered overhead. I hunched in my coat in a meager attempt to keep the rain off my neck.

"How long is the drive?" I asked, when we were on our way in Celia's tiny car.

"About three hours," Celia replied. "I'm sure you're sick of sitting."

I was sick of many things, but I kept quiet.

"Are you hungry? We could stop for something." She maneuvered through the streets of Paris, channeling the energy of a New York City cabbie. I found it amusing as she cursed in French when a bout of road rage overtook her.

"Sorry, that's the worst of it, I promise. The roads are a little wider once you get out of the city."

"No, I'm not hungry." I watched the countryside speed by. Everything was dull, and it was hard to imagine what it would look like dressed in the green of spring. I'd lived in gray, long before Mom got sick, trying to convince myself I needed everything on mute. Stupid, stupid, stupid. "Thank you, for letting me come here."

"You're welcome," Celia said. "Sometimes you need to get away."

I glanced at her. It was impossible to miss her tired, red-rimmed eyes. She was grieving too; for an old friend, or a future without my mother—I didn't know which. I turned my head, not wishing to see Celia's pain.

Mine was enough.

We drove in silence; it could've been a three hour or a twenty-minute drive for all I knew. In that moment I existed in a state of in-between, a misty nothingness.

Celia parked the car in a narrow spot across the street from the bed and breakfast. The lobby walls were whitewashed stone. It was quaint and charming in all the ways that weren't annoying. Guiding me past the spacious dining room, comfortable library, and surprisingly modern kitchen, Celia chattered about nothing. The property was surrounded by a ten-foot stone wall, and we trudged through the courtyard to a small cottage.

I walked inside and found myself in the living room. There was an unlit fireplace in the corner, and a rustic burnt-orange couch up against a wall. Just past it was a kitchen, small but serviceable.

"The staircase at the back leads upstairs to the bathroom and bedroom. Take your time, get situated. Come over for some food, if you want."

The door clicked shut, and I stood in the center of the room, attempting to adjust to the place I was now supposed to call home.

Thunder rumbled in the distance, and I went to the window and pulled back the curtain to reveal the dark sky. Threatening clouds curled and lightning flashed.

I watched the storm unleash Hell. It was strangely comforting.

There was a knock, and it took me a moment to realize I should answer it. I opened the door to a young man with a charming grin and ruffled sandy blond hair. He looked to be about my age, but his face was unlined, smooth and pristine. No grief had touched him. I felt so much older.

"I'm Luc," he said with a Gallic smile, which was a cross between a smirk and a pout. "Celia and Armand's son. *Maman* sent me to light a fire." He peered at me in curiosity.

I let him inside. Luc squatted by the fireplace, rearranging logs of wood into a pile. Striking a match, he lit the kindling, and soon flames were blazing. It felt homey—almost.

"Thanks," I said.

Luc stood and smiled. "You coming over later?"

"Don't think so." I was tired—I wanted to take a hot bath and then maybe try to sleep.

"You're not hungry?"

I shook my head. My stomach had withered—eating was a nuisance, and I couldn't remember the last time I'd had a solid meal, or wanted one.

"We'll have wine," he said, attempting to entice me. "From the vineyard. You won't be disappointed."

"Maybe," I said, though I had no intention of going. I saw him to the door and closed it after him. Grabbing my suitcases, I went up to the bedroom, and I could feel the warmth of the fire from downstairs.

I set my bags down on the double bed and opened them, staring at my clothes as if I didn't know how they'd gotten there. I shoved them into drawers of the dresser, not caring that everything was jumbled.

Dipping out into the hallway, I walked a few feet to the bathroom. In the linen closet, I found a set of faded blue towels that had seen many washings. Some things managed to last through time, no matter how tattered and faded they became. It made me wonder about people. How many tragedies did it take to tarnish them like old pennies?

I placed the towel that smelled like jasmine and mint on the counter and examined the tub. It was a porcelain claw foot and for some reason it made me weep.

I turned on the faucet and the sound drowned out my sobs. I don't know how long I sat on the edge of the tub, crying for nothing and everything, but eventually the tears subsided. Stripping off all my clothes, I sank into the scalding water, hoping it would do something for the chill that lived in my bones.

Chapter 7

Sage

The next morning, incessant knocking dragged me from a drugged sleep. Rising from the bed, I swiped a hand across my parched lips. I shivered as I pulled on sweats. Winter in the Loire Valley was not temperate.

I trudged down the stairs, noting the embers in the hearth. I had fallen asleep with the warmth of a raging fire, but now I was cold once again. I opened the door to Celia standing on the steps, holding a cup of coffee.

I let her in. Without a word, she handed me the mug and went to stoke the fire. As the flames came back to life, I shuddered with relief.

"You didn't make it over for dinner."

"Jet lag."

"I figured."

I sat on the couch and leaned my head back against the cushion. "What the hell am I doing?" I said, more to myself than to Celia.

Without hesitation, she sat and wrapped her arms around me. Burying my head in her shoulder, I began to sob. She made soothing noises against my hair, but then I realized it was the sound of Celia's own crying; we grieved together. When the storm of emotion passed, I pulled back and dried my face. She did the same and smiled in self-conscious understanding.

"You don't have to have anything figured out. Right now, all you have to do is come over and let me make you pancakes. Think you can do that?"

•••

I sat at the table, drinking another cup of coffee and taking small dainty bites of fluffy pancakes. In my state of grief, everything was muted; colors, tastes, smells. All my senses were drowning in an ocean of anguish.

"So, I run the bed and breakfast," Celia said, taking a seat. "Man the desk, cook, set up tours that sort of thing. Luc and my husband handle the vineyard. When you're feeling situated, would you be interested in helping? Might give you something to do."

"Sure." I stood up. "I need to send an email. May I use your computer?"

Celia led me to the front desk and logged on before stepping away to give me privacy, though I hardly needed it. Opening my inbox, I filtered through the junk mail, disregarding Connor's emails, pleas for me to return to him and my sanity.

I typed a message to Jules that read simply, *Arrived.* I pressed send and logged out. It wouldn't hold her at bay forever, but it would give me a momentary reprieve.

"I was thinking Luc could show you around *Tours*?"

"What can I do?" Luc asked, strolling into the room.

"Show Sage the town."

Luc looked at me. "Sure. That okay with you?"

I nodded. "Let me shower real fast."

We drove twenty minutes to downtown and parked in a narrow alley. I was tired, drugged, and spacey, so I let Luc lead me. He pointed out landmarks, the train station, and the university. We walked along the main drag, and he took me to a cell phone store, where I bought a serviceable phone as opposed to a gadget. I sent a quick text to Jules and then turned it off.

There weren't many people who needed to know my whereabouts. I liked being off the grid. I wanted simple.

"I've never been to New York," Luc said, attempting to engage me in conversation. "What's it like?"

Until a week ago, it hadn't just been a city—it had been my home, and a place to build memories. I'd become an adult there, yet the idea of ever returning burned a hole in the cavern of my belly. "It's a bizarre place."

He laughed. "How so?"

Tilting my head to one side, I thought about it. "I used to love the hustle—I thrived on the energy, but things change. What was it like growing up here, in this idyllic, postcard-perfect place?"

Luc smiled. "Couldn't imagine living anywhere else."

"Have you traveled?"

He nodded. "All over Europe. Australia. I've seen enough to know this will always be home."

It started to rain, and though I had an umbrella that kept me dry, the cobblestone was slick, and I slipped. I sat still, water soaking into my jeans, the cold of winter seeping into my bones.

"What are you doing?" Luc demanded. "Get up."

When I didn't move, he hauled me to my feet. Our umbrellas clashed against one another, dribbling rain on his coat and neck. "I think it's time to go home."

We drove in silence, and my eyes began to close. I was tired, always tired. When we got back to the cottage, I let Luc build a fire as I stripped off my coat and boots. I went upstairs to change into dry clothes, then came back and reclined on the couch, throwing a plaid blanket over my legs.

"Do you want to talk about her?" Luc asked.

"No." I glanced at him. What did he see when he looked at me? I knew the bags under my dull gray eyes threatened to take over my entire visage, and my wan skin was drained of the blush of life. My cheekbones were grotesque arrows pointing to my frozen anguish. I was a canvas of flaws. "You don't have to stay with me."

"I know," he said, "but I thought you could use some comfort."

Comfort. I'd forgotten the meaning of the word. Connor hadn't given me much in the way of it—he hadn't known how. And Jules…well, she had her own idea of what it meant.

My head throbbed, crammed full and threatening to burst open. Maybe I should talk about my mother. Maybe that would make me feel better, though I doubted it.

"I wish I had a drink," I muttered. "These things are easier with a drink."

"There's some wine in the main house."

I shook my head. "Wine will not do for this kind of conversation."

"What then?"

"Scotch. Or tequila. Something that numbs." I placed my head in my hands.

"Just talk, Sage."

I sighed. Defeat was ubiquitous. "I felt relief when she died. She was in so much pain; I just wanted it to end. We put pets to sleep when there's no hope, but we watch our loved ones linger in their misery. Her suffering became my suffering." I lifted my head, heavy with guilt. "I know how I sound."

"You sound human."

"Humans are heartless."

"Or, maybe, they have too much heart. Ever think of that?"

"She was a writer."

"I know. We have her books in the library."

"Ever read them?"

He shook his head. "Not my genre. *Maman* has read them, though."

"What did she think?"

"Good stories. Your mother was very successful."

"Yes, she was." I paused in thought before asking, "What is the one thing that defines you, Luc?"

"I'm not sure I understand."

"You're a winemaker. Is that how you see yourself?"

"Ah. No, I'm other things too."

I sighed. "I'm worried I'm only a writer—we define ourselves because we have to, and I don't want to be defined. If I say 'writer', what does it really mean?" I felt drunk, but I knew it was just exhaustion. I wished I was drunk, so drunk I couldn't form a coherent thought. "It's fitting, you see, that Mom died when she did."

"What do you mean?"

"The last book she wrote was her best work; she strived for it her entire life. It was the pinnacle of her creativity. After that, there's nowhere to go but down," I whispered. "It never would've happened for her again, and she would've spent the rest of her life cursing herself for that one moment of brilliance, because it would've set the bar so high she'd never be able to surpass it."

"You weren't lying, were you? About needing a drink?"

I couldn't swallow my startled laughter.

"Come on. That's enough for one day."

Tugging me off the couch, he led me to the door. We ran to the manor in an attempt to stay dry, entering through the back door. We went into the kitchen, where Celia was placing ingredients on the counter.

"How was your day?" she asked.

"Rainy," I replied.

Luc went to the cabinet and pulled out wine glasses. "Is *Papa* home yet?"

Celia nodded. "Showering, and then he'll be down."

"Good." He opened a bottle of wine and poured me an overly full glass.

I wanted scotch, but wine would have to do. I took a sip and choked in surprise. I wasn't expecting the sharp burst of fruit on my tongue. It made me think of hot summers, picnics under trees and the hum of bees. "Oh."

Luc grinned and shot his mother a glance.

I felt like I was borrowing a memory that didn't belong to me. "Wow. Just—wow." I used to have a way with words. How ironic that they failed me in that moment.

"Glad you like it," a man said, entering the kitchen. He had the same color eyes as his son, but he was a good five inches shorter. His face was weathered and ruddy, a testament to his time spent outdoors. "Armand," he introduced.

"Sage." I took another sip. "I've never tasted anything like this."

Armand grinned like he wasn't surprised, and then went to kiss his wife before pouring himself a glass. "It's good to be home. I'm tired."

"How's *Grand-mère*?" Luc asked.

"Stubborn, but settled in her new place. I wish she would move back."

"Never going to happen," Celia said. "Your mother is far too independent." She unwrapped a wedge of Camembert and placed it on a platter. Washing a cluster of purple grapes, she put them next to the cheese and then brought it to the table. Luc and Armand sat down while Celia stayed at the counter and began dicing an onion.

"Would you like some help?" I offered.

Celia smiled. "Sure." She pulled out a large pot and filled it three quarters of the way with water. After dumping in a palm full of salt, she covered it with the lid, turned the burner on high, and transferred chopped pancetta into a sizzling frying pan. She threw the onions into another skillet and slowly caramelized them, and then combined them with the crispy pancetta and stirred.

"What are we making exactly?" I asked as I watched her break four eggs into a bowl of cream and whisk them.

"Spaghetti Carbonara."

I paused. "Isn't that Italian?"

"It is," Celia agreed. "Oh, were you hoping for a French meal?"

I wasn't hoping for anything at all. And that was the truth of it. "No, it's fine. It smells great."

The timer buzzed, and she tested a noodle and then gave me one. "Al dente—perfect."

She divided the pasta onto four plates, added the cream of eggs, shaved Parmesan, and then cracked fresh black pepper.

"Where did you learn to make this?" I wondered aloud when we were all seated around the table.

"My mother," Armand interjected with a smile.

"Go ahead, everyone," Celia said.

I hesitated and then took a bite. The creamy, bacon and egg dish glided over my tongue, and I felt true hunger for the first time since Mom died.

As I listened to the laughter and conversation around me, I realized that life would continue whether I wanted it to or not.

I pushed back from the table. "Excuse me—I'm not feeling well." I ran from the room and rushed out the back door into the cold, rainy night, unraveling like a loose spool of yarn.

Ducking into the cottage, I stood in front of the fire as I dug into my purse for pills to help me sleep.

•••

It was still dark when I opened my eyes. The rain had stopped sometime in the night, and despite the medication, shadowy thoughts had moved throughout my subconscious and infiltrated my dreams. I was tired and shaky; it was a usual post-burial morning.

Trembling, I got up from the couch where I'd fallen asleep and wrapped the blanket around my thin, scarecrow-like frame. Since my mother's diagnosis I'd lost a good fifteen pounds, and I hadn't had it to lose in the first place. Every time I looked in the mirror, I bit my lip to keep from gasping—what I saw scared the hell out of me.

There was a soft knock on the door. I knew it was Celia; she seemed to be making it her mission to care for me, but I busy being at war with myself.

Celia came into the cottage and handed me a loaf tin covered in aluminum foil. "Homemade bread."

I sniffed, and my stomach rumbled. I was in momentary shock that my mouth filled with saliva, my taste buds enticed by aroma alone. It made me yearn for all the comfort that food gave. I could use the calories. Maybe I'd find a way back to life through my stomach, since it didn't yield to heartache—not anymore—it was an angry baby bird wanting to be fed.

"I'm sorry…about last night," I apologized, taking a seat on the couch and tearing off a corner of the warm, yeasty loaf. I stuck it in my mouth and chewed.

If only my misery wasn't worn on my face. I wished I could bury it deep inside.

"Don't apologize," Celia said. "You'll come out of your shell when you're ready. In the meantime, I plan on feeding you and checking in on you, whether you want it or not. I'm here as a friend."

Celia didn't ask anything of me, and I exhaled a sigh of relief I hadn't known I held. "Thank you."

"Get dressed. Armand wants to show you the vineyard."

•••

Thirty minutes later, I walked with Armand through acres of rolling hillside, covered in well-groomed rows of vines. The day was overcast, but it didn't look like it would rain. Everything was quiet, sleeping, awaiting the season of the sun. I wondered what the vineyard would be like in spring, ripe and in bloom.

What was it like to create something so beautiful? Armand was a maker of wine. My mother had been a maker of books. The need to create was inherently human, and strong within me. How I managed to settle for such an empty career was beyond me.

"How long has your family owned the vineyard?"

"Generations," Armand explained. "When my mother and father married, she moved here. After my father died, she returned to Italy."

"Italian to the core?"

"Without a doubt."

"What was my mother like? Back then?" I asked before I could take it back.

Armand looked at me. "Headstrong. Always knew what she wanted and where she was going. She's the reason I met Celia, did you know?"

I shook my head.

"It was their junior year of college. Summer. They were traveling all around Europe, and Celia wanted to go to Belgium, but Penny insisted on France. They got here, and the rest, they say, is history."

"Love at first sight?" I smiled.

"God no!" Armand laughed. "Celia detested me, but I knew what I wanted, and I pursued her— relentlessly."

"She finally gave in?"

Armand's blue eyes twinkled. "Celia saw me flirting with Penny one night, and it made her realize she wasn't indifferent after all."

I laughed. It sounded exactly like something Mom would have done, and in that moment I almost felt like she walked alongside us. Those we loved would be immortalized in our memories, until we too, were gone.

Chapter 8

Kai

I wondered where I was as the countryside whizzed by the train window. I unscrewed my flask, took a long sip, and tapped my foot to the beat I heard in my head.

The prostitute in the Red Light District had been nice. I'd paid her, only to realize I didn't want to sleep with her. Instead, we'd reclined in her bed, not saying a word. After my hour was up, I went down to a café, bought a blunt and smoked it.

Tristan would've told me I was crazy. Dream Tristan *did* tell me I was crazy. Dream Reece, softer, gentler, didn't judge me aloud.

I'd seen and done so many things after they died. I started with the Great Wall of China and then journeyed to Hong Kong. The pollution in the air made the sun appear blood red, and had made me feel like I'd landed on an alien planet. The Great Pyramids of Egypt were hot and dusty, and I'd almost gotten spit on by a camel. Camels were mean bastards. I drank beer in mass quantities to combat the dourness of Prague. One night I'd even stripped and went for a midnight swim in the Vltava River. I'd gone sport fishing off the coast of Croatia, fallen off the boat and almost drowned. Almost.

None of it had made an impact.

I hadn't made my way to South America yet. Maybe I'd go see the Mayan ruins and offer a blood sacrifice—to what end, I didn't know.

The train stopped, and I got off. It was raining. God, did every place I traveled have to rain so much? I should visit an island with nothing but sun and white sand, and an endless supply of rum.

My baseball cap was sodden, and my clothes stuck to me; it's what I got for not carrying an umbrella. Maybe I'd get pneumonia and die. A guy had to have dreams, didn't he?

I walked around the old cobblestone square, dried off in a pub, and then soaked my blood in alcohol. I supposed I should find a place to sleep, if I didn't want it to be a park bench.

Everything was written in French. I was in France, or so I believed—for the time being anyway.

•••

I picked up the mandolin and stroked its body like I would a woman. My fingers glided over the strings; it was familiar, comforting. It hadn't always been the case. My grandfather had been relentless when teaching me to play. I remembered the hours of practice, the anger when I couldn't move my hands the way they needed to, until one day everything connected.

My grandfather had been able to pick up any stringed instrument and master it, given enough time—it had been one of his many talents. I hoped I had inherited some of them, but I doubted it. The mandolin was the only thing I stuck with; nothing else held my interest. I was decent at many things, but proficient at few.

I was too smart for my own damn good—my parents had said it often enough. I'm not sure I believed them, since I felt steeped in mediocrity.

The moon shone through the window of the tiny studio I'd found in place of a park bench. No lights were on—not because I didn't have electricity, but because I found the dark comforting, like this little town somewhere in the Loire Valley.

The notes came out mournful, poetic—a eulogy for the friends I'd lost. I'd played them many eulogies.

I uncorked the bourbon and drank straight from the bottle. When I was drunk enough, I asked, "Tristan? Reece? It's your turn. Take a swig."

But there was no answer from the ghosts that followed me; silence was the only reply—the bottle of bourbon and an old, scarred mandolin my only companions.

•••

"How did you get a girl like Lucy?" I demand, casting into the lake. Tristan catches his first fish while I reel in my fifth.

"Son of a bitch," Tristan curses. "How am I supposed to win this competition?"

"My dream, my rules, remember?"

"Right."

"Tell me about Lucy."

"Fuck if I know. She's the perfect woman. Not only did she knock beer bottles out of my hands, but she knocked sense into me on more than one occasion." Tristan grins.

"You'll find it, you know."

"Will I? I'm not sure."

"You won't wander forever. You'll find a reason to stay somewhere."

"You were closer to her than you were to us, weren't you?"

"It's different," Tristan explains. "When you meet the woman you're supposed to spend your life with, you'll understand."

I shake my head. "You grew up, didn't you? I didn't even notice."

"Happens to the best of us. It's going to happen to you."

I laugh. "Not if I have anything to say about it."

Chapter 9

Sage

One night, when I'd been in France for a little over a week, Luc came to my door and demanded I get dressed. "Where are you taking me?" I asked, even as I grabbed my coat.

Luc grinned. "A dive."

Dive was a generous description of the bar. It was a seedy hole-in-the-wall with an old jukebox and a few scarred, un-level pool tables. It was stuck in the '80's, but as I was learning, *Tours* was a mishmash of culture from the past. That was part of its charm.

"What are you having?" Luc asked.

"How about a beer and a game of pool?"

"Rack 'em."

I kicked his ass in pool, or he let me, and I introduced him to "Eye of the Tiger". I didn't think I would laugh again, not so soon after losing my mother. But laugh I did when a ridiculously drunk Luc played the song over and over on the wailing jukebox, singing along off key and annoying the other patrons.

Taking pity on them, I selected a Tom Petty song, hoping Luc didn't know the lyrics. I set down the pool cue and headed to the middle of the dance floor. I wasn't a dancer by any means, but tonight, I wanted to move. It was probably the five beers I'd consumed, but still, I felt *good.*

I was paying homage to Mom. She had loved classic rock, and had hundreds of compilation playlists on iTunes. Some days it had been nothing but Zeppelin, on others it was Simon and Garfunkel. I could always tell her mood by what music was playing.

Neon lights from beer signs painted my skin in a medley of fluorescent glow. I drank and danced until the world spun, and then I let Luc cart me out into the crisp night.

"You're beautiful—did you know that?" he said, his hands steadying me while I stumbled like a clown on stilts.

"It's not polite to lie to a woman," I teased.

"I'm not lying."

"Thanks for being here. You're a good sport to put up with me."

He gazed down into my eyes. "Sage, I—"

I stopped him from speaking by placing a hand on his chest. "I just need a friend, okay? I'm not ready for anything else."

Luc squeezed my shoulder gently before turning me in the direction of home. "Okay."

•••

The next morning, I threw on a pair of old sweats and a sweatshirt, and went in search of coffee and Luc in the main house.

Luc seemed to be a relationship kind of man. Until recently, I had been a relationship kind of woman, but I had been down that road with Connor, becoming entrapped in a loveless relationship. I didn't want to make the same mistake again, and I needed time.

"Where's Luc?" I asked Celia, who was at the desk sending an email. After typing something, she looked up.

"He went to visit his grandmother early this morning."

I frowned.

"Do you want to tell me what happened? Don't think of me as Luc's mother."

I smiled. "But you are, and I'd never say anything that would make you—"

"Look at him differently? You think I'm blinded by the love I have for my son?"

"Not if you're anything like my mother."

My mother's revelations about me had often left me breathless, my feelings casualties in her war with truth.

Celia came out from behind the desk and led me into the kitchen. She poured me a cup of coffee and made me sit down. I began to talk. She had that look about her; her face was the blank page of a journal I wanted to fill.

I'd ruin Luc. My pain nearly smothered me—I wouldn't willingly invite him in to share the weight of it. He deserved a woman who had things figured out, and that wasn't me.

I never expected my mother's death to be my release from a life on autopilot. Why did it take her dying for me to realize what life *wasn't* about? Floating through experiences that failed to shape me was something I never wanted again. Would I ever want to be a writer? Did I really have a choice? The battlefield of life was strewn with shattered dreams. In my own war, would I triumph or fall?

•••

A week later, Luc still hadn't returned. Though he had been graceful about being denied, it appeared I had wounded him deeper than I knew.

I started helping Celia work the front desk, putting my fluent French to good use, answering emails and phone calls, and giving directions to guests. Nights were spent holed up in my cottage with a bottle of wine.

Some days, my sadness was an annoying buzz in the back of my head and I managed to compartmentalize it. On other days, it was an unchained beast snapping its ugly jaws around my heart. Tears caught me at strange moments, and at times I couldn't contain them. I lost hours trapped in sorrow with no hope for escape.

One afternoon, Celia said to me, "It's time for you to go."

Startled, I looked at her. "What?"

She grinned. "Go enjoy *Tours*. You've hardly seen the city. Don't you want to explore?"

"No, I don't. I'm not ready."

"Yes, you are. Go. I'm serious."

I'd been hiding, but it seemed I wouldn't be allowed to anymore. With no choice, I did as commanded.

•••

I wandered through the heart of downtown. Compact cars littered the main drag of the idyllic city.

The streets were nearly empty of pedestrians due to the impending rain, and it felt like I had the town to myself. I passed *pâtisseries*, and the tantalizing aromas of freshly baked goods pierced the damp winter air. I ambled along curvy, cobblestone streets, and found myself in front of an inconspicuous bookstore. Before I could stop myself, I went inside, and a tiny brass bell announced my presence to the shopkeeper. The aisles were narrow, and the store seemed to be bursting with books from floor to ceiling, yet there was a certain efficiency about the quaint shop. I spotted a section containing pens and notebooks, picked up a dark brown leather journal and held it in my hands. I brought it to my nose and inhaled the scent of *Tours*.

It was afternoon when I entered a café and sat at a small table, ordered a glass of wine, and pulled out my new journal and pen. I wanted to put down words, but nothing came. Had they finally abandoned me, or had I forced them away?

Staring out the window, I watched evening come. A waiter moved around the restaurant lighting candles on the tables. Customers, eager to be out of the cold, filled the doorway and began to take seats. I studied the menu and thought about ordering three entrees when I heard a voice in English say, "You're what Michelangelo hoped to create."

I looked up, a wry grin on my lips. I saw a stubble-spattered jaw, dark hair sticking out from under a University of Tennessee cap, and wounded blue-gray eyes. Sitting back in my chair, I projected lazy insolence, hoping it would scare him off. "Does that line *really* work?"

"You tell me." He plopped down in the vacant chair across from me without invitation.

I frowned. "I'm waiting for someone."

"No, you're not."

"I'm not?" I tapped the pen rapidly on the table.

"Nope, because I'm here." He pushed back his hat and smiled.

I sighed. "Why did you speak English?"

He plucked the pen from my fingertips and moved it through his knuckles like I'd seen musicians do with a guitar pick. I hated that I was mesmerized by the action. Shaking it off, I realized he was just another careless, handsome man who knew that he was universally adored by women.

But not me.

"Look around you," he said. "You dress differently than the rest of this lot. I took a gamble and spoke in English. And I was right, wasn't I?"

"So what? You spotted an American in France. Big deal."

His joking demeanor disappeared as he said, "You're sad."

His accurate assessment took me completely off guard. "No, I'm not."

"Yeah, you are."

"What makes you say that?" I crossed my arms over my chest in a subconsciously defensive gesture.

He peered at me before answering. "I've traveled the world. I know sadness when I see it."

All my effort at hiding my anguish in plain sight had been for nothing. Unbidden tears began to flood my eyes. I was starting to cry in front of a complete stranger.

His hand reached for mine in a gesture of comfort that Connor never could have mustered. Despite not knowing my new companion, I didn't pull away. I was lost in an ocean of feeling, but I managed to pull myself together. I finally withdrew my hand, grabbed my pen and journal, and shoved them into my bag.

"Wait," he said, realizing I was about to depart.

With great reluctance, I glanced at him.

"I'm supposed to play here tonight. Will you stay for just one song?"

Without waiting for my response, he rose and went to a stool at the back of the restaurant. He picked up a mandolin resting in the corner, and I watched his fingers press against the strings as he struck a chord. He began to play a song that made me feel more alone than I thought possible. It evoked a memory so powerful, that it made me rise from my seat and rush out into the night.

I was light-headed, shaky, and terrified.

The song was a trigger, a broken melody of a summer long ago in Prospect Park when Béla Fleck had given a concert. My mother and I had sat on the grass, a picnic basket between us, drinking wine out of plastic red cups. When I heard that song for the first time, it stuck in my mind, lingering like a hazy dream. For months after, I repeatedly listened to the song on my iPod while words spilled from my pen, forming into a manuscript.

It was the manuscript my mother had found.

Needing to escape my feelings, I walked through the rain, unmindful of where my legs carried me. I wanted to find a liquor store so I could drown my emotions. I entertained the idea of getting a bottle of my mother's favorite scotch, but this was no celebration. It was a time of forgetting, so a bottle of anything would do.

Back in the cottage I lit a fire, but left the rest of the lights off. I opened a bottle of cheap bourbon and didn't bother with a glass. I found my iPod, plugged in headphones and listened to the song on repeat. Grief was a strange entity, and like the moon it waxed and waned. I'd never felt more alone than in that moment, and I drank until I drifted off to sleep.

Chapter 10

Sage

I sat in the corner of the café, close enough to see the dark, careless stubble on his jaw. Sounds of the mandolin soothed me, like a salve reaching all the way to my bones.

He was talented.

When he played, he brought tears to my eyes, and I wondered what sort of magic he held, a true master of emotion. The song ended, and the sudden silence left me feeling empty.

I glanced up to find a blue-gray stare raking over me. The player inclined his head in acknowledgement. I did the same—and then, without hesitation, he began to play the song that had caused me to leave the previous night.

But this time, instead of running, I leaned towards him, wanting to soak up the notes. When he finished, he set his mandolin down in its case and walked towards me, dressed in faded, ratty jeans and a black t-shirt. I could see the tempest in his eyes. He sat on the stool next to me, a careless smile spreading across his face. I raised an eyebrow, his grin widening. He flagged down the bartender and ordered two shots of bourbon.

"Cheers," he said, holding up his glass. We clinked and downed them; I didn't even flinch.

"You're quite impressive," he murmured.

"Glad you think so." I ordered another round.

"So, stranger. You have a name?"

I bit my lip. To tell him would make me real. "Does it matter?"

"I can call you Lady Magnolia."

I stared at him for a moment. Suddenly, my name didn't feel like it belonged to me anymore, so I told him. "Sage."

He held out his hand. "Kai."

I took it, noting both the warmth and calluses. When I tried to pull away, he tightened his grip. "May I have my hand back?"

"In a minute."

His thumb weaved a sensuous stroke across my knuckles. He stared at me, but I didn't feel like squirming. The power of his eyes entranced me, and my heart pounded as he continued to hold my hand. He was a stranger in so many ways, and yet I saw something in him that I had in myself.

His sorrow was a mirror into my heart.

I knew instinctively that Kai was reckless, and I wanted to throw myself into the eye of his storm. I wanted experiences that would forge and inspire me, and I knew that could only happen with him, but I couldn't say why.

"Sage…"

"Yes?"

"May I kiss you?"

I couldn't speak past the emotion in my throat, so I nodded.

As Kai's face came close to mine, I thought he was going to kiss my lips—instead he pressed his warm mouth to the flickering pulse at my throat.

"Will you come home with me?" he asked.

"That depends."

"On what?"

Without taking my eyes off him, I plucked the glass from his hand and drank the bourbon in a few long swallows. Setting it down on the bar, I reached for my purse to pay for our drinks, but he stopped me by pulling out his wallet and throwing down some Euros. "How many women have said *no* to you?"

"None."

"You're honest."

"I don't think you're the kind of woman that can stomach lies." He stared at me. Relentless. Feral. "You're coming home with me, aren't you?"

"Yes." There was intensity in him, and I liked it.

His hand squeezed my arm. "Stay here—don't move."

I pulled on my coat while he went to get his mandolin. We left the bar and walked into the night. Without asking, he laced his fingers in mine.

"Have you ever been so cold, so weary, you wonder how you'll ever make it back?" His voice was soft, and I wasn't sure I heard him.

"What are you trying to come back from?"

"What are *you*?"

I didn't answer.

We stopped when we came to the *Tours* Cathedral. The old Gothic building was austere in the moonlight, and seemed to block out the entire sky.

"Have you been inside?" I asked.

He shook his head. "Look." He pointed in the direction of an ancient, knobby tree as we strolled towards it. Moonlight bathed naked, twisted branches in a silver glow.

"It belongs in the realm of fairies," I said. "Imagine all the stories that tree could tell if only it could talk."

I leaned over and pressed my lips to bark. I closed my eyes and leaned my forehead against it, wanting to pay respect to something that had withstood the test of time, far longer than any single human life. I glanced at Kai, and he watched me with a steady gaze. I gave no apology for my moment with the tree. Grabbing a low-hanging limb, I hoisted myself up into the canopy. "You coming?" I called down.

A moment later, he sat on a branch across from me.

"Do you have a place where time stops for you?" I wondered.

"I used to, but it's gone now." He turned his eyes to me; they were haunted with despair.

I hadn't expected the weight of his emotion, and so I jumped down to escape the moment. Kai followed, landing next to me. Without a word, he took my hand and led me away.

•••

We arrived at a narrow door on a cobblestone street, lined with dull grass peeping between the cracks. I trailed after Kai up the stairs. Jiggling the key in the lock, he let me inside. The studio was sparse—twin bed in the corner, a rickety circular table with two wire chairs, and a small refrigerator making a faint humming noise, attesting to its age.

Kai set his mandolin case down as I walked to the window and looked out over the quiet path. I could almost imagine the color of the flowers that would appear in spring. Turning back to him, I smiled.

"What?"

"It seems just the sort of place a musician would live."

He grinned as we perched on the bed. Holding my hand, he traced the back of it. "Anyone tell you that you have elegant knuckles?"

I laughed. "No."

He brought them to his lips. "This—," he gestured to the studio, "is just a place out of the rain."

"You don't like being owned by things, do you?"

He shrugged. "Obligation is a bitch. What about you?"

I thought of Connor; I had let myself be owned by people. I nodded.

Kai reached out with his free hand to touch my face. "Where's your home, Sage?"

"I don't have one." My voice was full of bone-jarring loss, an endless reservoir of sadness.

Further words were unnecessary as he turned his body towards me. Sinking his fingers into my hair, he pulled my face close to his. His mouth covered my lips in an urgent kiss, and I gave into his need, fueling my own. With gentle insistence, he pushed me back, and his body melted over mine. His hands and lips were everywhere; it was a struggle to breathe and when I did, the scent of sunshine and pine filled my nose.

Perhaps I didn't have a home, but in that moment, I felt like I did. In his arms, my aching spirit calmed. He was summoning a feeling I had long thought dead.

We struggled out of our clothes, and I watched as Kai's eyes roamed over me in reverence. I touched him, my fingers colliding with an angry scar on his chest. It looked like a burn.

"What is—"

"Not yet," he interrupted. "I'll tell you, but not right now." He silenced me with a kiss.

I swallowed questions as my hands glided over his skin and played with the dark hairs on his chest.

His fingers tickled their way down my body, and I shivered in delight, not wanting to wait any longer. The aching loneliness disappeared like mist late in the morning as our bodies joined as one.

I rocked against him, my mouth seeking his. I bit his lip and then soothed the pain with my tongue.

He groaned, but it wasn't in despair.

Everything made sense, and the only thing that mattered was Kai's mouth on mine and the feeling of his warm, flushed skin against me. We moved in a frenetic pace—a moment too brief in time.

Our breaths mingled as our hearts beat in a synonymous, steady rhythm. Kai's face nestled into the crook of my neck, and my hands gripped his hair as we attained the deepest release possible. I was fulfilled and at peace, but when Kai eased out of me I felt empty again.

"Come on," he said, taking my hand and leading me towards the tiny bathroom. The narrow shower stall would force us to remain close.

We showered in easy silence, our hands still finding a reason to touch one another. I pressed a kiss to his scar, which I could now see in the light.

"It looks like a brand." A tragic T&R marked forever on his body, remembered by his flesh.

"It is."

I didn't ask about it again.

The hot water beat down on us, and I closed my eyes and leaned against his slick shoulder. His arms came around me and squeezed. I fit into him—I belonged. We dried off, and Kai gave me one of his t-shirts.

"You're staying."

"I am?" I asked, even as I reached for the shirt and pulled it over my head. "You don't seem the type that spends a whole night with a woman."

"I'm not," he admitted, "but I want to spend tonight with you."

I did as I was bid, climbing into his bed and scooting over, making room for him. He slid in next to me, putting a warm, heavy leg across mine. My eyes drifted closed, even as I thought again that I shouldn't stay.

Comfort is a powerful sedative.

Chapter 11

Kai

I bolted up, gasping, my body slippery with sweat. I had dreamt of the crash again, the smell of burning metal in my nose, the taste of it at the back of my throat, threatening to choke me.

I looked over at Sage. It was strange to see her there. I'd never brought a woman home with me. I'd left all of them in the middle of the night at apartments or houses I'd convinced them to bring me to, but this was a woman I didn't want to leave.

I wasn't sure why.

Her hair flowed across the pillow like a mermaid under water. Her face was turned away from me, and her breathing was even and deep. Sage was exceptionally beautiful, but it wasn't her looks that intrigued me.

I got out of bed, careful not to disturb her.

When Sage came into the café for the first time I thought she appeared tragic. I noticed a sadness about her, and wanted to play her a song that would make her smile. I had no idea the song I chose would cause her to leave.

When she came back the following night, I felt something. Hope, maybe.

I'd been traveling for years, with no desire to stay put. One woman had been as good as the next, but I wanted Sage for more than a single night.

I scratched my chest as I opened the cupboard, pulled out a cup, and filled it with water. Taking a drink, I turned when I heard footsteps behind me. My shirt covered the tops of Sage's thighs and clung to her breasts, and I could see her nipples, the color of a coral starfish. Her long hair hung down her back in soft waves, fair skin flushed pink. She walked to me, and I wrapped my arms around her as she placed her head in the crook of my neck like she was made for the spot. I breathed her in—she smelled warm, like a spring afternoon in Monteagle.

"Did I wake you?"

"No," she mumbled into my chest, her mouth close to my brand.

All the women I had slept with asked about it—I gave them different answers every time, but for once, I wanted to speak the truth, wondering if I still could. But not now.

I cupped her head in my hands, tugging on her hair to make her look at me. My mouth claimed hers; I needed to feel her moving beneath me as I lost myself in her. Only then were my demons at bay.

I wondered about hers.

I took her back to the twin bed, laid her down, and covered her with my body. Her fingers trailed down my arms and gripped my shoulders as I thrust into her, making us one.

This time, we made love, the savage beast of guilt slumbering. This time, it was just for us.

•••

"Don't you guys get bored?" I ask.

Tristan and Reece exchange a look as Tristan passes Reece the hand rolled cigarette. "Bored?" Tristan queries. "What do you mean?"

"I hate shoes," Reece grumbles, wiggling his bare toes.

"Why do we keep meeting here?" I wonder aloud.

"You tell us," Tristan says.

"I thought this was your favorite place?" Reece points out. The sun glides up over the mountains. It's quiet, serene—the silver lake is always placid.

"It is," I state. "But it's—"

"A painful reminder of home?" Tristan finishes.

I nod, picking up a twig and snapping it.

"You going to tell us about the girl?" Reece demands, taking another long drag of the cigarette.

Tristan raises his eyebrows. "Yeah, is it serious?"

"We just met."

"That's a 'yes'." Tristan grins.

"Think she'll make you happy?" Reece asks.

"Yeah."

"Think she'll make you a better man?"

"Hopefully."

"Does she make you reflect?"

"She is my mirror."

Tristan is thoughtful, and then he smiles. "I don't have a reflection anymore."

"Time to go," Reece says, rising. "Take it easy, Kai."

I watch my two best friends walk down the path, their bodies disappearing before my eyes. Sighing, I look at the sky and then descend the mountain.

Chapter 12

Sage

We were a mesh of tangled limbs. Kai's leg was thrown over mine as he held me in his arms. We faced one another, my head resting underneath his chin. I traced a finger in the dip between his collarbones and wondered about the illusion of intimacy. I had never had a one-night stand before, and I had been prepared for awkwardness, yet all I felt was comfort.

He sighed.

"You awake?" I whispered.

"Yeah."

I pulled back, wanting to look in the direction of his eyes. One of his hands came up to caress the curve of my cheek. He kissed me. It was a feathered dance across my lips, but not a plea for more. It was a statement of feeling, of knowledge that I rested next to him.

"Am I hogging the bed?" he asked.

I snorted. "It's barely a bed. How can you hog it?"

Kai attempted to move over. "I'm not used to sharing a bed."

Not to sleep, I thought dryly, but didn't reply. His statement made me think of Connor—the last person I wanted in bed with me. But still, I couldn't expel him from my mind. I'd broken our engagement only a month ago, and I was already in bed with another man. I shoved thoughts of Connor aside, and the guilt that came with it.

"What are you thinking about?" Kai asked quietly. His hand ran down the knobs of my spine, lingering at my tailbone.

"Nothing."

"I don't believe you."

"What are you thinking about?" I countered.

"Fishing."

"Fishing? I feel like I should be offended."

I could hear the smile in his voice when he said, "If I was back home, this is the time I'd be getting up. I'd put on my waders, grab my pole and head out to the lake.""I've never fished before."

"No?" he asked in clear surprise.

"I'm from Brooklyn," I said as if that explained everything.

"Aren't you close to water?"

"The East River doesn't count."

He laughed.

"Actually, you can fish in Prospect Park. Have to throw the fish back though. Seems kind of like a waste."

He made a vague noise of agreement. "I always eat what I catch. Are you tired? Do you want to go to sleep?"

"I'm kind of hungry," I admitted. As if on cue, my stomach moaned.

"Come on, I have some food, I think."

We got up and he slipped into boxers and I threw on his discarded t-shirt. Kai opened the refrigerator and pulled out a block of cheese, smiling in triumph. I peeled an orange that rested on the counter and set it onto a plate.

"Want some cider?" he asked.

"Sure."

He opened a bottle of brut cider and poured it into one glass. He gave me a lopsided grin as he handed it to me. "I figured we could share. I don't have cooties. Promise."

My lips twitched into a grin. "I don't believe you."

We took our snack to the kitchen table and ate in comfortable silence. The crisp cider went down a little too easily, and soon I was feeling drowsy. I got up, set the empty dishware in the sink and turned to him and smiled.

"Are you any good? At fishing, I mean."

"Not bad," he said, though it sounded like feigned humbleness.

"How many fish have you caught in one trip?" I asked as I climbed into bed. Kai got in next to me and settled the covers over us before spooning me.

"Ten. All before dawn. Once the sun comes up, it's like the fish know you're trying to catch them." He swept his lips across the skin below my ear. "Good night, Sage."

"Good night, Kai."

I dreamed of lakes.

•••

I woke just as the sun was rising, but when I attempted to get out of bed, Kai's arm shot out and grasped my wrist.

"Don't even think about it," he mumbled into the pillow.

"Think about what?"

"Leaving."

"Wasn't planning on it."

He chuckled as his arms wrapped around me, and I turned towards his embrace. His eyes were open; they were clear, serene, magical. "You're a shitty liar, you know that?"

"Let me up," I protested, struggling against his arms.

"Not until you promise you won't bolt."

"I promise. Now let me make some coffee, or you'll wish I had left. You do have some here, right?"

"Yeah." He released me, and I scrambled out of bed, giving him a view of my backside. He pulled on a pair of shorts, but left his chest bare. "You don't do this a lot, do you?"

I moved around the kitchen and made coffee as we conversed. "What, sleep with strangers? How could you tell?"

"Just knew."

"Am I just another notch on your belt?"

"Would it bother you if you were?"

I shrugged. "What can a girl hope to expect? It's not like we spent a lot of time getting to know one another."

He smiled. It was slow, heated. "I know you fine, but I'd like to know you better."

I looked at him, amusement stamped across my mouth. "We don't have to do this."

"Do what?"

"Let's call this what it is and leave it at that."

"Are you telling me you used me for sex?"

I laughed. "What if I did?"

"I feel so used," he teased.

I pulled out two mugs and handed him one. I had no idea how he liked his coffee, and I didn't want to pretend I did, so I poured it black.

"Let me take you to dinner."

"Are you promising to buy me food before we have sex next time?"

"Well at least I know there will be a 'next time'." He grinned. "I win."

I looked at him for a long moment, sipping my black coffee. It was hot, and it scalded my tongue, so I set it down. I went to grab my belongings, shimmied into my clothes, and then put on my coat. I was willing to give him the benefit of the doubt—at least for one more night. "Come to the *Château de Germain* tonight. I live in the small cottage behind the bed and breakfast."

"You live on a vineyard?"

"Yes. Bring a bottle of bourbon. I'll take care of the food."

"Can't argue with that."

•••

"Someone got in early this morning," Celia said with a wry grin as I joined her at the front desk.

My face heated, but I said nothing.

"It's okay, you know."

"What?"

"Moving on with your life."

"Is that what I'm doing?"

"Don't think too much about it," Celia said, pulling me from my thoughts. "Enjoy it."

Even after my night with Kai, I was still in a river of grief. What did I expect after a month in France? A miracle?

"What's it like for you?" I queried. In all this time, I never thought to ask how Celia was dealing with the loss of her oldest friend—I felt heartless.

"Nothing like what you're going through," Celia said. "Losing a friend weathers differently; losing a parent…nothing compares."

"Loss is loss, isn't it?"

"I suppose so. You want to tell me about the guy?"

"Nothing to tell. A ship in the night—he'll be gone before you know it."

"Don't be so sure." Celia sounded like a cryptic fortune-teller.

"What do you mean?"

"Things have a way of finding us and sticking when we least expect it."

•••

I pulled the door open and stood back, letting Kai inside. I wore a pair of black leggings, a slouchy white sweater and house slippers. The roaring fire swallowed the chill from the air, lending a comfortable ambiance to the room.

"Cozy," he said, leaning in and grazing my cheek with his lips.

"Let me take your coat."

He shrugged out of it, and I hung it on the rack as he set a bottle of bourbon down on the coffee table.

"What have you got planned?" Kai asked, his gaze straying to the pillows and blankets in front of the fireplace. The coffee table was set with two whiskey glasses and platters of cheese, bread, olives and fruit. "Is that going to be enough for both of us?"

"Used to bigger portions?" I teased.

"Yup. Must be the Southerner in me."

"Ah, I had an inclining you were from the South. You've got that lazy drawl—it's like whiskey and lemonade on a hot summer day."

He grinned. "You like my accent?"

"Maybe." I paused. "Where are you actually from?"

"Monteagle, Tennessee. What about you?"

"I'm from New York."

"Yankee!" he said, feigning shock. "Don't worry I don't discriminate." He winked.

"Thank goodness for that. Take off your shoes. Stay a while."

He grabbed the bottle of bourbon. "Ready to crack this open?"

"Sure. Ice?"

He nodded, and I went into the kitchen with the two glasses. A moment later, I returned and we sat down on the pallet and took a sip of our drinks.

"Hi," he murmured, leaning closer.

"Hello." I let him kiss my lips, enjoying the warmth of the fire and him. He pulled back, picked a grape off one of the plates, and popped it into his mouth.

"I was surprised you opened the door."

"Were you?"

"I thought I might've scared you away. I'm glad I didn't." Though his tone was light, his eyes blazed with intensity.

I took a large swallow of bourbon, but said nothing.

"It feels easy, you know? I want to be myself around you."

"Thank you for that," I said in sincerity. Unveiling ourselves to strangers was never an easy task. There was always the fear that the other person wouldn't like what they saw.

I picked up the bottle and topped off our drinks.

"Are you ready to tell me why you ran out of the café when I played that song?"

I peered at him over my amber liquid. "Only if you tell me about your brand."

"I was going to tell you about that anyway."

I raised an eyebrow. "You first."

Kai clenched his glass, turned somber eyes to me and said, "Two years ago my best friends died in a plane crash. Now I wear their initials."

The air left my lungs, and I blinked several times—whatever I had been expecting, it hadn't been that. We were both fluent in the language of grief.

His hand came up to stroke the side of my cheek. "What happened to you?"

I sighed. "The first time I ever heard the song you played was at a concert with my mother. And she died—a little over a month ago."

It was his turn to be speechless, and then he cleared his throat. "A month? Wow."

I nodded. "Ovarian cancer."

"Fuck." He shook his head. "What brought you here?"

"My mother's oldest friend married the man who owns this vineyard."

"Had to get away?"

"Yeah, you?"

"I left home right after they died, and I haven't been back since."

I leaned into his touch. "Have you been in France the whole time?"

Kai shook his head. "I started in Asia, and I go wherever, whenever."

"Playing your mandolin in cafés?" I smiled. His hand moved to my hair, and he twirled a strand around his fingers.

"That's a fairly recent thing."

"Is it?"

"Only since I came to France."

"Which was when?"

Kai laughed. "About a month ago."

"Interesting timeline," I noted.

"Isn't it?"

I kissed him, and as I did there was a knock on the door, startling us apart. "Sorry, I don't know who that could be."

"No?"

I stood, and answered the door with a slight smile on my face, not at all prepared for Luc to be on my front steps. "You're back?" I blurted out.

He nodded. "Just now. Listen, can we talk?" His eyes widened when he saw Kai, who rose and came to stand behind me. I felt Kai's heat through his shirt, and I wanted to press into him, but that would give them both the wrong idea.

"Now is not really a good time," I said.

"No kidding," Luc replied, his gaze trained on Kai. "Who are you?"

Luc asked the question like he had the possessive right, but I didn't know how to get around introducing them. "This is Kai. Kai, this is Luc. He's the son of the owners."

Kai held out his hand, ever the Southern gentleman. Would Luc be as refined? He was French after all.

When it was clear that Luc was not going to take Kai's hand I asked, "Can we talk tomorrow?"

"Sure. Whatever," Luc said before leaving.

I closed the door and turned to face Kai. His blue-gray eyes narrowed and his jaw clenched.

"Did you sleep with him?" Kai asked, his voice tight.

"Not so good with beating around the bush, are you?"

"Sage…"

"If I did?" I challenged.

Like a jungle cat, he was on me, pushing me against the door, his mouth covering mine. It was a brutal tempest of emotion, and I held onto him like a castaway in a life raft.

"I didn't," I murmured once Kai's kisses calmed. He bathed my forehead with tender lips as if apologizing for his irrational behavior.

"What happened between you two?"

"Is this really any of your business?"

"I'm making it my business. What happened?"

"Nothing."

"It doesn't look that way."

My sigh was weary, but I gave in. "I didn't lie to you."

"Do you want him?"

"No," I stated. His eyes poured into me, filling me up with the depth of his feelings. I wanted to shake in fear. "Don't make claims, and don't ask for promises."

"Okay," he said in reluctant acceptance.

I raised an eyebrow. "You ready for dinner?"

"No."

"More bourbon?"

"No."

"Should we go upstairs then?"

"Yep."

•••

I watched Kai sleep on his stomach, like a baby that wanted for nothing. The fairy moon outlined his fair skin in a silvery glow, a demigod gilded in shadow. He stirred. Pain rarely slept, even in dreams, but tonight we'd both rested peacefully. I had awakened only moments ago, needing to see him with my own eyes, to remember he was there.

"We should get candles," he mumbled into the pillow.

I trailed a hand down his back, loving that he shivered at my touch. "Candles? Candles are cliché," I whispered, placing my head next to his so our breaths mingled.

"I want to see you golden." He rolled over. "That first night you came to the café, I couldn't help but notice how you looked in candlelight."

"You're like a wandering bard, you know."

"I'm no bard."

"But you *are* a wanderer."

We never made it back downstairs for dinner, choosing instead to spend our time in bed—touching, sharing, exploring.

"Would it really have bothered you if I'd slept with Luc?" I asked.

He inhaled deeply as if he was stalling for time so he could choose his words carefully. "I know it's hypocritical since you know my history, but yeah, it would've bothered me."

"Luc? Or the idea of Luc."

"I don't know," he admitted, "but I'm glad nothing happened between you two. It's one thing to know you've been with other people—it's another to have to see them."

"That's fair, I guess."

I kissed his collarbone and wondered how he'd played his way into my blood. He held me like his mandolin, cradling me so that I felt like a cherished possession. Kai had learned the corners of my soul, and it had occurred in the darkest part of the night, when the stars peeked out from the clouds and a sliver of moon rode high in the sky. I felt both aged and reborn.

He would have to leave me in the morning, when the sun would rise and time would start again. But for now, the sleepy minstrel sheltered me in warmth. I fell asleep with a smile on my face.

•••

The next morning I was not at all surprised to find I was alone in bed, but I was stunned by the wash of bereavement. I was supposed to be glad I had my space back, but when I breathed in, I no longer detected the scent of sunshine and mountains—the smell of Kai.

Stumbling downstairs, I halted. Kai was in the kitchen, standing at the counter having a cup of coffee, like he belonged there—like he lived with me. Taking a moment, I consumed him with my eyes. He wasn't very tall, close to five-ten maybe. His body was sturdy, almost compact, and when I was in his arms, I didn't know there was a world outside just the two of us. His hair was dark brown and a bit too long; it fell into his face. I didn't know if he owned a razor, but I liked his gritty jaw. He was careless with his appearance, but it didn't matter; all I saw were captivating eyes and a kindred spirit.

I moved behind him and pressed my cheek to his back. He stiffened and then relaxed. Setting down his coffee cup, he turned to me, pulled me into his arms and lifted me onto the counter. He stood in between my legs, which I wrapped around him. He was in boxers and a white undershirt, his hair sticking up on end. I smiled and smoothed the most endearing, irreverent cowlick I had ever seen.

Placing my hands on his chest, I closed my eyes. "You're still here."

"Where else would I be?" His voice was husky with sleep and something else. Desire, maybe.

"I don't know," I answered, talking into his neck. "None of this seems real."

"The most surreal moments are often the most genuine."

"I didn't believe it when my mother died, but it turned out to be the only truth of my life."

"This is truth, too."

"Is it?" I still wasn't sure.

His arms tightened, but he didn't speak. I let him hold me before pulling back and stealing his coffee. Touch of cream was how he took it, I noted.

After we showered and dressed, Kai walked me to the back of the bed and breakfast, kissing me on the lips and saluting before walking away. He didn't tell me he'd see me that night; it was already a forgone conclusion. Whether I wanted him or not.

Ship in the night, I reminded myself, seed in the wind. And I'd let him go when the next place called to him.

•••

I spent the morning at the desk with Celia, but by the time afternoon rolled around, I knew I couldn't put off the confrontation with Luc any longer. I found him drinking a beer on the balcony that overlooked the vineyard. It was cold and quiet, but the sky was clear.

He didn't turn as I approached. Perhaps he was expecting me all along.

"You're with Kai."

"No," I said.

"Certainly looked that way to me."

"I was engaged, Luc. Not long ago."

"Oh. I didn't know."

"That's why I'm telling you. I don't know what I want," I admitted. "All I know is what I *don't* want."

"And that's me?"

"This isn't about you. This is about *me*. Let me breathe, Luc."

He picked at the corner of the beer label and peeled it. He still wouldn't look at me.

"You don't want me, not really. You think you do because you don't know the real me."

"Do *you* even know the real you?"

I glanced at the vines, my gaze landing on a rut of dirt. "No, I don't. I thought I did, once. It was all a lie. Do you want me to lie to you, Luc?"

When he wouldn't answer, I walked away.

•••

"I haven't talked to my family in two years," Kai said. His voice was quiet, his hand sliding up and down my arm. Lying in the double bed, my head resting on his chest, I stroked his brand. It was jagged, like my heart.

"Do you miss them?"

"No."

"Liar."

"No, it's true."

"Do you miss anything?"

"My favorite fishing hole," he admitted. "I miss the hours I'd lose up in those mountains. I miss Reece and Tristan, but that goes without saying. I miss Alice and Keith, Reece's parents, who are more my parents than my own. I miss my grandmother. But I don't miss my Mom and Dad, or brother."

"Why not?"

His sigh was labored. "My parents want me to be a certain way, and Wyatt…"

"Wyatt?"

"My brother. He's everything I'm not."

I mulled over his words before asking, "Do you plan to go back?"

"No. What about you?"

"What about me?"

"You ever think of going back to New York?"

"To what?" I sat up, my tangled hair falling across my shoulders.

"What did you leave behind?" He sat up too, the moonlight turning his skin silvery blue. Somewhere far away the sky rumbled.

"Nothing—there's nothing there."

"A girl like you always has someone waiting."

Without thought, I glanced at my ring finger.

"Sage, are you married?"

"Would it bother you if I was?"

He didn't answer, he just continued to stare at me.

I sighed. "No, I'm not married."

"Engaged?"

"I was." There was no apology, no sadness in my voice. It all seemed so long ago, my relationship with Connor. "None of that matters now."

"How could it not matter?"

"The same way it doesn't matter that you've been with a bunch of women."

"It's different," Kai insisted. "I wasn't planning to share a life with any of them. Did you leave him?"

"Yes," I explained. "It needed to end. So I ended it." I examined him, trying to see all the little parts that made him who he was. "You're afraid I'm going to leave you, too."

"No, I'm not." He climbed out of bed and went in search of his pants.

"Like hell you're not," I said, watching him. "You think I abandon people."

"Do you?"

"No. It looks that way, maybe, but it's not true. I know what you're doing."

"What?" His voice was strained with hurt and rage.

"You're leaving me before I leave you, before you're in too deep."

"Don't you get it?" He stalked to the side of the bed and hauled me into his arms. "I'm already in too deep."

"This has to be enough," I begged, "please, this has to be enough." It was a broken plea.

"For now."

His mouth came down to claim mine in fierce possession. I ripped at his clothes, tearing into him, wanting him to brand me until I knew him in my bones. It scared me—our intensity. I wondered what we would leave in our wake, but I was straining towards it anyway.

Maybe not a passing ship after all.

Maybe the seed had settled and taken root.

Chapter 13

Kai

I came to, knowing it was morning. I inhaled—Sage was near; she shifted closer, and the tickle of her long brownish-red hair joined her smell.

"You want a lot from me, don't you?" she whispered.

"Yep."

"Why?"

"It would terrify you if I told you."

"Get out," she commanded.

I forced her to meet my gaze. "No."

"What do you mean, *no*?" she demanded, throwing her legs over the side of the bed.

"Exactly as it sounds. I'm not going anywhere."

She moved away, and I watched her from the confines of the covers, staring at the woman who was doing everything in her power to retreat. It was too late for that; I'd follow her. Maybe I could be relentless when I wanted something. Who knew?

"I'm not ready for this—whatever *this* is."

"Okay."

"I mean it, Kai. Don't placate me. I'm not ready for anything serious."

"Is that what you told Luc?"

She didn't reply.

"Why did you come home with me that night? There was a guy right under your nose you could've been with."

"I knew Luc would want more. I didn't think you would."

"You thought you were safe." I sat up and stretched, glad she watched my every move. "Hate to break it to you, darlin', but you're not safe. Not from the way I make you feel."

"Stop it."

"Stop what? Do you think I like knowing I want you, and there's nothing I can do about it?" Tears fell down her magnolia cheeks. "Your mother just died," my voice was a whispered caress, "let me be here for you."

She collapsed onto the floor, and I went to her, wrapping my arms around her. Leaning against me, she shook with sobs. When she cried, she put her whole body into it—nothing about Sage was passive.

"How can you be here for me? You're not even here for yourself."

Was she right? I'd been running for so long I didn't feel winded anymore.

"I was drinking a lot," I admitted, "before we met." It was an extreme understatement. How would she react if I told her there were weeks, months that were nothing more than a blurred recollection?

"It's only been two weeks since we met, Kai. Do you see such a drastic change in yourself already?"

I cocked my head to the side. "Do you?"

We were at a standstill—she wiped her face, slid out of my embrace, and stood.

"Nothing can be resolved in a day, Sage."

"So what do we do?"

I grinned. "We eat breakfast."

•••

I didn't want to leave, worried that if I did Sage would disappear like a thought just out of reach. I needed her.

I loved her.

When her hand lingered on my shoulder and she leaned into my mouth, I swallowed the words and almost choked on them. They didn't go down easy. I touched her hair and then left.

The winter day was crisp but clear as I walked to my studio. Grabbing my mandolin, I went into the café, ate a croissant, and washed it down with an espresso. I played until late afternoon. As I packed up, a man in his late twenties approached me.

"You're good," he said in an Irish lilt.

I looked at him. "Thanks, but why did you speak to me in English?"

The man gestured to my University of Tennessee baseball cap. I wondered if I should start carrying around a hotdog, so I could drive home the point that no one could be more American than me.

"Dorian," the man introduced, and I shook his hand. "A friend of mine and I have a band. Wondering if you wanted to jam with us."

"Two man band? What kind of music?"

Dorian grinned. "Irish, of course."

"Of course," I said with a smile.

"I play the guitar, and Finn plays the fiddle. I thought a mandolin might be a nice addition."

I didn't have to think about it. "Sounds like a good time."

"Do you know McCool's on *La Rue du Commerce*? We jam there. Patrons are pretty forgiving, especially on the weekend. You free tonight?"

"I am."

"Seven sound good?"

"Sure."

•••

I wander through the forest, the sound of trickling water reaching my ears. Leaves crunch under my feet and my hands are cold as I shove them into pockets. The trees are slick with frost, but the familiar noises I associate with nature don't exist. No chirping birds, no humming insects—only my breath. When I come to the clearing, I stop.

"About time you got here," Reece says.

"Sorry, this is a new path."

"You were annoyed that we kept meeting at the lake."

"True. This is a nice change of scenery." I take a seat next to my old friend, blood turning to ice—my heart is in danger of bursting. "Were you afraid?"

"Of death?"

I shake my head. "Of life."

"The unknown scares you, doesn't it?" Reece hops off the rock and walks around barefoot, the cold not affecting him.

"What's the point of it all?" I ask him.

"Going all existentialist on me?"

I laugh. "It's been on my mind lately."

"Tell me about the girl."

"Sage."

"Tell me about Sage. She's different, isn't she?"

"Very."

"So you meet this woman, and suddenly you're wondering what life is about?"

I breathe deeply. "I feel like I've found someone special, and I'm worried she's going to leave me."

"You're allowed to be happy. Don't waste time worrying about things you can't control."

"Is that what I'm doing?" My tone is callous.

"Just live, Kai."

Chapter 14

Sage

I couldn't stop the grin from spreading across my face as I stepped into the Irish pub. It looked like a bar straight out of Dublin, yet it was nestled in the Old Square of *Tours* in the heart of the Loire Valley.

I was ordering a glass of Bushmills when I felt a body sidle up next to me. Swiveling my head, I smiled. "Hello, stranger."

Kai greeted me by pulling me close and running his hand along my jaw. His blue-gray eyes were flinty with promise. Our familiarity knew no bounds—eyes and bodies spoke when words weren't enough.

"I wondered when you'd show up. We're almost ready to go on."

I looked past him towards the two men on stage. I had met Dorian and Finn a week ago; they were charming Irishmen with easy smiles. The crowd was growing eager, and I didn't want to keep him. "Maybe I should find a seat?"

He winked. "I found a spot for you, come on."

Grabbing my drink, I followed. He sat me at a small table off to the side of the stage so I would have a perfect view of the band. I kissed him and whispered, "Break a leg."

While the musicians were tuning their instruments, my gaze wandered around the bar. A young man with a group of friends peered at me with unconcealed interest. I broke eye contact, focusing my attention on Kai. I was grateful when the music started.

Kai's smile brought a pool of tears to my eyes—I felt his joy. This moment, this happiness, was all for him. Was this how he looked when he was fishing, or when he was with his two best friends, who were now gone? When we were together, did he feel the same way?

The band played a fast paced jig, and the crowd roared in delight. Dorian, the singer, had a strong, clear voice. Throughout their set, Kai's gaze would find mine and linger, making me warm all over.

In the middle of a song, I rose to fetch another drink. I attempted to catch the bartender's attention, but he was busy flirting with a blonde at the other end of the bar.

"Buy you a drink?"

I turned to the voice—it was the young man who'd been watching me. He was tall and thin, with a wide, crooked smile. His brown eyes looked their fill, and liked what they saw.

"No, thanks," I dismissed.

"You have a boyfriend?"

"Yes." It was a lie. Kai and I hadn't talked about it, but even if we had, Kai didn't encompass the word—he was more, but I wasn't ready to admit that to myself, let alone to a stranger.

"I don't believe you."

"Your choice."

"Let me buy you a drink," he insisted.

"I'm just here to enjoy the music."

"Dinner then—let me take you to dinner."

His persistence annoyed me. Resolute that I wouldn't be able to get another drink, I went to leave, but the man grabbed me by my upper arms. "What the hell?" I yelled, attempting to fight him off. He kissed me, and I gagged on the taste of beer and street vendor food.

The young man pulled back, looking pleased with himself even as he swayed, barely able to stand upright. "Now you want to go out with me, don't you?"

The band played on, but the sounds of Kai's mandolin were suddenly absent. Before I could register why, a fist came out of nowhere and collided with the Frenchman's jaw. My head whipped around to find Kai shaking out his hand and cursing under his breath. The drunken Frenchman slumped against the bar, his tongue lolling in his head. I might have found it comical if I hadn't been in outright shock.

The bartender started yelling for us to leave, and I managed to coerce Kai out of the pub before the Frenchman's friends came after us. "What the hell were you thinking?" I demanded, my voice booming across the cobblestones.

"I wasn't."

"Clearly." I glared at him. "I was about to slap his face."

"Really?" Kai raised his eyebrows, the set of his shoulders taut with anger.

"Really. I know you're Southern, but *come on*."

"His lips were on yours," Kai said through a clenched jaw.

"I'm well aware of that fact, and I didn't like it any more than you did."

He took a step closer to me, his face harsh, almost grotesque in the moonlight. "Don't pretend to be offended by what I've done. Do us both a favor and admit you liked it—liked me fighting for you."

"Fuck you!"

He yanked me into his arms and kissed me. The breath left my body, and I wrapped myself around him, hating him for speaking the truth, and hating myself for knowing it. I shoved him away and wiped my mouth with the back of my hand, as if I could remove the taste of him. I had pieced a life together around a man, and I hadn't been aware I'd done it. I'd stopped thinking of Kai as something temporary. When had it all changed?

He took my chin in his hand, compelling me to look at him. Kai with a steady gaze was more unnerving than Kai with unknowable intensity. Unable to say all the things I wanted to, I said instead, "You're were supposed to be a seed and blow where the wind carried you. You weren't supposed to stay."

"I wish you'd show me what you write in those journals. The ones you talk to when you can't talk to me."

"Why?"

"I want to know you."

"You know me fine."

His stare was unflinching. "I want to know your heart, and I think you put it in those pages."

I took a deep breath and forced myself to admit, "I'm not some great mystery, Kai. My mother's death wrecked me, and I barely survived. You'll wreck me, too. Maybe forever."

"You think I'll continue to wander, don't you?"

"When was the last time you felt the urge to stay?"

"I've never spent more than one night with the same woman. Don't you get that?"

I couldn't tell him he was a love ballad, a song that would play in my blood long after he'd left me for someone else.

"I need some ice," he muttered.

"Don't you have to go back in there and continue?"

"I effectively ended the set. Besides, I don't think I can flex my fingers to play."

We began to walk in the direction of my cottage.

"You're falling in love with me," he stated, putting his arm around my shoulder. "That's why you're upset. Not because I punched some guy who deserved it."

I didn't reply because I wasn't falling in love— I'd crashed into it, and it gripped me in an unyielding embrace.

I was already there.

•••

Kai was on the couch, cradling his hand in his lap while I filled a bag with ice. Handing it to him, I sat and stared into the blazing fire I'd lit upon arriving home. The bottle of bourbon on the coffee table was open; we didn't bother with glasses. I took a swallow out of it and then handed it to him.

"It's a good thing people can't die from guilt," he said.

"You don't have to feel guilty anymore—I forgive you for treating me like a trophy." My tone was full of brevity.

He grinned in sardonic humor. "I'm not talking about that." He took a long drink from the bottle. "I was supposed to be in the plane."

"What? What are you talking about?"

Kai was silent for so long, I didn't know if he'd speak again. "It was a little two-seater, and Tristan was flying. We were celebrating because he'd gotten his pilot's license. I won *rock, paper, scissors*, but Reece looked so depressed I let him go instead of me."

"Holy shit," I whispered.

Flames danced in his eyes as he leaned over and pressed his lips to my throat, saying words against my skin. "Please don't leave me out here alone. Let me in."

I placed a hand on his chest, the steady beating of his heart solid and reassuring. Kai covered my hand with his and then brought it to his lips. My breath hitched, and I tried to hide my tears, but they came and I couldn't stop them. "I already have, Kai."

He pulled me to him. "Damn, what you do to me."

"Do you regret leaving?"

"I regret *how* I left."

"What do you mean?"

"I didn't even leave a note. I just…left. Do you judge me for that?" His gaze was open, honest, and he hid nothing, including the blackest parts of himself.

I shook my head. "I'd be seven shades of hypocrite if I did. I haven't spoken to my best friend in weeks. I silence her calls. I ignore her emails."

"Do *you* have any regrets? About leaving New York?"

"No. I left a job that meant nothing. I couldn't stay with Connor and pretend my mother's death didn't change everything," I touched his face, "but you left behind your entire family. How are you supposed to come back from that?"

"I don't know. I don't know who I am anymore," he said, like it was a revelation.

"Would your friends want this? You feeling guilty because you lived and they died?"

"Don't tell me they would have done any better if I had been the one who died. You'll never know them, and they'll never know you."

"Tell me about them. It will only give me a vague idea, but tell me anyway."

He took my hand. "Reece was quiet until you got to know him. He liked to watch things…people. Tristan though—that kid jumped in knee-deep before any of us decided to follow. He got into so much trouble."

"What kind of trouble?"

"He smoked and drank—bought a motorcycle, that sort of thing. Ran around with a bunch of women, but then he fell in love with Lucy."

"Lucy?"

"His wife. Life is so unfair."

"It is," I stated. "How did she manage to get Tristan to settle down?"

Kai laughed; it was the first genuine sound of happiness that had come out of his mouth all evening. "We met Lucy in fourth grade. She was this gangly girl with freckles covering every inch of her face, huge glasses, and hair more orange than red. But she got super hot around the time we were in high school, and she understood Tristan like no one else. She didn't berate him for drinking or smoking, and when he found acceptance in her, he fell hard and fast. I didn't understand it…not until now." He touched my cheek and smiled. "If this is what healing feels like, I'll take it."

I wanted to crawl into him and bury myself. I could no longer hold back the tears.

"Ah, darlin'," he mumbled into my hair, letting me sob out my anguish.

Hope, tinged with despair permeated my voice as I asked, "Do you think we have a chance at happiness? We've both lost so much."

He smiled before capturing my lips, demanding and greedy. We were rough, clawing at each other in zealous passion. It was devastating, so complete, leaving nothing but heated breaths and desire. When we lay together, spent and exhausted, Kai pulled the blanket from the couch over us.

"Tell me," I demanded, knowing he would know what I needed.

"I love you."

His declaration was my salvation.

Chapter 15

Sage

"Where are you going?" I whispered the next morning.

Kai grinned and pressed a kiss to my exposed shoulder. "My, how the tables have turned since we first met."

"I don't know what you're talking about," I teased as I stroked his face. "Don't even think about shaving."

"Yes, ma'am."

"So where *are* you going?"

"I want to track down Dorian and Finn and apologize for last night. See if I ruined our place to jam."

"Can I convince you to shower first?"

He raised an eyebrow. "Will you join me?"

After, I kissed him on the lips and saw him off, then went in search of Luc. We would have to coexist, and I refused to avoid him any longer. I found Armand instead.

"Walk with me," he said. We ambled through vines that were still quiet, still waiting for spring. I rolled my shoulders, wanting to stretch and open like a new flower.

"How are you settling in?"

"It's weird. I feel like I've been here forever."

"Magic of this place," he agreed with a grin. He turned serious. "You can talk to me. I mean, I know it's probably easier with Celia, but I knew your mother, too."

It was a knife to my heart, a reminder that I'd gone on living. I'd told Kai that Tristan and Reece would want him to find peace, find happiness. Would my mother have been any different?

Death was hardest on those left behind.

"Tell me a story about my mother."

"Did she ever tell you about the time she wanted to learn to work in the fields?"

"No, she didn't."

"She got so sunburned, she looked like a crispy chicken."

We laughed, and I sighed knowing I had people to help me remember her.

"Is my son still avoiding you?"

His question jarred me. "You know about that?"

"Celia might have said something, and Luc isn't here."

"Where is he?"

"Visiting friends in *Marseilles*. You didn't notice he was gone?"

My cheeks bloomed. "Ah, I've been sort of…occupied."

"We've noticed. You both should come to dinner tonight."

"Dinner?"

He nodded. "I think it's important we get to know the man you've been spending time with."

"Wow."

"What?"

"I have a family."

Armand grinned. "Whether you want us or not."

"I do want you," I said, not at all surprised to find my eyes burning with emotion. "It's nice to be cared for."

"Not cared for, Sage. Loved."

•••

"This isn't 'meet the parents'," I explained.

"It feels that way," Kai said.

"I don't have parents, remember? But Celia and Armand have become family to me."

"And what am I?"

"Too soon to tell," I lied.

We walked into the kitchen; Celia covered a pot of water with a lid, and Armand sat at the table with a glass of wine.

"Do you ever cook?" I asked Armand, who grinned at the question.

"Not if I can help it." He stood and went to shake Kai's hand. "Get you a glass, Kai?"

"Sure. Thanks."

Celia watched Kai with an unnerving stare, and I had a brief glimpse of what it would have been like if my mother had met him. Mom had barely been able to tolerate Connor. Would she have accepted Kai? Would she have liked him?

The tension grew insurmountable until Celia said, "Kai, how are you at making salads?"

"Can't hurt to give it a try." He went to the sink and washed his hands.

"Stuff's on the counter." Celia's gaze slid to the doorway. "What are you doing here?"

"I live here." Luc sauntered into the kitchen and looked at Kai. After a moment he glanced in my direction and asked, "Can we talk?"

Impeccable timing.

"Please?" he pleaded.

Kai's face was unreadable. Shrugging, I followed Luc into the courtyard. The sun had set and it was cold, so I wrapped my arms around myself and bounced from one foot to the other.

"I'm sorry, I've been an ass."

"Yes, you have been," I agreed, "and you've been avoiding me."

"You're happy with him, aren't you?"

"Yes."

"Then I'm glad for you."

"*Really?*"

He shrugged. "Not yet, but I'll get there."

"How long do you expect that to take? Kai's in your kitchen."

"So he is."

"I don't need you to like him, but what about us? Can we be friends?"

His eyes were hopeful. "I didn't blow it?"

"Of course not. We were well on our way. I emoted all over you when I first got here, if you recall. That makes us friends, right?"

He laughed in relief. "Do you mean it?"

"I do. Let's just forget everything, okay?"

"You can do that?"

"Why not? What is there between us, Luc, except friendship? In time, you'll realize I wasn't right for you."

"Don't patronize me."

"I'm not trying to."

We stared at each other, and Luc's shoulders lost their tension.

"Let's go eat. Maybe pretend you like Kai?"

We went back inside to a quiet kitchen. Kai diced vegetables, and the only sound in the room was of the knife hitting the cutting board. Celia enjoyed a glass of wine while Armand rubbed her shoulder.

Luc and Kai stared at one another, not saying a word. My eyes dodged back and forth between the two of them, wondering how things were going to play out. Luc inclined his head, and Kai did the same. I didn't know what it meant, but they seemed to have come to an understanding.

"How long have you been traveling?" Celia asked Kai.

"Couple of years."

"And you've been in France how long?" Armand pried.

Somehow I'd acquired surrogate parents. I smiled into my wine.

"Close to two months now."

"Plan to stick around?" Luc wondered.

Kai glared.

"I'm asking as a friend," Luc defended. "Sage has had a rough go of it. I don't want her hurt."

I raised my eyebrows and looked at Kai inquisitively.

Kai took my hand and grinned. "Just try and get rid of me."

•••

"Have time for a quick chat?" Celia asked me the following morning.

"Sure." I poured myself a cup of coffee and sat at the kitchen table. Armand and Luc were running errands around town, and Kai had already left.

"I like Kai," Celia began.

"Oh, boy. I'm sensing a *but*."

"Not a *but*," Celia said with a shake of her head.

"You're worried."

"Concerned."

"Same thing in the eyes of a parent."

"I'm not trying to replace Penny."

"I know."

"But, I've come to know you, Sage. And not just as my friend's daughter. I want to look out for you."

I smiled. "I know."

"This thing with Kai is happening really fast."

"It is."

"You just lost your mother, ended things with a fiancé, and left your entire life behind. Are you ready for this?"

I tapped the rim of my mug. "I've felt more alive in two months with Kai than in one year with Connor." I stood, wanting to put an end to the conversation. I respected Celia, but this was my decision to make. "I know how this looks, but you don't know what's between two people unless you're one of the two. Do you know the things we say to each other late at night? Do you know what it's like to wake up in the morning and feel like you've been given your life back? I do."

"You're angry."

"I'm not," I said, meaning it. "I appreciate everything you have done for me. Letting me come here, giving me your shoulder. But I love him."

"Is he a crutch?"

"I don't know. Maybe. Probably. But my heart went to him before I could consciously give it."

Celia stared at me for a long moment, her eyes full. "Will he hurt you?"

"No."

"How do you know?"

I smiled. "I just do."

•••

We were lying in bed, the clear night shining through the window when Kai said, "I was thinking...I should move in here."

I snorted with laughter.

"What?" he demanded. "The idea of living together is *funny*?"

I laughed harder and threw a hand in the general direction of the corner. "That's your mandolin, right? And those are your pants? When was the last time you went to your studio?"

He laughed, too. "I guess you're right."

"Might as well move in the rest of your things."

"There's not a lot."

"Makes packing easy."

"Can we have a party?" Kai asked.

I turned in his arms and pressed a kiss to his collarbone. "Any kind of party you want."

His lips touched mine. It didn't seem to matter, day or night, I wanted him. I wondered if it would ever wear off.

I hoped it wouldn't.

"Tell me—what kind of foods will we have?"

"Sweet things," he said as he nibbled my shoulder.

"What else," I demanded.

"Will you let me distract you already?" he pleaded, his voice husky.

Desire fizzed under my skin like a thousand champagne bubbles popping.

Later, when he climbed out of bed and went in search of his clothes, I asked, "Where are you going?"

"To get the rest of my things."

"Now?"

He grinned. "There isn't much. I want to live with you, Sage."

"I'm coming, too."

When we were strolling hand in hand towards his studio, I took a deep breath and said, "Smell that?"

"What?"

"It will be spring soon."

"How can you tell?"

I smiled. "I've lived in New York my whole life, I know the scent of snow. There's no bite to the air right now. Spring is close." I felt joyful, young. But when was the last time Kai had been carefree? His guilt tethered him like a kite.

"I can't wait to walk around barefoot," he said. "It's been so long since I've felt the grass between my toes."

"Wild child," I teased.

"You never walk around without shoes?"

"In New York? And get hepatitis?"

We laughed, and it warmed the dark corners of my heart. We arrived at his studio a few minutes later and climbed dingy stairs toward the front door. Kai slid a key into the tattered deadbolt, turned it sharply and eased the door open, letting me through. The refrigerator hummed in the corner of the small kitchen, drawing attention to its chipped, enameled body. Everything was bathed in fluorescent light, and as Kai began to gather his things I realized that this place had never been Kai's home—and he had never wanted it to be. I crossed the room to help him pack and he looked at me, his smile wide and easy. And in that moment, without a word, I knew we were both thinking about starting a new life together.

"What was it like? Living with your fiancé?" Kai asked, jarring me out of my thoughts.

"Why do you want to know?"

"I'm curious about Connor and your life before you came here—tell me about it," he demanded.

"What am I supposed to say?"

"I don't know."

I bit my lip in thought. "I hated his socks and all they stood for. Rigid, confining. When he proposed, I should've broken it off, but I didn't. Instead I complacently accepted him." I stared at Kai, my mouth tight with remembrance. "I don't want to talk about who I was. I was scared to dream. Scared to think I could be different, or have something different. I settled, and I don't want to talk about it."

"It's the flaws that make us truly love someone."

"That's far too poetic, even for me, Kai."

He smiled.

"Can I tell you some things I want you to know?"

Kai nodded.

"I love that we stay awake late into the nights, learning the outlines of one another. I love that I've learned you by touch. I love that the small crinkles at the corners of your despondent, troubadour eyes tell your life story. And when I'm in your arms and you're inside me, I feel a connection deeper than words can describe."

He embraced me as I continued to speak, "I know your heart has been broken, but I want to help you stitch it back together…Will you let me?"

Kai's hands cradled my cheeks as he stared into my eyes. His lips covered mine, and we fell into the moment—and each other.

Chapter 16

Sage

Winter turned to spring, and the grapes in Armand's vineyard ripened. I helped out around the bed and breakfast, deriving a primitive joy from being productive. I didn't think about the future—choosing instead to live in the present, wanting to soak up every experience, every moment.

Most of my reflections found their way into a journal. Every once in a while I'd share something I wrote with Kai before putting it under the mattress, like I had been doing for years. It was the only routine I followed.

One warm May afternoon, I was manning the desk alone when Kai tore into the foyer, animated and happy. "I have a surprise for you. Can you sneak away this weekend?"

It was the sort of spontaneity I'd grown to love. "I don't see why not."

Twenty minutes later, we were packed, seated in a small black rental car, and driving out of the city. "Will you tell me where we're going?"

"Nope."

"Will I like it?"

"Yep."

"How long do I have to wait until I find out?"

"About three-and-a-half hours. Turn on some music."

"What do you want to hear? Jazz? Bluegrass?"

Kai grinned. "How about some Creedence?"

I smiled back. "Perfect road trip music." I peered out the window, enjoying the scenery. The countryside was in bloom, and the lush rolling hills reminded me of a postcard.

"It doesn't look real, does it?" Kai asked.

I glanced at him; he smiled, but his eyes were on the road. "I still can't believe I get to call France home. Is it home for you?"

"Home is wherever you are, Sage. Does that scare you?"

"Not anymore," I admitted. "What are your dreams, Kai?"

"To feel the way I feel right now—forever."

I caught my breath. "And you call me the writer."

He sighed. "I never thought this was going to be my life. I didn't think I deserved this; to feel all I feel for you, to want to laugh and cry in your arms." His throat tightened with emotion.

I brushed tears from my eyes. I could tell he was trying to shake off the heaviness of our conversation. We needed light, so I steered the dialogue somewhere else. "Favorite Ben and Jerry's ice cream flavor?"

"Phish Food. You?"

"Boston Cream Pie."

"Hmm," he said, running his tongue across his lips. "Favorite book?"

"*The Thornbirds*."

"Never read it. What's it about?"

"Forbidden love, for one. The story follows three generations of women. They made it into a really good miniseries."

He snorted with laughter. "I'll read it if you read my favorite book."

"And that is?"

"*A River Runs Through It,* by Norman Maclean."

I smiled in arrogance. "Already read it."

"Have you now?"

"Okay, next question, if you threw a dinner party, who would you invite?"

"Do I have to cook?"

"No."

He furrowed his brow. "Do the guests have to be living, or can they be dead?"

"Either."

"Fictional or real?"

"Just answer the question!" I said in exasperation.

"Captain Hook."

"Captain Hook? *Really?*"

"Yeah, I bet his side of the story is more interesting."

I chuckled.

"How about you?" he asked.

"Wild Bill Hickok. I want to know if he really had a premonition that he was going to die, and if he did, why he didn't try and change his fate."

"Can you really change your fate?"

I shrugged. "I like to believe anything is possible. If you could be Scarecrow, Tin Man, or Lion, who would you pick?"

Kai thought for a moment. "Scarecrow. He has the best song. You're Tin Man though."

"How do you figure?"

"You're all heart."

Three-and-a-half hours later, we reached our destination, and I pressed my nose against the car window. "A vineyard? We *live* on a vineyard!"

"It was Armand's suggestion. Welcome to the *Château La Piolette*."

Kai parked, and we walked into the *château*, where we met the owners, a middle-aged husband and wife, who reminded me of Celia and Armand. It made me wonder about the institution of marriage. Was it another box I tried to fit into? Another lie I'd been told I wanted? I looked at Kai as he conversed with the couple. His smile was deep and hearty. I wanted him, any way I could have him—odd, how that became the only truth I knew.

After we set our bags down in our room, I asked, "What should we do first?"

"We have a few hours before sunset. Want to walk around?"

"Yeah, let's eat and then explore."

He called and requested a picnic basket. We found a pristine spot underneath a large tree, spread out a blanket, and began to unpack. Kai pulled out a small half bottle of wine and twisted off the cap.

We laughed and talked, late afternoon sinking into twilight. Moments like these made me feel suspended in time, like there was no other place I was meant to be. Everything before Kai seemed so far away, so trivial. He heightened all my senses; for the first time, I tasted life, and I wanted to chew it up like a ripe, sweet peach.

My thoughts drifted to Kai's home in Monteagle, wondering what it would be like to go there with him. Would I ever find out? Did I want to? Would he consider returning if I said I'd go with him? Did I have the right to ask?

Wanting to change the direction of my unspoken questions, I leaned in to kiss him, cutting him off in the middle of a word. I knew his lips like they were my own. His hands were in my hair as we strained closer to one another. Desire whirled through me, awakening everything inside—I was consumed and reborn in my passion.

I led him back to our room. I undressed him and ran my fingers along the planes of his body. The sheet was cool beneath my heated skin. I grazed my fingertips along the slope of his back, and his shallow breathing turned heavy. His desirous eyes peered into mine, and I gave a part of myself to him I didn't want back. I cried out as Kai filled me—I wasn't cold, not when he was with me.

Lying in bed with our arms and legs entangled, I closed my eyes. Kai rested his chin on my breastbone. It was dark, and the curtains were pulled back to reveal the face of the moon.

I traced his ear with my finger. "My thoughts and feelings, they're all of you. I'm sad for what I've lost, but knowing I have you makes it bearable—so bearable." I kissed him. "I think we are what ballads are written of, what bards sing of. We are epic, you and I." I sat up and put on a shirt over my naked body.

"What are you doing?"

"Come with me." Holding hands, we walked into the intoxicating evening. Countless stars hung in the net of the endless universe. I picked out Orion, wondering what it would be like to be forever in the sky, watching, waiting.

Kai pulled me into his arms and I placed a hand on his heart, my face in the crook of his neck. "You remind me of this poem I read once," he whispered.

The smell of him was in my nose, my brain smoky with comfort and peace.

"How familiar are you with Yeats?"

"A little."

He told me about "The Song of Wandering Aengus". It was about a man who had caught a silver trout that turned into a beautiful woman. She disappeared, and he spent the rest of his life wandering the hills in search of her.

"That will not be us," I said when he finished. "I will not leave you in the night, and you will not have to look for me."

"It was dark for so long, Sage, but you're my light."

I pressed a kiss in the dip at the base of his collarbone.

"How long will it last?" I asked.

"What do you mean?"

Staring up into his eyes, I wished I could see the stars reflected in them. "The light goes out, Kai. Always."

•••

"Wake up, darlin'." Kai brushed his lips across my cheek as I struggled to open my eyes.

"What time is it?"

"Just before sunrise."

I rolled over and hugged the pillow. "Wake me up in a few hours." I attempted to go back to sleep, but with gentle insistence, Kai tugged on the sheet, so I was nothing more than skin.

"Come watch it with me."

Growling like a bear cub, I searched for his t-shirt. We sat outside, my legs thrown over his while I yawned. The sun crept up, lighting the dew-covered leaves, making them sparkle.

"You are so beautiful when you first wake up," Kai said. "Your skin is flushed and you smell like powdered sugar."

I smiled. "That just tells me that you want a donut in the morning."

We laughed, the air teasing the hair at our temples. After a quick breakfast in the main house, we visited a bee farm, then rented bikes and rode to the small town that hummed with life. We walked hand in hand as timeless lovers.

When we returned to the vineyard it was evening, and a celebration was in full swing. Musicians with guitars and hand drums were playing as people danced. Children ran around, engaging in games and trickery. Bottles of wine were broken out and flowing. Laughter blanketed us in a joyful sound.

His hand was warm and steady at my waist, and I longed to breathe in the scent of him and touch his skin. When the moon was at its zenith, I felt like a fairy woman; my chestnut hair shining in the moonlight, and Kai, my human lover, entranced by my beauty was caught in my magical web. I led him back to our room, needing to possess him and lose myself.

Unable to unbutton his shirt fast enough, I pulled it apart, small white buttons scattering like seeds in the wind. Kai pushed me against the wall, lifted my skirt, and sank into my depths.

I welcomed him home. His hands wove into my hair, and his breathing became labored. As I scraped his back with my nails, I felt the sob of release in my throat. Our hearts beat in a codependent cadence, and still he stayed against me.

Kai looked into my eyes, lifted himself off me, and moved us to the bed. We lay down face to face. "I'm sorry—did I hurt you?"

Shaking my head, I put a hand to his cheek. "I needed you, like I've never needed anything."

He caught my escaping tears with his lips, kissing the corners of my eyes. His voice was a distant magical chant as he said, "You're enough to make me believe there's a God."

I smiled, listening to the night settling down, inhaling the fragrant breeze drifting through the room. I didn't want to move, wishing to remain frozen in time, my lover next to me for all eternity.

•••

"This was a perfect weekend," I said the following morning as we loaded the car. "I'm glad we came. I love living life in the moment."

"You've never done that before, have you?"

I shook my head.

"But you left New York and moved to France."

"That was different—it was not a whim. It was necessary." Kai started the engine and I buckled myself in and said, "It's how you live your life, though, isn't it?"

He shrugged. "For a while, it was the easiest thing to do. No demands, go where I wanted, when I wanted."

"Do you ever plan?"

"I planned this trip, sort of. What would you do if money was no object?"

"Money isn't really an object for me. My mom did okay as a writer, you know, and she left me everything. And I haven't figured out what I want in life."

"No?"

"Have you?" I asked.

"Can't say that I have," he admitted.

"You and me. That's it, that's all that matters."

"You don't want more?"

"More what? I had the career and the guy. Both were the *right* ones, I guess, but I'd lie awake at night feeling empty. I didn't know what I was supposed to do about it, so I did nothing."

"What about writing?" he asked. "You ever going to pursue it?"

"I don't know. It's all wrapped up with my mother. Like my talent is tainted. What happens if I give in?"

"What happens if you don't?"

I was silent as I pressed my head to the window. "I used to laugh at all those women who wanted nothing more than a house, a husband, and kids. I thought they weren't ambitious, and I could never understand why they thought that stuff was enough. Now I'm thinking they might be on to something. It's the simple things, isn't it? When your days are spent laughing and loving, what more is there? What are we supposed to need?"

"If your mother hadn't died, would you feel this way?"

I shrugged. "I don't know."

"I've been wandering for years. I have no drive, no ambition except for the next beautiful place, the next breath of peace."

I stared at him, and a missing key of understanding sank into its lock. "You come from money, don't you? Serious money. That's what this is about?"

He nodded, his mouth full of resentment. "Are you angry?"

"Why would I be? It explains how you've been able to travel the world without worry."

"I didn't share it with you. Should I have told you sooner?"

I shook my head. "I don't think so."

"It doesn't change anything for you?"

I smiled. "It doesn't change how I see you."

"Coming from a family with money is such a burden. There was always this expectation that I had to do something with my life. Go to law school, become a doctor—live the dream my parents hoped would come true for me."

"You never wanted that life?"

"No. Not before Tristan and Reece died, and definitely not after."

"Strange, how you recognized it for what it was. I never saw things clearly. My mother always wanted more from me—for me to publish my works, but I didn't see it like you did." I was thoughtful. "Are you ever going to face your family?"

"Don't call me a coward."

"I wasn't."

"You were."

"I don't think you're a coward," I insisted, "but you've got to deal with this, Kai. If you don't, it's going to swallow you—swallow us. Is that what you want?"

"I didn't know I could live again. *You* make me live again." He paused. "Marry me."

"*What?*" I asked, startled. "You don't mean that."

"I do," he said. Then in a stronger voice he said again, "Marry me." He pulled over onto the side of road and cut the engine. With an intense look, a fire in his eyes, he dragged me to him, his fingers in my hair, and his mouth close to mine. "I can face anything knowing I have you. I *will* face it," he vowed. "Marry me, Sage."

I traced his jaw with a finger. The stubble was rough, like the sandpapery tongue of a feline. Tears welled in my eyes.

I nodded, and Kai smiled deeply. It was pure, effortless, like I had given him the world.

Chapter 17

Sage

"What was your wedding to Connor going to be like?" Kai asked, later that night when we were in bed.

I sighed and snuggled into his arms. "Big, grandiose. It was supposed to be on Long Island."

"That doesn't sound like you."

"It wasn't."

"What kind of wedding *do* you want?"

"Small, and over fast."

He chuckled. "Think I'm going to run?"

"It actually has nothing to do with you. A wedding isn't what's important. It's the marriage."

"Wise words. Are you going to invite Jules?"

"I don't know; I haven't spoken to her since I got here. Do I want the first conversation to be, 'Hey, I'm getting married, and, no, I'm not crazy'?"

"Valid point, but she is your best friend."

"I want to be happy on my wedding day, Kai. I'm not sure I can be if Jules comes. I don't want to have to explain myself. Even to her."

"I can understand that. What happens when she finds out, though? After the fact?"

"I'll deal with it, but for now, I want to revel in us, and continue to shut out the world."

"You're a bad influence," he teased.

"Let's hope."

"Were you planning to take Connor's last name?"

"Yes."

"Are you taking mine?"

Reaching up, I stroked his hair. "Yes."

"Would your mom be mad about that?"

"No. She took my dad's name. Even though she already had a successful writing career by then." I laughed in wry humor.

"What?"

"I'm thinking about a fight we had—she told me to publish under a different name if I didn't want to be associated with her. I can do that now, if I ever…" I shook my head and kissed his brand. "Irony, huh? Life's a satire."

"A series of them," he agreed.

•••

We were married a week later, standing among the vines and tucked away in a pocket of serenity. I wore a simple white gown, the sun heating my skin, a crown of dandelions resting on my head—it was a crown of wishes yet to be made.

The lines around Kai's eyes wrinkled as he smiled, and I envisioned how he'd look in middle age. It was a moment of my life I'd remember forever—those lines would become deeper and more meaningful as the years went on, like a mountain pass forged by a river.

Kai clasped my hands and vowed to be my roof out of the rain, to keep me going when I didn't have the strength, and to be everything to me when I felt like I had nothing.

Only Luc, Celia, and Armand attended. When we toasted to our marriage, Kai and I looked at one another and silently gave tribute to those we'd lost. This day that meant so much to us was tinged with unspoken sadness, the beauty of our marriage smudged with darkness like the corners of an old photograph.

We sat outside at the table that had been set with simple china. I touched Kai's hand, loving that when we retired for the night, I would be sleeping next to my husband.

"I found something, and I'd like you to have it," Celia said when the wine bottles were empty and day descended into night.

It was a discolored Polaroid placed in a thin black frame, a portrait of my mother and Celia in their early twenties. The girls had their arms around each other's shoulders, looking jubilant, hopeful, before they knew what life would throw at them. In the background was the vineyard.

"You said no presents," Celia remarked as I continued to stare at it, "but I found this in an old shoe box."

I looked at Celia, who peered at me like a mother. "Thank you."

"She would be proud of you for living your life and finding love."

I was about to answer, but emotion gripped my throat, so all I did was nod.

"Sage?" Kai called. "You ready?"

Embracing Celia, I closed my eyes. I wished Mom had lived long enough to see this milestone. But if she had, would I even be here, or would I be married to someone else, trapped in a life of my own foolish, rebellious making? Something to think about—later, when I was ready.

We walked into the cottage, breathing in the night air wafting through the windows. I set the frame on the mantle, took off my wreath of wishes, and placed it next to the photo.

"You look like her," Kai commented.

"I know." I smiled. "Genes don't lie."

"I'm sorry she couldn't be here."

"I'm sorry they couldn't be here, either."

I reached for him, not wanting to think about our pasts and all we'd lost. I wouldn't think about our future either—I only needed time in the present, because it too, would flee from us before we were ready. "Take me to bed, Kai."

He did exactly that.

•••

"Good morning, darlin'," Kai whispered.

I rolled over, my arms encircling him. I snuggled into his chest and kissed his skin.

"Morning," I answered, opening my eyes and smiling. "We got married yesterday, didn't we?"

He looked smug. "Yep. Tricked ya; now, you're mine."

I laughed as he pressed his lips to my ear and then moved his way to my mouth. "We get to do this every morning," I said.

"How lucky are we?"

"Promise not to get sick of me?"

"Stupid promise to make, Sage. I could never get sick of you."

"You say that now, when we're fresh and new. What happens after fifty years? You may hope to go deaf so you never have to listen to me," I teased. He ran a hand across my body, making me tingle from his touch. I wanted him to sink into me and stay, so we'd never be separated again.

"Fresh and new are for others. Others without pasts, others without heartache. You and I, we're old already. We'll grow older still—and maybe a little wiser."

"Do you feel wise now?" I asked. "Can I borrow some of that wisdom?"

He raised an eyebrow. "Married you, didn't I? That may be the wisest thing I've ever done."

•••

"Go to Paris for a few days," Celia said.

"Maybe."

"You should have a honeymoon—even if it is a short one."

"We live in France. Every day is a honeymoon," I said with a laugh. "When was the last time you went on a vacation?"

"Valid point."

"I'm enjoying living in the present. If we go on a honeymoon, we'll just pack and head to the airport and decide our destination when we get there."

Late that afternoon, Celia left to begin dinner preparation. I was getting ready to head back to the cottage and wait for Kai, who was helping Luc and Armand around the vineyard. The front door of the bed and breakfast opened. I looked at the entrance, expecting to see guests returning for fruit and wine.

I gasped.

Jules' long, black curls were cut into a bob, and her blue eyes stared at me with resolute intensity.

"What are you doing here?" I gaped like a fish.

"Some greeting after five months of no communication." Jules crossed her arms over her small frame.

"Sage?" Kai called as he came into the lobby from the back.

Jules' gaze snapped to Kai, who was covered in sweat and dirt. "Who's this?"

"Kai," he said, putting out his hand. He looked at it, saw the grime, and pulled it back.

"Kai, this is Jules."

"*Jules* Jules?"

I nodded. "This is Kai."

Jules rolled her eyes. "Yes, I know, he already introduced himself."

"My husband."

The ticking of the grandfather clock let me know time passed, even as Jules continued to watch me in mute horror.

Kai made an instinctive and hasty retreat.

"*Husband?*" Jules squeaked. "You got *married*? To a fucking stranger?"

"He's not a stranger," I said, my voice rising.

"What did you do—marry the first guy you got into bed with?"

My hand reared back, and I slapped Jules across the cheek hard. I didn't know who was more surprised. I looked at my palm, wondering if it had found a mind of its own. My gaze snapped to Jules, and my voice shook when I said, "You don't know shit. Don't pretend otherwise." I turned to stalk out of the room.

"Sage Eleanor Harper. Stop. Right. There."

"My last name is Ferris, and what have I told you about calling me by my full name?" I yelled, spinning around. I didn't care if anyone heard us.

"You slapped me!" Jules bellowed, a bright red handprint across her face. "You fucking slapped me!"

"Why are you here?"

"What reason do you want? You wouldn't answer my emails or calls, so I came, knowing you'd have to talk to me if I got in your face. And then you *slapped* me. Who the fuck are you right now?"

I didn't want to explain myself, so I said nothing.

"Have you told Connor?"

"Why would I tell him anything?"

"You don't think you owe him any sort of explanation?"

"No, I don't."

"How long have you been married?"

"Stop hurling questions at me!"

"Answer me!"

I felt weary and defeated. "Few days."

Jules' voice softened, "Can we do this sitting down?"

"You think I'd invite you into my home? Now?"

"I flew across an ocean to see you."

"I didn't ask you to do that."

"Just…let's sit down. Please?"

Once we were seated in the cottage, two glasses of bourbon poured but untouched, Jules said, "I can't believe you got married. I can't believe you got married without *me*."

I heard the distress in her voice; it cleared the last of the anger from my mind. "I'm sorry."

"Are you?"

"Yes. I didn't do it to hurt you." I was adamant. "And I'm sorry about the slap."

"I deserved it—I was mean."

"Astute of you." I smiled and took a sip of my drink.

"Was marrying Kai another one of your so-called symptoms? Are you still reeling?"

"*This*—this is why I didn't invite you. You think I'm broken and damaged, and moving to France was a mistake." Jules opened her mouth to speak, but I silenced her with a hand. "Don't bother. I'm well aware of how this looks. I didn't want to hear it—not from you. I still don't."

Upstairs, the bathroom door opened, and Kai's footsteps echoed across the wooden floor. I looked up as if I could see him through the ceiling. A smile with a volition of its own drifted across my face, like a puffy white cloud making its way in the blue sky.

"Holy shit."

My attention snapped back to my friend, and the smile faded from my lips. "What?"

"You're really in love with him—in a way you never were with Connor."

I paused. "Yes."

Jules stood, walked to the mantle, and stared at the photograph. "Is this Penny?"

"And Celia, from days gone by."

"She'd be happy—that you married Kai after such a short time."

"You think?"

"She was always worried you'd find yourself trapped in a loveless marriage. Worried you loved the idea of security more than you'd love the man you chose. She would've approved of you marrying for love."

"Kai and I, we're real."

She caressed the drying dandelion crown.

"I wore that at my wedding," I said.

"You *are* different. New York Sage would never have worn such a thing."

"New York Sage wouldn't have done a lot of things."

Jules took up residence in the chair again and said nothing. When Kai came down the stairs, he seemed hesitant. I scooted over on the couch, making room for him and patted the seat cushion. He sat next to me, lending his silent support. I curled into his side and then looked at Jules, who watched us with keen interest.

"I don't forgive you, you know," Jules said, pretending Kai wasn't there. "For ignoring me these past few months, and for not inviting me to your wedding."

"But you understand?" I asked.

"Yes."

"I apologize, but I stand by my decisions."

Jules nodded. "Okay then."

"I'm glad you're here."

"No, you're not."

"I am," I said, "but I was afraid."

"Of what?"

"I thought if I saw you, I'd feel my mother's death all over again."

Jules picked up her glass of bourbon on the rocks and took a sip. "This is terrible."

"Careful," I warned. "You've got a Southerner sitting not five feet from you." Jules held the cold glass to her cheek, but I was the one who winced. "I'm a shit."

"Yep, my cheek is throbbing."

"You deserved it."

"Yeah, I did."

"You guys act like you're sisters," Kai noted.

Jules and I laughed. "You have no idea," we said at the same time, and then laughed again.

The three of us talked long into the night. After a few hours, Kai stood up and kissed me on the forehead, leaving Jules and me alone.

"More tea?" I asked, grabbing our cups. We had switched from bourbon to avoid getting too drunk.

"Sure," Jules said, looking thoughtful. "Your life is here now, isn't it?"

I nodded as I filled our mugs with hot water.

"What about Kai?"

"What about him?"

"Will he ever visit his family?"

"I don't know. I won't force him."

When we were too tired to carry on, I made up the couch and Jules settled down for the night. I crept upstairs and slid in bed next to Kai, who snored lightly. In his sleep, he wrapped his arm around me and patted my rump. I smiled, scooted closer and fell asleep.

Chapter 18

Sage

The following morning, we took Jules to the main house and introduced her to the Germains. Celia insisted on making a breakfast that lasted until lunch. Armand left to tend to the vines, but Luc lingered, and I didn't miss the interested glances in Jules' direction. It reinforced what I already knew; Luc had never had any real feelings for me. If she found him charming and interesting, then I'd give them my blessing. Every woman needed to have at least one torrid love affair while in France.

"Where are we going first?" Jules demanded after we finished eating.

"How about a tour of the vineyard?" Luc asked.

Jules smiled and took his arm. "Lead the way, and thanks for speaking English for my benefit."

I watched Luc guide Jules outside and then glanced at my husband. "That looks promising."

"I'm glad he's over you."

I stifled my laughter. "There was nothing to get over. Not really."

"Didn't he go to Italy for two weeks because you shot him down?"

"Jealousy becomes you," I teased. "Luc didn't know any better."

Kai looked thoughtful. "I bet Connor is still tortured."

I sighed. "Do you think Jules is right? Should I contact him?"

"Do you respect what you had together, even though it didn't work out?"

"I suppose so."

"There's no good way to tell him, but yeah, I think he deserves to know. If a woman I loved broke off our engagement, moved across an ocean, and remarried before the year mark, I'd be a wreck."

"*Any* woman, or a specific woman?"

He looked at me. "You. He's not the same after you; he can't be."

I smiled. "Are you the same?"

"Not even a little bit."

"Did I make you a better version of yourself?"

"Maybe," he joked. "Maybe even the best version of myself. How do you like that?"

Sighing, I tugged on his arm. "Come on, let's catch up with them."

"Think they'll do something crazy?" Kai gestured with his chin.

"Who knows?"

"How did you guys forgive each other so easily after not speaking for so long?"

"How did you and your friends handle stuff?"

"We punched each other."

"Well, I did slap her, but I apologized. I guess, sometimes, friendship is more than just years of history."

After the tour of the vineyard, we hopped into Luc's compact car and drove to downtown *Tours*. We walked around the Old Square, eating gelato, and Kai pointed out the Irish pub where he played.

"Will I get to see you in action?" Jules asked.

Kai smiled. "Absolutely."

Before the sun set we ducked into a café, squeezed ourselves around a small table and ordered two bottles of wine.

"How is it that the table wine in France is better than most wines in the U.S.?" Jules wanted to know.

"Because Americans don't know the first thing about wine. Among other things," Luc said with a grin.

"Your mother is American," Jules pointed out.

"But she married a Frenchman and became an expatriate."

"Touché."

Kai whispered to me, "I bet you five bucks he'll get her into bed by the end of the week."

I turned my head, my lips grazing his ear. "You kidding? She'll get *him* into bed by the end of the night."

Kai pretended to be scandalized. "You New Yorkers move really fast."

I put a hand on his leg and grinned. "*We* move fast? When did *you* propose?"

"Point taken."

•••

Three days later, we were in McCool's watching Kai and his band play. A smattering of empty glasses sat in front of us, attesting to the length of time we'd been there. I had a nice buzz going, and I was getting itchy feet, wanting to dance.

"Your husband is kind of hot," Jules commented.

"Tell me about it," I said.

"You know, I'm sitting right here," Luc said, his arm around Jules. She looked up, smiled, and moved closer to him.

I grinned into my pint of cider. I'd been right about their timeline for getting together. Jules was only in town for another week, and there hadn't been time to wait—Luc wasn't complaining. I was happy for them, and I wondered if it would turn into something more permanent.

When the band stopped for a break, Kai sat down next to me and took a drink from my glass.

"You guys are good," Jules commented.

"Thanks."

"Do you plan on doing anything with it?" she pressed.

"Doing anything? I don't follow."

"Is this for fun, or are you hoping it goes somewhere?"

"God, you New Yorkers are so driven, aren't you?" Kai laughed. "Whatever happens, happens."

"How Southern of you." Jules stood up. "I need another drink."

"I'll come with you." Luc trailed after her.

"Ah, drive. I wonder what that feels like," Kai joked.

"I'm not sure it's all that it's cracked up to be," I answered.

"What do you mean?"

"Driven people always want more. They never know contentment."

"You sure about that?"

I smiled. "Nope."

I thought of my mother. She hadn't been happy unless she was writing, and even then her happiness was tainted with frustration and insecurity, wondering if she was going in the right direction. Maybe there was no *right* direction, only forward.

Jules and Luc returned, and I kicked Kai out of the booth. "I want to dance," I said. "So make it a quick jig."

Grinning, he rose. "Whatever you say, ma'am." He touched the brim of his hat, sauntered to the stage, and picked up his instrument. I stood and chugged the last of my pint.

"What are you doing?" Jules asked, when I grabbed her hand and tugged her towards the floor, forcing her to relinquish her newly acquired drink.

"We're dancing," I informed her.

"Who the hell *are* you?" she shouted over the din of music, but she was smiling. "You hate dancing!"

"Not anymore."

Jules must have learned her lesson—she no longer asked questions about my newfound sense of crazy, she just went along with it. The crazy wasn't going anywhere.

•••

I dropped the letter into the mailbox before I could think better of it. I sighed, wondering how it would change Connor's life. I hoped it liberated him.

"He'll appreciate the gesture," Jules said, linking her arm through mine. We walked to a café for a quick bite alone before Luc drove Jules to Charles de Gaulle for her evening flight.

"You think? After he reads it, there's a very good chance he'll be performing Voodoo on a doll that looks like me." We settled into chairs, and I ordered for us in rapid French. "I'm sure he gave up thinking he'd hear from me ever again."

"Ah, no, he hasn't." Jules stared at a spot on the table, running her thumbnail in a groove of a wood seam.

"You talk to him, don't you?"

Jules continued to evade my gaze. "Every now and then. He's called to ask if I've spoken to you."

"You told him I'd come back, didn't you? That's why you've been on my ass to contact him."

"I'm sorry," Jules said, finally looking at me. The waiter dropped off our coffees. Jules reached for her cup, took a hasty sip, and then made a noise.

"Scald your tongue?"

"Little bit." Jules sighed. "What did you say in the letter?"

I rubbed a tired hand across my face. It had been a late night, but after everyone else had gone to sleep, I picked up a pen and wrote to my ex-fiancé, thinking uncomfortable words might be easier to write in the dark. Turns out it wasn't the dark that helped, but the liquor.

"I'm not sure it was entirely coherent," I admitted. "There was an apology woven in there—about breaking the engagement, but I also wrote that I should never have accepted his proposal in the first place."

"Oh, Sage…"

"Yeah, I was a little too honest, maybe. I told him he was a wonderful person, and he would make someone else very happy—though hopefully it wasn't as generic as all that."

"Did you tell him about Kai?"

"I told him I found someone, but not that I got married. I didn't think it would be nice to clobber him with that information. Maybe that can come later."

"You mean from me?"

"If you're so inclined. I'm sure he'll contact you as soon as he gets the letter."

"I'm sorry for this mess, for making him think you were just on a bender and you'd return to your senses."

I waved my hand, dismissing Jules' apology. "How were you to know? How were any of us to know? I should've contacted him long before now."

"Can I change the subject?"

"Please."

"Luc wants me to come back. Maybe at the end of summer. Is it okay that I'm with him? He told me he had thing for you when you first came here."

I smiled. "It was fleeting and nonexistent. He's a good guy, and you're a better fit for him. You both have the same outlook on life. You get each other. Just makes sense, y'know?"

"You mean that?"

"I do. Without a shadow of a doubt."

We finished our meals, and when it was time for Jules to leave, Luc loaded her bags into his car and got in to start the engine. Jules hugged Kai goodbye and whispered something in his ear that made him nod solemnly. I opened the passenger door and then put my arms around my oldest friend.

"You better email and call more, or I'll fly back over here just to kick your ass," Jules threatened.

"I promise." As they drove away, Kai and I watched them disappear down the road towards Paris.

"Everything okay?" Kai asked, rubbing a hand across my back.

"I miss her."

"She'll be back."

"I know."

"We can visit her in New York. Any time you want."

"You're so good to me."

He smiled, but it was sad. "I know what it's like to have friends that mean the world to you."

"Things are changing, aren't they?"

Kai took my hand and squeezed it. "Haven't they changed already?"

I squeezed back. "Yes. I suppose they have."

•••

"Happy Birthday, Sage," Kai whispered. The windows were thrown wide open, and the June country air swirled around the room. After a light supper of fruit, bread and cheese, we had gone to bed but not to sleep. We had stayed awake, laughing and talking, not caring that dawn was close.

I snuggled deeper into his arms, relishing the feel of his warm skin beneath my cheek. "Twenty-seven. Wow."

"Do you feel old?"

"No. I feel like I'm getting younger. Is that weird?"

"Kind of. You ready for your present?"

"You didn't have to get me anything." Kai moved, and I groaned. "Come back." I heard the bedside table drawer open and the clanking of metal, and then Kai handed me a set of brass keys. Sitting up, I looked at him for an explanation. "What are these for?"

"I bought us a house."

My eyes widened. "*You bought us a house*—just like that?"

His smile faltered. "I wanted to surprise you."

"You bought a house? Without even consulting me?" No matter how many times I repeated it, I couldn't believe it. I shot out of bed and reached for my clothes. "I want to see it. Now." People didn't just buy a house on a whim, but Kai was a whim kind of man. I loved that about him—but a house?

Kai didn't argue. We borrowed Celia's car and drove in silence for twenty minutes before pulling up in front of a modest stone farmhouse. Most of it was swaddled in darkness.

I strolled to the quaint, red front door and touched the golden lion knocker, curious about my new home. Using my shiny new key, I stepped into the foyer, fumbled for a light switch and watched as the hallway blazed to life.

I ambled through the house, learning it like a lover. Kai followed at a discreet distance, allowing me time. I ran my hands over the whitewashed walls of the living room, noticing the open feel of the home. I went into the modern kitchen and marveled that it didn't detract from the rustic beauty of the rest of the house. Opening the back door of the kitchen, I saw moonlight glinting off a small lake and watched grass dance in the gentle summer breeze.

I took the spiral stairs to the second floor turret and found a large bay window that overlooked the property. It was the perfect room to write. Writing for me was inevitable now, like taking my next breath. To keep denying it would be to deny myself. Maybe I would get a typewriter, an old one. It would mean more when I finished whatever I decided to create. I would feel like I'd earned it through each punch of a sticky key.

When I came to the master bedroom, I pulled open the French doors and went out onto the balcony, cool predawn air caressing my skin. I sat on the stone floor, stretching my legs out. Kai crouched next to me.

"It's—"

I held up a hand, willing him silent. We sat in quietude, long enough for our bodies to grow numb, but still we didn't move.

By the time the sun crept up on the horizon, I had managed to find my voice. "The sky looks different here—it's golden. No, not golden exactly, butterscotch. And lavender, the color of cotton candy." I smiled in whimsical thought.

"Sage?"

"It's perfect." My voice turned to a muffled whisper. "You didn't ask me because you knew this house was perfect for us—it's a dream."

Moments we hadn't had yet flashed in my mind. Making love by the fireplace on cold winter nights; Kai standing in the doorway of the nursery while I watched him soothe our child in his arms. And years later, his temples stained gray with age and wisdom as he chased our children around the lake. Would five be too many?

"Do you want kids?" I blurted out.

He looked at me. "I think so, but I never thought much about it."

"I know we should've probably talked about this sooner, long before we got married."

"I always assumed I would, but it was a vague idea. What about you?"

"I thought I had a lot of living to do before I made that happen. The idea used to terrify me."

"And now?"

I shrugged.

"I'll give you anything you want. Making you happy is my reason for living." He took my hand and brought it to his lips. "Let's make a baby."

I inhaled a shaky breath. "We already have—I'm pregnant."

•••

We drove back to the cottage in silence, the shock of my news infusing the air. It wasn't until we tumbled back into bed and held each other that he spoke.

"How far along are you?"

"Six weeks." I sighed.

"Why didn't you tell me sooner?"

"I wanted to be sure. I didn't plan this."

He laughed and laughed until he cried.

"What?" I demanded. "What's so funny?"

"You and me. Flying by the seat of our pants. Of course this would happen to us."

"You're unhappy about it, aren't you?"

He shook his head, pulling me close, so I couldn't leave. "No, I'm sorry, darlin'; you misunderstand. Did you plan to marry a man you'd only known for a few months?"

"What does that have to do with anything?"

"Look at our relationship up until this point. Should I really be surprised you're pregnant?"

"I didn't trap you, I swear—"

"Oh, is that what you think this about?"

I nodded.

"I know you'd never do something like that."

I exhaled in relief.

"Things change all the time, Sage."

I looked up into his eyes; they were soft with emotion though there was nothing soft about him.

His hand touched my belly. "I didn't think my life could be this full. It all seems possible, now."

"What does?" I asked.

"Everything."

•••

We moved into the farmhouse that week. I sat on the bank of our property, my bare feet in the cool water of the lake. Tilting my face up to the sky, I felt the sunbeams mark me. I could already feel my skin turning pink, but I didn't care. Let the perfect day stain my body.

"You look like a Baroque painting," Kai said from somewhere behind me. I turned my head and looked over my shoulder at him. He was shirtless, his red brand bright against the fair canvas of his chest. He wore a pair of old khaki shorts and his baseball cap; his hair was long and falling into his eyes, and he hastily brushed it off his forehead.

"What would the title of the painting be?" I asked, as he came and plopped down next to me, sticking his feet into the water and brushing my toes with his.

"*A Content Woman.*"

"Hmmm." I leaned my head against him. He was warm, familiar, like I had known him before this life. "We are defined by the joys as much as the tragedies."

"I want to give you so much joy you forget you ever had any tragedy. Fill you with so much light that it shoots out of your fingers and toes."

"Now, that would be an amazing painting."

"Maybe we'll have it commissioned, and we can hang it over the fireplace in the living room."

"And when our children ask what it means, what will you tell them?"

He pressed a kiss to my collarbone and said, "I will tell them you are my sun and the keeper of the light."

I sighed. I was a yellow balloon in danger of floating away. "Content doesn't seem right."

"No? What then?"

"*A Woman in Joy.*"

"*A Woman in Joy,*" he echoed. "A true masterpiece."

•••

We were naked on a pallet of blankets in front of the unlit fireplace of the farmhouse. It was early evening, just past twilight. We owned a bed, but I was a bigger fan of the floor at the moment.

"Is this what you had in mind when you saw the house?"

I grinned. "Maybe. I definitely thought we'd be doing this in winter." Kai's fingers drew circles on my belly. "I was thinking we could paint the nursery green. None of that pink or blue crap."

"Green is good."

"Not mint green—forest green."

"Sage green?" he teased.

I laughed. "Do you want to find out the sex when it's time?"

"I already know."

"Do you?"

"It's a boy," Kai stated.

"You seem pretty sure of that fact. What happens if it's a girl?"

"Then it's a girl. I'd be happy with that, too."

"You want a son though, right? Don't all men want a son? A legacy?"

"Some legacy I am," he said, bitter resentment coating his tongue.

I touched his arm, but did not placate him with empty words. I doubted he'd listen to them anyway.

Kai sat up and gazed at the mantle. "I think I have to go back."

I stared at him; his revelation was a hammer on a glass window. "How long have you being thinking about this?"

"Ever since you told me you were pregnant. It changes everything. I can't look our kid in the eye and tell him I was a coward. I've got to go back and deal with things—finally deal with things."

I'd been dreading and hoping for this moment. How long could we have kept pretending that we were enough for each other? I wanted to tell him I was afraid, that our life wouldn't be the same after we went to Monteagle, but what did we have if we couldn't face his past? It would be a labyrinth, hedged with brutal emotions and unspeakable truths, but at least we'd find our way together.

"Okay." I wished I felt stronger. "We'll go."

He leaned over and placed a kiss on my stomach before wrapping his arms around me.

"It's always something, isn't it?" I said.

He pulled back, brushing his thumbs across my cheeks. "I think they call this *life*. I have to do this."

"I know." There wasn't just one moment that defined adulthood. Our lives were a series of rebirths. Some of us were born with indomitable spirits that ensured we got up, checked for broken bones and then started again.

He made me proud.

With one arm around me, Kai reached for his cell phone and held it, weighing it in his hand. He took a deep breath and dialed. After a few moments he said simply, "It's me. I'm coming home."

Chapter 19

Kai

Sage rested against my shoulder, sound asleep, and I brushed my lips across her forehead. We were somewhere over the Atlantic, and I knew that if I opened the airplane window shade, all I'd see would be darkness and gray clouds.

I felt like I was returning to my own funeral, so heavenly judges could weigh the balance of my life. I wondered if my faults outweighed the good deeds.

Sage made a whimpering sound and twitched before settling down. It'd been a week since we decided to face my family. Celia had put up a fight, telling us that Sage could travel now, but when she was in her third trimester it would be unsafe. I told Celia we'd be back long before then—I didn't want to linger in Monteagle. My life was in France with Sage, and soon our child, but I had to face my family.

My guilt had been a constant companion, and though I thought I had shut the door on my past, it came at me with a vengeful axe. It would find me no matter where I went. I couldn't run anymore; I had to stand and accept it. It would be harsh and ugly, but maybe it would give me peace. Maybe it would give everyone peace.

Sage finally stirred and awakened. Turning to me, she offered a sleepy smile. It seemed the woman held secrets and mystery in the corners of her mouth—more so than even the Mona Lisa. I didn't think I'd ever fully understand the quirk of those beautiful lips, even if I had years. And I would have years. *We* would have years. So many.

I wanted to protect her from everything, even myself—and most definitely my parents. I was about to subject Sage to my family—they were like angry bears. *Don't feed the animals, folks; they aren't tame!*

"Want some water?" I reached up and pressed the flight attendant call button.

Sage nodded. "I cried most of the way to France, you know."

"I'm crying on the inside," I drawled. "I wish I didn't feel compelled to do this."

"Blasted adulthood."

"Blasted reevaluation," I said. The flight attendant came, and I requested a bottle of water.

"Maybe some pretzels?" Sage asked. "Please?"

The woman turned off the call light and left.

"Are you going to tell me the plan, or are we winging it?"

"We're seeing Reece's parents first."

"It doesn't seem fair to just show up on their front porch."

I paused. "They know I'm coming."

"Yeah, I know you called them to let them know."

"I called them again."

"Oh. Do they know about me?"

"No, not yet."

"What about the baby? Are we going to tell them?"

"Eventually."

Sage turned her eyes to the closed window and lifted the shade. "I wish we were already there. The waiting is killing me."

"They'll love you."

"Will they?"

"Of course."

"What about your family? And don't lie to me."

"My grandmother, father, and brother will adore you."

"But your mother?"

"My mother hates *me* right now, so there's a good chance she'll hate you too." My tone and words had the desired effect I wanted—Sage laughed. I was kidding, sort of. I hadn't spoken to my mother, but I didn't need a crystal ball to know how she would react.

•••

It was just past lunchtime when we climbed the porch steps of Reece's parents' ranch house. We were tired and nervous. I'd had so much coffee I was jittery, but Sage remained calm.

The screen was closed, but the main door was open; I could hear pans clattering in the kitchen and running water in the sink.

I stared at nothing for a long moment, Sage's hand gripping mine. I wondered if I ever would've found the courage if it hadn't been for her. Probably not.

With a deep breath, I finally rang the bell.

A middle-aged woman with graying blonde hair and a flour-smudged face appeared through the

164

screen. She opened the door and then threw herself at me, the sound of her crying in my ears. I hugged and patted her back as I rested my cheek against her head, closing my eyes. She dropped her arms and swiped the tears off her cheeks as she turned her curious gaze to Sage.

"Alice, this is my wife, Sage."

Alice blinked. "Wife?"

"It's nice to meet—" Sage began, but was clearly caught off guard when Alice enveloped her in a strong hug.

Pulling away, Alice smiled. "It's wonderful to meet you, Sage. Go on into the kitchen. I'm going to run out to the barn and grab Keith."

"No doubt to warn him," I said. Alice threw me a look, raised an eyebrow, and went to find her husband. It was good to know that some things hadn't changed with time. She still had a sense of humor after everything she'd been through.

"What was that?" Sage demanded. "I expected anger when you told her about me."

"She doesn't think it's out of character," I explained with a wry grin, "even for me. I'm the kind of guy that leaves in the middle of the night on a whim, remember? It almost makes sense that I'd return with a wife."

We walked into the kitchen, and Sage settled into a worn chair while I opened the cupboard. Taking out two glasses, I went to the refrigerator and pulled out the carton of orange juice.

Sage laughed. "You're certainly at home here."

I smiled; it was both in pleasure and pain. The back door crashed open, and Keith Chelser stormed into the kitchen, his face wreathed in disbelief as if needing physical proof of my existence. The man was huge, a modern John Wayne, filling the kitchen with his height and breadth. He was what a cowboy hoped to look like.

When I was a kid, I thought he could crush me. But I'd seen his bear-paw hands deliver foals. I'd wanted to be him. Keith had heart and a moral code that ancient warriors could have lived by. Being near him now made me realize my own code was at the bottom of a lake. I'd have to hold my breath, swim down to the dark muddy goop and retrieve it if I wanted it back.

Keith embraced me, and then promptly withdrew and decked me across the jaw. I collapsed on scarecrow legs, but he immediately reached down to help me off the floor. I staggered like I was drunk, and Keith steadied me like I was a toy.

There was that moral code.

Looking at Sage, I grinned. She hesitantly smiled back, but then she stared at Keith, shooting him an angry glare.

She stood and craned her neck to peer at him. The cowboy towered over her, and it made me swallow a laugh. A fight between Sage and Keith? I'd bet on Sage—always.

"You punched my husband."

"Yep," Keith said without apology. "Sage?"

"Yeah?"

He grinned. "Welcome to the family."

●●●

After a dinner of meatloaf and potatoes, and many hours of talking, Alice insisted we stay with them. She didn't take *no* for an answer. I didn't want to stay anywhere else anyway.

The window drapes of the guest room were open, letting in the moonlight. Sage burrowed close to me.

I inhaled deeply, and the muscles of my back relaxed as I exhaled. "You smell that?" I mumbled, pressing my head against hers. "It smells like sugar and nutmeg. It smells like home."

"It wasn't as bad as you thought it would be, was it?"

"No. They make it easy. Well, not easy, but they don't make it worse." The shock of seeing Alice and Keith had nearly felled me. I hadn't been prepared for the tiny lines of pain at the corners of Alice's eyes, put there by the grief of losing her only child. But she was like a rapier forged in fire now, hardened and almost unbreakable. Keith, on the other hand, looked like a tired, worn out saddle at the end of its life.

"When are you going to see Lucy?"

My voice was laced with guilt when I answered, "Soon. It's going to be rough. I left her alone to deal with everything—she doesn't have parents like the Chelsers. There's no home for her like this…she's alone."

"What about Tristan's family?"

"The Evanstons are proper, concerned with appearances. They're the kind of people that retreat into themselves when bad things happen. Lucy might as well have been by herself."

"I can't imagine what that must have been like for her," Sage said. "I don't think I could've been that strong."

I pressed my lips together in bitterness. "She shouldn't have had to be that strong. I should've stayed."

She ran a hand through my hair, but said nothing. Sage didn't try to absolve me, and I doubted I would've accepted absolution anyway.

•••

The next morning, Sage lifted her head from the toilet and glared at me. "You rat bastard."

"I asked if you wanted me to hold your hair— you said no."

Rising from her spot on the bathroom floor, she went to the sink and washed out her mouth. "It's bad enough I've had to give up coffee and scotch, but the constant puking? Not fair. I feel like I have chronic sea sickness."

"You're beautiful."

"I'm green," she snapped. "I look like Kermit the Frog."

I rubbed a knuckle against my lips, trying to hide my smile.

"Fuck you."

I laughed.

We went downstairs to the kitchen, and Sage sank into a chair. Alice was at the stove, flipping bacon. Keith sat at the table, enjoying a cup of a coffee and reading the newspaper.

"Good morning," Alice said. "You guys hungry?"

"Famished," Sage said. I stared at her and raised an eyebrow. She shrugged.

"Famished?" Keith asked, lowering the newspaper. "I could've sworn I heard you throwing up right before I came downstairs."

Alice looked over her shoulder at Sage. "You feeling okay? Are you sick?"

Sage glanced at me, and I nodded. She announced, "I'm pregnant."

Alice made a noise in the back of her throat, and Keith's eyes widened.

"Can you not tell my parents?" I asked.

"You sound like a teenager," Alice said with a grin.

I rolled my eyes. "I'd just rather tell them in person."

"Like waiting to tell us about Sage until you were on our doorstep?" Alice teased. She patted Sage on the arm, and I knew I was right. Alice and Keith liked her. How could they not?

Alice set a plate of food in front of Sage. "Congratulations, but eat slowly. Trust me."

Keith laughed. "Congratulations—to the both of you."

After we ate, we showered and headed out. When we were on our way, Sage looked at the colored bruise on my jaw and said, "God, he really decked you."

"Yeah, it hurt like a son of a bitch. He didn't hold back."

"It gives you a dangerous look. Not going to lie; I kind of like it."

"Then it was all worth it," I said with a wry grin.

Lucy lived in a small cottage along the edge of a glade in the house she had shared with Tristan. We parked the rental car and got out, but before we even reached the front door, it opened. A tall, slender, red-haired woman stepped out onto the porch.

She held a toddler.

My steps faltered. The baby made a noise, a cross between a squeal and a gurgle. His brown hair was mixed with traces of red, but his eyes were green.

Like his father's.

"Hello, Kai." Lucy's voice was weary, resolute.

I tried to speak numerous times before finally spitting out, "Why didn't you tell me?"

Lucy's face was pale, her eyes wide. "I didn't know for sure until after you were gone, and then there was no way to find you."

The guilt of leaving washed over me, compounded by coming face to face with Tristan's son for the first time. Lucy had needed me, and I'd left her. It was another reason to hate myself.

The toddler reached out, and without saying a word Lucy plopped him into my arms.

Tristan's son.

I looked into the boy's eyes, and my heart shattered into tiny shards of glass.

Fuck.

"You must be Sage."

"News travels fast," Sage said.

"Alice called, but I didn't believe her at first," Lucy explained. "Come in."

"Christ," I muttered. "If Alice called you, then she definitely called my mother."

Sage took a seat on the couch, and Lucy made her way to an old scarred recliner and collapsed into it. I saw exhaustion in the grooves around her mouth, the bags under her eyes. How much of it was heartache, and how much of it was raising a child alone?

I bit my tongue hard, stopping myself from asking her all the questions I didn't deserve answers to. "What's his name?" I sat down next to Sage with the baby on my lap.

"Dakota." She peered at her son. "He doesn't usually take to strangers."

I stared at her—I wasn't supposed to be a stranger, yet I was. "I should've been here."

"Yeah, you should've been," she stated. Dakota cooed and turned big green eyes to Sage, luring her attention.

"May I?" Sage looked to Lucy, asking for permission to hold Dakota.

Lucy nodded and without hesitation, I handed Dakota to Sage. I became mesmerized by the sight of her entertaining the toddler. It gave me a glimpse of our future—it was closer than I thought.

"So you're back."

"We are, but only for a little while," I explained.

Lucy closed her mouth, but her cheeks suddenly flushed red with anger. "Damn you."

I looked at Sage, who nodded in tacit understanding, stood up, and took Dakota out onto the porch. The front door clicked shut, and I was left alone with Tristan's widow.

Widow.

The word was supposed to be reserved for old women, wrinkled by time and with many years of love in their lives. Widow was not a word for Lucy. Vibrant, passionate, warrior—those were the words I would've called her.

"I'm so mad at you I can barely see straight," she seethed. "How could you—"

"I had to."

"You have no idea what the last two and a half years have been like for me."

"You have no idea what they've been like for me either."

"You should've stayed."

"Why? To be constantly reminded that they're gone?" I stood and faced her, no longer shying away from Lucy and all that I had run from—we dueled with words and hurt feelings. The years of grief burdened us both, but I wanted to claw my way out— I had too much to live for.

"When they died, everything was dark. All I saw was the next bottle of bourbon, the next place to move. I never thought I'd meet a woman I wanted to marry. She's more than that, Lucy. She's the reason I came back." I sighed wearily. "She's pregnant."

Lucy's ire diffused, replaced by shock. "You're kidding?"

"Nope. We're going back to France."

"Why?"

"What do you mean, *why*?"

"What's keeping you there?"

"We bought a house."

"So sell it. *This* is your home."

"No." My voice was unyielding granite. "I can't, Lucy. I can't walk around every corner expecting to see my two best friends. If I moved back here, I'd never sleep well again. I don't get how you can stand it here."

"Where else am I supposed to go?" she demanded. "Take my son away from his grandparents? Away from the Chelsers? Away from—"

I looked at her, sharp and assessing. "Away from who?"

She took a deep breath. "Wyatt."

The name was like being thrown into an avalanche of snow; the air left my lungs and I felt cold and buried. "Wyatt? My brother?"

Two patches of red appeared at the top of her cheekbones, only this time it wasn't anger coloring her. "Yes."

"I'll kill him."

"I love him, Kai."

"You love *Tristan*," I gritted out.

The sharp contours of her face softened. "Of course, I do, but am I supposed to be alone the rest of my life? Am I supposed to never love again?"

"How long?"

"*What?*"

"How long did you wait before you got together?"

Her blue eyes were stormy. "Fuck you, Kai."

"How long, Lucy?"

"None of your goddamn business!"

We glared at one another. I wondered if learning to love again was a betrayal. But Tristan was dead;

he'd left behind a wife and a son. Didn't Lucy deserve some measure of happiness? If I'd been here, would it have happened? Thinking about the what-ifs of my life would sink me. I couldn't change them.

"He's loved me for years. Did you know?" Lucy asked.

"No, I didn't."

She paused before saying, "A year—nothing happened for a year. Dakota was sick and in the hospital. Wyatt had been coming around, checking in on me. I called him, and he came. I could depend on him; he's been solid, steady."

It didn't sound at all like the kind of love she'd had with Tristan. Theirs had been a wild, tempestuous, burn-everything-to-the-ground kind of love.

Which kind meant more?

While I reeled from revelations, she wasn't through giving them. Lucy took a deep breath. "He's asked me to marry him—and I've said yes."

•••

A car door slammed, and a moment later, I heard my brother's voice on the porch. I stalked outside, ignoring Sage and Dakota, eager for a confrontation with Wyatt.

"You," I fumed, the full force of my wrath directed at Wyatt. I heard Lucy moving behind me.

"He knows?" Wyatt peered at Lucy for confirmation, his face wreathed in calm acceptance.

"Yes." She strode towards Wyatt to stand near him in a show of solidarity.

"Knows? Knows what?" Sage asked in confusion, handing off Dakota to his mother.

"Wyatt asked Lucy to marry him." My voice was full of outrage on behalf of my dead friend. I took another menacing step towards Wyatt, my fists clenching for a fight.

Sage moved between us to ease the tension. Her voice was low, but solid like steel as she said, "Don't do it. It'll make things worse."

I glared down at Sage, "Lucy is—"

"Not yours to defend."

I was in no mood to be placated. Cursing violently, I stalked past my brother and trekked into the woods, wanting to leave it all behind.

"He just needs some time," I heard Sage say right before I was out of earshot.

I wanted to hit something, but I was afraid I'd never stop, so I let my feet carry me instead. The sound of swishing trees filled my ears, the smell of warm earth in my nose; I knew where I was headed.

The cemetery was empty of mourners as I strolled to Reece's modest headstone. Next to it was Tristan's, and I grimaced when I looked at it—it was a monument, colossal and grotesque, nothing like Reece's. *Appearances*, I sneered. The Evanstons would never have let their son's death go unnoticed.

My friends should've been buried in the mountains in unmarked graves, part of the earth they came from. It's what they both would've wanted, but at least their parents had done something right, and had laid them to rest next to one another. It made it easy for me when I paid my respects. I snorted. *Easy.* Nothing about this was easy.

"What the fuck," I said to the ground, knowing I wouldn't get a reply.

Wyatt would marry Lucy, and he would be the only father Dakota would ever know. My brother was a good man, but could he love Lucy the way a woman with heartache and darkness needed to be loved?

I swam through my thoughts with a powerful breaststroke, but I didn't find any peace.

Afternoon wore on, and I did not return. Instead, I took up vigilance, sitting with my back against a tree. The sun traveled across the sky as I talked to the ghosts of my two friends, trying to rectify my past so I could have a future.

I wondered how Sage was getting along with Wyatt. What was he telling her? Scaring her, no doubt, about what she was about to endure when she faced our parents.

A car door slammed in the distance, and a few moments later Sage ambled through the cemetery. The headstones looked bare, solemn in the green lawn. Gold rays glinted off the leaves, aiding in the serenity where bodies rested eternally, their souls long gone.

Without a word, she eased down next to me and plucked at the grass. A slight breeze played with her hair. "How are you doing?"

I shrugged, surprised that I no longer felt anger. I was resigned. "Life's odd, you know? I should've been prepared for things to be different when I came back. My life is different, why wouldn't Lucy's be? Wyatt's?" Looking at her, I grinned in wry humor. "Time didn't stop while I was away."

She stood up and reached a hand down. I grasped it, rose, and pulled her into my arms. "Be happy for them," Sage whispered.

"I am—sort of."

I hoped that Wyatt loved Lucy the way I loved Sage. Perhaps Wyatt and I were more similar than I had thought, and maybe our tension had no place in adulthood. We were men now, hardened in the fires of life.

Sage laughed. "No, you're not."

"You've got to understand... Wyatt is my brother. A brother I never got along with, never felt any sort of kinship with. He's in love with Lucy, Tristan's wife. Tristan—my brother in every way except blood."

"He loves her, and he loves Dakota too," she pointed out. "If you can't be happy for Wyatt, be happy for them. Wouldn't Tristan want this for her, for his son?"

"Part of him would want her to move on, find someone, love again," I conceded.

"But the male part of his brain would demand she love and pine for him forever?"

"Something like that. You understand them, don't you? My friends you've never met."

"You've painted a vivid picture of them." She stared into my eyes. "I'd want you to find someone."

My arms tightened around her, unable to fathom such a horrible idea as living a life without her. "Nothing is going to happen to you."

"You're right." She pressed her lips to mine. "We're going to grow old and wrinkly together."

I sighed in contentment.

"I told Wyatt I'm pregnant. Think he'll tell your parents?"

"Not if he knows what's good for him."

She smiled. "He picked Lucy. I think he has a fair idea of what's good for him. He invited us to a family dinner with your parents."

"When?"

"Tomorrow night."

"You mean we've got a whole day before entering the lion's den?"

"That gives us twenty-four hours to prepare."

"Hate to break it to you, darlin', but twenty-four hours isn't enough. I've had twenty-nine years, and I'm still not ready for this moment."

"It's time to face them," she said. "You can do this; I know you can."

The faith she had in me was staggering. *Nothing like the love a good woman, right?* I didn't know why she loved me, but I'd take it. "You don't know what you're getting into," I warned.

•••

I open my eyes, watching the sun rise over the lake as I perch on a rock. Tristan is on the bank, fishing pole in hand, casting away.

"Any luck?" I ask.

"With life, or fishing?" Tristan answers with a question.

"Aren't they the same thing?"

Tristan's smile is wide, devilish. "No point in life if you can't fish."

"You're so Norman Maclean right now."

"I prefer David James Duncan."

"You would."

"So Lucy and Wyatt..."

"Ah, you know."

"I do."

"You're not mad."

"I was, for a while. Reece got to hear all about it. I'm okay with it now."

"How?" I demand. *"How can you be okay with it?"*

"You wouldn't understand."

"Explain it to me."

Tristan's gaze is steady. *"You left voluntarily. You just...up and left. You went somewhere else, and you didn't look back."*

"I didn't have much to keep me here." I defend myself, but there's no anger in my voice.

"But still, you left. I was forced by fate. I left a wife behind. She was alone, terrified, grieving—and pregnant. If she'd been the one to die and I had to go on..." He shudders visibly at the thought. *"There were countless nights she cried non-stop, curled up in our bed. Do you know what it's like to leave the woman you love, and watch her live without you, hoping she finds the strength because you're not there to give it to her? Only death was powerful enough to make me leave her."*

Tristan's haunted eyes lock on mine, and I see my own heart reflected in them—twisted, ravaged, then stitched back together but barely beating.

"Wyatt gives Lucy the strength she needs to go on. He protects her, and loves my son as his own. Life never looks the way you think it will. Never in a

million of my dreams did I think my wife would end up with your brother. But I never thought I'd die, either—unable to touch her, hold her, wipe the tears from her eyes. I don't get to be there when our son grows into a man. Wyatt will have that honor. Do you know what that feels like?"

"Are you in Heaven?" I wonder, my voice gritty, my throat tight with regret and pathos.

"Technically, spiritually, or hopefully?"

"All of the above."

Tristan's mouth curves into a ghoulish, gruesome smile. "I'm in limbo, waiting until I can see Lucy again. But she has a long life to live first. A life without me."

"Do you know that for sure?"

He laughs in sardonic humor. "Nothing is for sure, Kai."

Chapter 20

Sage

The Ferris' library was quiet, the air salted with strain and implied accusations. I sat next to Kai on a black leather couch while Claire Ferris stared at her wayward son as though she didn't recognize him. To his credit, Kai didn't wear the University of Tennessee baseball cap that was usually glued to his head. He had even combed his hair for the occasion. I wanted to mess it up. It made him look like someone else, someone orderly, not my Kai.

Wyatt was in the corner, clutching his drink and sending me subtle looks of support. I liked Wyatt. I liked any man that went after the woman he wanted, despite insurmountable obstacles.

George stood by the liquor cart, putting ice cubes into glasses. I studied Kai's father and I struggled to see any family resemblance. It was Wyatt who favored George in looks—blond hair, blue eyes. Kai really was the black sheep of the family, it seemed.

I turned my attention to George's mother. She smiled wide, and I felt myself relax a bit. I recognized that smile instantly. It was Kai's. Memaw just might be a kindred spirit.

"Can I get you a drink, Sage?" George offered.

An entire bottle of scotch, I wanted to say. Instead, I said, "Club soda, please."

"Kai?"

"Bourbon on the rocks."

After George handed us our glasses, he took a seat next to his wife on the couch facing us. I was in the front row for the Ferris family fight.

"So, you're staying with the Chelsers?" Claire asked, smashing the silence.

Maybe I can hide behind that big desk over there…

"You already know the answer to that, Mom."

"And you've seen Lucy?"

Kai's sigh was labored. "Yes."

"So, we were your last stop?" Claire's voice was frosty, like Superman's Fortress of Solitude.

"Saving the best for last," Kai said in a sarcastic voice.

Memaw almost spit out her drink, but managed to contain her laughter.

"What took you so long to come back?" Claire demanded, ignoring her mother-in-law.

"Claire," George warned.

"No. I have the right to know why my son decided to visit everyone before his own parents."

"Yeah, I know this is bad—" Kai looked pained.

Claire glared as she went on, "And why he stayed away without a single word for two-and-a-half years before coming home."

"Home—is that where I am?"

My husband could play mean when he wanted. This wasn't going well. Not at all.

"Kai," I pleaded.

"No, let him speak. Are you planning on continuing your little jaunt across the world, or are you going to stay in Monteagle, be an adult, and live up to the Ferris name?"

"I *am* an adult."

"Well, you're not acting like one," Claire snapped.

"We bought a house in France."

"Doesn't make you an adult."

"We are going to raise our baby there."

It was like a vacuum had sucked all the air out of the room. The ice in the drinks clinked against glass. Kai's breathing was heavy, like he'd run some great distance.

"Baby?" Memaw asked. "You're having a baby?" She looked at me, and I nodded slightly. All at once they seemed to remember that I sat among them.

"Did you know about this?" Claire stared at her oldest son. Wyatt's jaw clamped shut, but he inclined his head. Claire turned her attention back to Kai, her eyes narrowing. "You can't live in France. Especially not now. Now that she…"

I wondered why Claire couldn't finish the sentence. She didn't believe it, maybe, or didn't want to believe it. Well, if I had any doubts about what she thought of me, I didn't need to wonder any longer. The woman couldn't even say my name. We'd just told her she was going to be a grandmother, and yet there was no joy in her voice. If my mother had been here, there would've been hugs, tears, and celebration. There would've been so much happiness it would've felt like a gift from the stars.

Mom. Someone would be calling me that one day. One day soon.

"Why can't we live in France?" Kai demanded.

Claire made a sound of exasperation. "What will you do there?"

Kai shrugged. "Whatever I want."

I was exhausted, even though it was Kai fighting each round. No matter how many verbal fists he took to the jaw, he got up, ready for more. I fell deeper in love with the tortured man I had married. The father of my child. My husband. My strength.

"Sage, do you want to come sit outside with me?" Memaw asked. I looked at Kai who nodded and squeezed my hand. A reprieve. I'd take it.

"I'll just…" Wyatt said, moving towards the door. "Oh hell, I'm getting out of here."

I snorted with surprised laughter as I let Memaw lead me out of the library and through the house. The photographs on the walls were exhibits of memories from Kai's childhood. As we walked past a pristine kitchen occupied by a private chef, I understood more about the Ferris family than I ever would from any line of questioning.

"Let's go out back," Memaw suggested. "It's the only redeeming quality of this otherwise cold house." Once we were on the porch, we settled into plush chairs and looked up into the dark purple sky; the sun had set, and the night was soft and quiet. "So, you're pregnant."

"I am."

"Are you excited?"

I looked at her, and Memaw shrugged.

"Inane question, I know."

"I am excited." It was the truth—children no longer terrified me. I had Kai. What did I have to be scared of? I rested a hand on my belly, breathing in the heady mountain air.

"Y'all didn't wait…"

"Ah, no, we didn't."

"Planned?"

"Nope."

"Most things aren't."

"Death never is, so why should conception be any different?" My voice came out hard and warped, like twisted steel. I didn't mean it to, but I felt I had the right to be defensive.

Memaw glanced at me. "I wasn't judging you—either of you."

"Okay."

"As long as you're both happy."

I smiled. "My mom used to say fitting yourself into a box is like wearing shoes that are too small. Convention is a box people put themselves in because they don't know where else to go."

"Your mother sounds like a wise woman."

"She was."

"Was?"

"She died—not even a year ago."

"I'm sorry."

"I know what you're thinking."

"Do you?"

"You think we jumped into this too soon, don't you?"

"That's Kai."

I looked at her in confusion. "You're not upset?"

Memaw chuckled. "Let me guess; he decided he wanted you, whether or not you wanted him back."

I laughed. "You know your grandson."

"I do."

"I chose him, too. Not right away, but—"

"He's Kai."

"Exactly." I had been cold before I met Kai—barren, empty. He had been the sun, and I the dying bloom. Maybe we were both and neither. I rubbed my stomach in thought. I didn't like to think about what turns my life would've made if Kai and I hadn't found each other, but we did.

"The baby sparked his conscience," I went on. "He didn't want to be known as a coward, so he came back to face…everything."

I had never called Kai a coward. That was his own word for himself. Another box.

"Part of him died when Reece and Tristan did," Memaw said.

"I know. You can't outrun your past, no matter how hard you try, and believe me, Kai tried. But he can't live here. As much as he loves it, it would be a constant reminder of all he's lost, and he wants to look to the future. Will his parents understand that?"

Memaw gazed into the sky, as if she'd find the words written in the stars. "I don't know. Kai has never done anything they wanted him to do."

"Maybe they should stop expecting him to be who they want and just let him be himself. They see him as a disappointment, the screw up, don't they?"

Memaw's non-reply was her answer. We sat in silence for a time before she finally said, "Kai never sought his parents' approval—for anything. He had Tristan and Reece and they were the only people he was accountable to, the only people he *wanted* to be accountable to. George and Claire never really understood that."

"And Wyatt? Did he understand it?"

186

"Wyatt grew to understand and accept it because he didn't have a choice. It's hard for him, even now, knowing he and Kai have never been close."

Resigned, I stood. "Should we go back in there? See if the smoke from the dueling pistols has cleared?"

"Are you going to rescue him?"

"You think he needs it?"

"Without a doubt."

•••

Dinner was a silent, stunted affair; there was no attempt at polite conversation. There was plenty of alcohol consumption, long disdainful looks, and enough tension to gorge on. I stared at my plate most of the time, enjoying the duck in a fig reduction sauce. I didn't miss the irony of being fed a decadent meal, all the while Claire making me feel like I didn't deserve it. She observed me through dinner; her eyes trained on my hands, examining me while I ate the main course with a salad fork. I did it just to piss her off. It was cheap, but it felt good.

The minute dessert was over, we rose to leave.

"You aren't taking a plane out tonight, are you?" Claire asked.

Kai threw his mother a look and said, "No, Mom. We bought one way tickets so we can leave whenever we want."

"You might as well take your car back. While you're here," George said. "Keys are on the front table."

Kai looked at his father in surprise. "Thanks." We walked to the garage and Kai's black Mercedes sat in its spot.

"You weren't lying, were you? About the money."

"The car was a college graduation present." Kai plopped the car keys into my hand, and I had to admit I was itching to get behind the wheel. "I'm too buzzed to drive."

"Lucky bastard. If I wasn't growing a human, I'd be hammered."

Kai laughed and then hugged me. "God, I have no idea what I'd do without you."

"You never have to find out. What are we going to do with the rental?"

"Return it tomorrow. Get in."

Once we were on our way back to the Chelsers', I said, "Tell me about the showdown."

"Dad let my mother do most of the talking. She asked if you married me for my money."

I snorted.

"You're not surprised?"

"Not at all—Wyatt warned me."

"Did he? When?"

"When you were at the cemetery. He told me more about your parents than you did."

"So you didn't walk in totally blind?"

"No, I knew it was coming." I laughed.

"What?"

"Our mothers are complete opposites. My mother lived in truth. Your mother lives in denial." I pulled into the gravel driveway and parked next to Keith's green truck.

"Yeah, when she was talking I could see the disappointment on Dad's face. Doesn't matter, though; I feel great. You know why?"

"Bourbon?" I smiled. I loved this giggly drunk version of Kai. Usually, when we drank, we suffered great melancholia. Not tonight, apparently.

"Partly. But I faced my parents, told them what I wanted, and I didn't care if they supported me or not. And the thing is, I meant every word." We got out of the car, and Kai grabbed my hand and led me to the stables.

We ducked into the barn; a few horses neighed in greeting, but most ignored us. Finding an empty stall, he grabbed a couple of horse blankets, threw them onto the straw and pulled me down. I cuddled into his arms. I was drowsy from food and the smell of him. He was better than a sedative.

"I just want some time with you here."

Before I knew it, my eyes were closing, and I was falling asleep, wrapped in security and warmth.

•••

"My mother wants to throw us a wedding reception," Kai said two days later. He poured a cup of coffee and sat down at the kitchen table. Keith was already tending the horses, and Alice was collecting eggs from the chickens.

"No." I eyed the coffee in forlorn longing. "I will not be paraded around in her social circle so she can pretend to accept us."

"I told her we weren't going to be in town long enough for her to put it together."

I raised my eyebrows. "I bet she didn't take that excuse."

"She had the nerve to say that I was ashamed of you; otherwise, I'd want to show you off and tell everyone we're happy and expecting a baby."

"She's good." I sighed. "You agreed, didn't you?"

"Call it a gesture of goodwill."

"Did she give you a time frame for this event?"

"September."

"That's over two months away!"

"I know, but Mom wants to have the party at the Hermitage Hotel in Nashville. It's the earliest available date."

"Joy."

"Black tie."

"Didn't doubt that for a second."

"She wants you in a wedding dress."

"*Absolutely not,*" I declared. "I'm not going to be the pregnant girl in a big poofy dress. I will not look like a frosted cupcake."

Kai's lips twitched.

"This isn't funny, Kai."

He stared into his cup before peering at me with an abashed look. "I sort of already told her she could take you dress shopping."

We gazed at one another and I said, "If you weren't the father of my child…"

"Okay, I get it, I owe you big time."

"Yeah, you do."

•••

I sat in the passenger side of Claire's car as we drove in silence towards Nashville. Stifling my disdain for the situation, I was determined to get through this with whatever grace I possessed, but I didn't have a lot of reserves left.

Kai had volunteered to go with us, but I refused. I wouldn't let him be the buffer—I had to endure this; I would endure this, no matter the cost. I wouldn't cower or hide, and certainly not behind my husband. He'd been through enough.

"Why are we doing this?"

"Because we have to." Claire glanced at me from behind black Dior sunglasses.

"Says who?"

"Me."

Claire was all about appearances—that much was obvious. I didn't miss her snide look as she took in my messy bun and lack of makeup. I was wearing a pressed white button-down, skinny jeans, and black flats.

I can't be that embarrassing, can I?

Ignoring her, I lost myself in thoughts of *Tours*. How were Armand and Luc doing? The vines needed pruning, no doubt. And Celia? Was the bed and breakfast full of eager guests looking for new experiences?

"You manipulated him into marrying you."

Hurled in a quiet tone, the accusation was more powerful for it. It ricocheted off the glass windows, landed in my lap, and now I'd have to deal with it. Keith had reconciled his anger with Kai by using his fist. Claire, Southern belle that she was, delivered blows in the form of verbal lacerations.

I would've preferred the fist.

I went from simmer to boil in moments. "Have you ever even met your son? He's got a will of his own—he's not a marionette on strings."

"He's a runner. He'll leave you."

I fingered my wedding ring, a simple thin band that meant more to me due to its simplicity. Every time I looked at it, I thought about how far we'd come, how far we still had to go. I knew deep inside that Kai would never leave me, no matter what anyone thought.

"You have no faith in him, do you?"

"He's proven that when things get hard he can't handle it."

"People change. I understand why you're upset. Your son left you for two years." I studied her. Her face was pinched with tension and pale with pain. "You're waiting for him to leave home again."

"He will," Claire answered tightly. "You'll go back to France and raise your child there. I'll never see my son. I'll never see my grandchild."

"Do you really think I'd keep you away?"

"I don't know. I don't know anything about you."

"All you need to know is that I love your son."

Claire pulled in front of the Hermitage Hotel, a beautiful, architectural gem in downtown Nashville. A valet took the car and drove off, and I followed Claire into the lobby. A short woman with hair in a no-nonsense bun held a clipboard and a pen, waiting for us. Claire greeted her and then turned to introduce me.

"Charlene, this is my daughter-in-law, Sage."

I wondered if part of Claire died admitting it.

"Pleased to meet you," Charlene said, shaking my hand. "If you two will follow me to the Grand Ballroom, we have some table settings for you to pick from."

The room was dimly lit; dozens of tables were adorned with different china sets and flower arrangements. I didn't pay attention to the mindless babble between Charlene and Claire as I walked around, hoping instead for one beautiful table to appeal more to me than another. It reminded me of a time, not so long ago, when I was with Connor choosing the menu for our wedding. The memory sat like curdled milk in my stomach.

"Sage, what do you think of this one?" Claire called out.

I strolled over to a round table laden with a white tablecloth and white china with gold accents. The stemware was fine crystal, and had an elegant gold band around the lip to match the china, and the silverware gleamed in candlelight. It looked royal and out of touch. I shook my head in disapproval as we moved from table to table. After a few minutes I watched as Claire and Charlene exchange a look, and Charlene walked off, leaving us alone.

"You don't like the settings?" Claire asked, her voice tight with impatience.

"No, I don't."

"What are you looking for?"

"Not these. They all look the same to me. It's all too formal."

Claire raised her perfectly sculpted eyebrows. "What would you have us do? Remove all the tables and have a picnic?"

"Sounds great to me."

I watched Claire's face turn the color of a plum tomato as she attempted to keep herself under control.

I crossed my arms over my chest. "Look, I don't care. This is *your* party. This isn't us—this is *you*, and we're doing this for *you*."

"Then why are you here? I could've made all these decisions without you and not gone through this."

"Go ahead," I allowed. "Save us both a headache; this was *your* idea."

"This was not my idea—none of this was my idea. You think I wanted this? My son married to a stranger?" Claire shouted.

"What's wrong with you? We're happy. Don't you want that for your son? What did you expect, Claire?" My emotions were cranked up high with a little help from pregnancy hormones.

"Well, I didn't expect for him to come back with a wife!" Claire's face was pinched in rage.

"But he did! And no matter how terrible you are to me, I'm not going anywhere!"

Tears of anger filled my eyes as I spun on my heel, eager to be out of the ballroom. Somehow, I found my way to the bathroom and collapsed on the long white couch. Grabbing a couple of tissues, I blew my nose. The tip turned red when I cried. It would take hours for it to return to normal. Everyone would know my mother-in-law had caused me grief.

The bathroom door opened. Claire came in, approaching the sink. She washed her hands with her back to me but said nothing. She seemed composed, calm, like we hadn't just been screaming at one another. I didn't have the strength for another confrontation, and would save my energy for the things that mattered—the wedding reception wasn't one of them. I wouldn't bother talking to her about anything else. She had her opinions and puffed up rhetoric wouldn't sway her anyway.

"The white table cloth with gold accents is fine," I said.

Claire did not reply as she wiped her hands dry.

"I'll even wear whatever dress you want," I relented.

"You will?"

"One condition—Kai and I get to have a bluegrass band for the party."

"Any dress I choose?"

"Any dress you choose."

Claire nodded. "You have a deal."

Four hours later, I cursed myself as I stood on a platform in front of three mirrors and a handful of bridal boutique attendants. My mother-in-law sipped champagne, looking very pleased with herself.

I was in a strapless ball gown with a satin corset, a full tulle skirt and tulle overlay. On the back of the dress was a peplum of organza petals. I looked like I belonged miniature sized on top of a wedding cake, but I turned to Claire and managed a smile, even though I wanted to throw up—and it had nothing to do with pregnancy.

For the wedding day, she would groom me into

what she wanted. And I would let her because I loved Kai.

"Perfect," Claire said with a smug grin.

That night, I crumpled onto the couch and refused to move. Kai sat down, picked up my feet, and let them rest across his lap. "You're a sport," Kai said as he began to rub my toes.

I purred in delight. "Your mother is pure evil. You won't believe the dress she picked out. Tell me about your day. Distract me from the memory of all the tulle."

Kai laughed. "I helped Keith with the horses and tried to get Tristan's father on the phone."

"Any luck?"

"No. I left messages, but he hasn't called me back. I think he's avoiding me."

"It's all *Alice in Wonderland* right now."

"What does that mean?" he asked.

"You know when she falls down the rabbit hole and then goes through the hourglass and turns upside down? That's what you've done, coming back here—turned everything upside down."

"I should be patient, shouldn't I?"

"Yes, and you should keep rubbing my feet."

Chapter 21

Kai

I slipped out of bed, watching the rise and fall of Sage's chest. She slept soundly; I touched her hair and leaned over to kiss her forehead before I left the guest room. I drove on autopilot on a road I had driven a thousand times. The terrain steepened as I entered the mountains, and twenty minutes later I pulled into the driveway of my grandmother's small wood cabin.

Cutting the engine, I got out of the car. The stars were bright, and the night was warm—I loved summertime in Monteagle. I missed this place more than I had thought.

I tread quietly, not wanting to scare the crap out of Memaw, but then the front door opened, and she stood in the doorway.

"What are you doing here?" she demanded.

"Couldn't sleep."

"So you thought you'd pop by for a midnight chat?" She smiled.

"You're awake, aren't you?"

"I am." She pulled the sash of her bathrobe tighter across her body. "I was going to make some tea. Want some?"

I sat in the kitchen as she heated water, and when she was done we took our mugs out onto the back porch to watch the stars. "It's nice out here," I said.

"Reminds me of all those nights in your childhood when you came to stay here with me and your grandfather."

"Those were the best." My voice was tinged with fondness. "Ice cream sundaes for dinner; pitching a tent in the backyard and pretending to go camping." I sighed. "This was more than my home—it was my haven."

"What about the Chelser ranch? You spent a good amount of time there, too."

I grinned. "That was the club house."

We laughed, and Memaw reached over to touch my arm. "I'm glad we could be there for you."

"You really have no idea what you've done for me. I wouldn't have survived without you and Grampy. I'm sorry we lost two years."

"But you're not sorry you left."

I shook my head. "I met Sage."

She smiled. "We all have our own journeys, Kai. Never apologize for where yours takes you."

"How did you go on after Grampy died?"

"The same way you did. I chose life."

I took a deep breath. "I thought I had lost everything when I lost Tristan and Reece, but now I have Sage, and I'm afraid all the time. I can't lose her too."

"That's how you know you have something truly beautiful, Kai. That's how you know your love will last a lifetime."

•••

I crept into the Chelsers' house, surprised to find Keith in the kitchen, heating something on the stove.

"I thought you went to bed hours ago," Keith commented as I sat at the table.

"I did—couldn't sleep, so I went for a drive. What are you doing?"

"Warming some milk."

"No bourbon?"

Keith smiled and went to the cabinet. He pulled out two cups, poured the milk into them and handed one to me.

I took a sip of warm milk and grimaced. "This is terrible."

"Yep," Keith agreed, sitting down with his mug.

"You don't sleep well?"

Keith shrugged. "Not anymore. Doesn't matter how long or how hard I've worked, I still wake up in the middle of the night."

"And the milk helps?"

"No, but it's habit now. Sometimes Alice is awake, too, and we have a nice long talk."

"Ever try pills?"

Keith made a face. "Poison."

I was silent and thoughtful. Pills had never been my choice to help me forget. Bourbon seemed destructive enough—and the women before Sage.

"What's on your mind, son?"

"I've tried getting in touch with Tristan's dad, but I haven't heard anything."

Keith's lined face looked resigned. "Alexander and Evelyn are separated."

"What? When?"

"For about a year, now," Keith admitted. "They had problems long before Tristan died."

"Shit. Why didn't Lucy tell me?"

"She doesn't know."

"Are you kidding me?"

Keith shook his head. "They don't want anyone to know."

"How are they keeping it a secret?"

"They still appear together in public but live separately."

"Appearances, huh? I can't believe it."

"Some people can't survive the tragedy of losing a child."

"You and Alice did."

Keith smiled, but it was buried by sadness. "You haven't been here to know what we've gone through, son, and I'm glad you weren't."

"Really?"

"Yes. You can't look back." Keith shrugged. "It was rough for a while, like living with a stranger."

"You guys were stronger than the tragedy."

"We're stronger in spite of it. I wouldn't wish losing a child on my worst enemy. It goes against the laws of nature—we were supposed to go first." He sighed. "Go to bed, Kai. Crawl in bed next to your beautiful wife and hold her."

Taking Keith's suggestion, I did exactly that, and wrapped my arms around Sage, who instinctively rolled towards me and whimpered in her sleep. I felt joy mixed with sadness, and pondered if life would ever be one without the other.

•••

"Do you ever wonder what your life could've been?" Reece asks.

"Sure, who doesn't?" I answer.

"Are there moments in your life where you knew that if you had taken a different path, everything would've been different?"

"I almost went to Italy instead of France."

"Really? What made you decide?"

I grin. "Train leaving first."

"That's it?"

"That's it."

"Damn." Reece pauses. "I almost didn't graduate high school."

"I know."

"If it wasn't for you and Tristan, I would've never gotten through it."

"I know that, too." I toss a pebble into the lake. "I wonder how Sage will look in fifteen years."

"Content," Reece predicts.

"I don't know if Sage and I are meant to be content—it may not be for us."

"It'll be what it'll be."

"I really miss you guys. I miss drinking beers on Tristan's porch, talking about women and life."

Reece laughs. "You never talked about women."

"Tristan's women," I correct. "Until he fell in love with Lucy. I haven't asked her if she's happy."

"Must be hard to look at Dakota and see Tristan peeking out from his eyes."

"Might give her comfort."

"It might—doubt it though," Reece says. "It's nice knowing there's a piece of him left."

"What's left of you?"

"You remember me, don't you?"

Chapter 22

Sage

I opened the door and blinked. Memaw stood on the Chelsers' porch, blue eyes twinkling, her smile wide.

"Sorry, did I wake you?"

"How could you tell?" I asked, my voice raspy. I'd been enjoying a nap on the couch when the knock sounded. Kai was with Keith, helping with the horses; it somehow gave him comfort to come home with dirt under his nails and sweat on his brow. Alice was out running errands, and I'd had the house to myself.

"First trimester. Besides, I see a pillow crease on your cheek."

I laughed, reaching up to touch my face. Sure enough, I felt a little groove.

"You want to come with me?"

"Sure." I slipped on my tennis shoes and sent a quick text to Kai. We drove into the mountains and I asked, "Where are we going?"

"I thought I'd show you the property."

"Property?"

"Mine."

We drove for a while and then parked at Memaw's cabin and climbed out the car. The day was bright and warm as we hiked, and soon I was wiping my forehead with the back of my hand. My grogginess melted away, leaving me restored. Memaw shot me a look and said, "You aren't winded are you?"

"Like I'd admit it to you?" The woman was downright spry, youthful.

Memaw chuckled. "Well, what do you think?" She gestured to the land, filled with trees, serenity and the most incredible panorama I'd ever seen.

"To say it's beautiful doesn't do it justice. Hand carved by Mother Nature herself."

"Must be strange for a city girl like you."

"I'm not a city girl. Not anymore," I said. "Hard to believe I ever was."

"You miss France."

"So much. Not just *Tours*, but the Germains, too." They'd been there for me, given me a place out of the storm, a place to weather the grief. *Family.*

Memaw touched my arm in tacit understanding. "How are the plans for the party coming?"

"You'll have to ask Claire. I'm out of it." Thank God, too, because I was fairly certain one of us wouldn't have survived. I went to fittings when she told me to. I nodded in agreement when she talked. I didn't hear anything.

We continued to walk until we came to a clearing, and then sat on gray rocks that were almost large enough to be boulders. I asked, "How are they dealing with Kai's homecoming?"

"They're not. George spends most of his time at the office, and Claire…"

"Claire is very free with her opinions."

"Don't let it get to you."

"I'll try. How did Claire wind up with George?" I wondered aloud.

"My son met her when he was too young to know any better."

"Does he love her?"

"Yes, but he also likes a challenge. It makes him feel like he's constantly earning something."

I snorted in laughter. "How like a lawyer to enjoy the take down."

"Were you a challenge?" Memaw asked.

"Maybe. Not really, I don't think. I had put up walls, but to Kai they were made of glass. He saw right through them. He was very persistent."

"He knew what he wanted," Memaw commented, "and he went after it."

"Yes, he did."

"Most of us see the truth between you and Kai. Claire will either climb on board or she won't. It's that simple."

I let out a breath, along with some of my tension. "It would be easier. On Kai that is, if she could just learn to accept me."

"It would be easier on all of us, honey. How is Kai?"

"He's okay."

"What's going on between Kai and Wyatt?"

"Not a lot. Both are in a state of mutual avoidance." I shook my head. "I like Wyatt. I like him a lot. And Lucy. I'm glad they're happy." I stood and stretched my back, unable to hide another yawn.

Memaw laughed. "Come on, I'll take you back to the Chelsers'."

I put a hand to my slowly rounding belly. "I feel like I'm sleeping all the time."

"Do you believe it yet?" She glanced at my midsection.

I shrugged. "Not yet. I don't think I'll believe it until I push the thing out of me."

She laughed. "You have such a way with words, Sage."

•••

I was setting a basket of newly-gathered eggs on the counter when my cell phone buzzed. Answering it, I heard Jules' voice on the other end just as the doorbell rang. "Hold on a second," I told her.

Throwing open the door, I stared at my best friend, who grinned, held out her phone and then hung up. She held a wrapped present under her arm and her suitcase rested on the porch.

"What are you doing here?" I asked, even as I enveloped Jules in an exuberant hug.

Grinning like an imp, Jules stepped into the foyer. "Kai and I planned this—thought you might need some reinforcements for this party you told me so much about."

"Best surprise ever!"

"Where is he?"

"With Keith, leading a group on a horse-back riding trail."

"Say what, now?"

I laughed. "He spends most of his days outdoors, getting his hands dirty."

"How Clint Eastwood of him."

"You have to stay here."

Jules set her bag down by the door. "Really?"

"Are you kidding? Alice will insist. This place is like a youth hostel." I pointed to the box. "What's that?"

"A gift for you."

"For me?"

"Well, for my niece or nephew."

I grinned and took the present into the kitchen. I tore off the wrapping paper, opened the box and pulled out a stuffed giraffe. "Could this be any cuter?"

"I got it from one of those really expensive baby boutiques."

"Upper East Side?"

"You know it."

"Thanks, Jules." I set the giraffe down on the chair. "I love it."

"There is a basket of eggs on the counter."

"Observant of you," I teased. "They have chickens."

"Chickens?"

"You know, *cluck cluck cluck.*"

"I know what a chicken is."

"I collect the eggs."

Jules laughed. "Dorothy, I don't think we're in Brooklyn anymore."

"Haven't been for a long time. You hungry?"

"Starved."

I made us sandwiches and then sat at the table. "Kai's mother continues to hate me."

"Has she spent any time with you at all?"

"As little as possible."

"I really wish you weren't knocked up. What's gossiping without a bottle of wine?"

"How about some chocolate?"

"Guess that will have to do."

"I'm glad you're here."

"I wish it was under better circumstances."

I sighed. "You know when you walk into your home and take a deep breath and feel the sanctuary of it?"

"Yeah."

"Being here feels something like that, but also like I'm hopping from one rock to another, trying not to fall into molten lava."

"That makes absolutely no sense."

"There's peace here, but there isn't. I don't know—maybe it's the hormones. Or this is the place where it all collides, and when it's over, I'm left with nothing but broken pieces."

"You talk in riddles; you didn't used to do that."

"Sorry, my brain is scrambled."

"Scrambled brains, yum. What do they taste like?"

"A little bit salty. From all the tears." Shaking my head, I smiled. "Come on, let's see if we can get Memaw to bake us something. You're going to love her."

•••

Kai and I had booked an expansive, cream-colored suite at the Hermitage Hotel, so we could get ready before the reception. Afterward, we'd come upstairs, soak in the Jacuzzi, and wash away the ordeal that would be this night. Kai, looking handsome in his tuxedo, had left thirty minutes ago.

He was probably at the hotel bar having a drink. I was alone with Jules, who was helping me with my hair and dress.

"Stop laughing," I demanded as I ran a hand down the ridiculous tulle skirt. I turned back to the mirror and stared at my reflection. I looked like a doll—lifeless and cold. "Why did I decide to do this?"

Jules sobered, rose from her chair and tied my sash into a bow. "Because you love Kai."

"It's that simple? I love him; therefore, I suffer?" I groused.

"Just wait. You'll see."

"See what?"

"I can't tell you. It will be worth it, though."

"He planned a surprise? Another one? He's full of them." I couldn't help the smile that tugged across my face.

"He did good with the farmhouse, didn't he? Trust him."

I reached for Jules' hand and squeezed it. "Can you tell I'm pregnant in this dress?"

"Yes," she said.

"Sometimes I wish you'd lie to me."

"No, you don't. Then you couldn't trust anything I said."

"There is that."

"You look beautiful," she went on. "You've got that pregnant glow."

I shot her a look, and she shrugged.

"The dress really isn't that bad, just not your style—you can do this."

"I don't want to leave this hotel suite. It's gorgeous and safe, and down in that ballroom, I'm going to have to talk to people I don't know and smile until my face hurts."

Jules linked her arm through mine and led me to the door. "Just think about what happens after the party."

"It's not appropriate to talk about."

"*Ga-ross!*"

We laughed as we got into the elevator. I fell silent, listening to the sound of my own heart. There would be people I knew, and I'd take comfort in the small dose of the familiar. Most of my life had become the unfamiliar, but I'd deal with that, too; I always did. I was nothing, if not adaptable.

I searched for Kai, wondering why I couldn't find him in the crowd. Letting Jules guide me, I didn't know where we were going until I saw the stage. Kai sat on a stool, a mandolin across his lap.

His blue-gray eyes were devouring me, and I didn't care that everyone could see. His face was a canvas, painted in shades of love and hope. My gaze slid to the lone man walking onto the platform. He carried a banjo and sat in the other chair.

I recognized Béla Fleck, whose song Kai had performed the first night we'd met—the song that always hummed just below the surface of my skin.

They played it for me.

When they finished, they moved into another song, something I'd never heard before. I knew it was written for me, for us. Kai stared at me, his heart in his eyes; mine was in my throat.

●●●

I leaned into Kai, pressing myself against him as we swayed on the dance floor, our arms wrapped around each other. I sighed in dreamy contentment. "You are an incredible husband." I stared at him as I brushed a hand down his tuxedo-clad arm.

Kai smiled, the corners of his eyes crinkling. "Award-winning?"

I laughed. "Yes. When did you write that song?"

"You nap a lot now—I had some time."

"That simple, huh?"

"Ever hear of a little thing called inspiration?"

I grinned. "Starting to." My journal writings had diverged onto a new path, paved with thick mossy trees and speckled with sunlight. I wondered where it would lead, and if I'd follow.

"So how'd you get him here?"

"Béla Fleck?"

"Yeah."

"My secret. Just know that there isn't anything I wouldn't do for you."

"Good to know."

I brought his mouth close to mine, getting ready to ask him if he wanted to leave when George appeared next to us and asked, "Can I cut in?"

I swallowed my sigh of disappointment. I wanted to be with Kai, and only Kai, but our time alone would have to wait.

"Sure. I'll go dance with Memaw." Kai brought my hand to his lips, his eyes promising me joy and other things, before walking away.

George held out his arms and I stepped into them. "Thank you," he said.

"For what?"

"For going along with this."

"Did it make Claire happy?"

George's lips twitched in humor. "Does anything make Claire happy? No, I was thanking you for myself. It made my home life far more enjoyable this past month."

I chuckled. "You're welcome."

George looked over my shoulder and stared at Kai. "He used to be so restless. Now he looks happy."

"He is."

"We have you to thank for that."

"Me?"

"I don't know how I can ever repay you. What you've done for Kai, for our family…"

My eyes misted. "We're family, George. You owe me nothing."

George was about to reply when there was a shout from across the room. I turned at the sound, wondering what was happening. I saw Wyatt kneeling on the ground next to a form I couldn't make out. Breaking free of George's embrace I ran, shoving people out of the way. The crowd parted as I approached, and I saw a pale and unconscious Memaw on the floor. She looked small and frail, and the pulse at her neck fluttered like the beat of a dragonfly's wing.

Kai yelled for someone to call an ambulance. His eyes scanned the guests, and I knew he was looking for me. When he saw me, he reached out, grabbed me by the hand and pulled me to his side.

I placed a hand on the frantic beating of his heart.

•••

The mood in the Ferris library was somber. George's eyes were empty, his face painting a picture of disbelief. Memaw had had a stroke. By the time the ambulance had arrived, it was too late. Her life had slipped away, like soil through a closed hand.

Everyone was still in their formal wear, a painful reminder that hours ago we had been celebrating. Now, we would have to plan for a funeral.
Is this life? From happiness and health to death in one breath?

I glanced at Kai. Solemn face, haunted eyes, but his grip was strong in mine.

"I need to lie down," George announced, his voice broken. Standing, he set his bourbon on the end table. He paused, looking unsure before leaving.

"Should we start thinking about the funeral?" Wyatt asked.

Claire nodded. "I'll start the arrangements."

George wasn't in a mental state to see to it, and now Claire was the matriarch of the family. She had duties and impossible shoes to fill.

Lucy spoke up, "Please let me know what I can do to help."

Wyatt and Lucy left, and the room was quiet with loss.

Claire looked at her son before her eyes darted to me. "Will you leave? After the funeral I mean? There's nothing keeping you here anymore."

Kai was about to answer when I interjected, "We haven't talked about it yet, but I think we'll stay for a few more weeks, at least."

He gazed at me, tracing a finger over my ear, his eyes saying everything his mouth couldn't. Turning his attention back to his mother, he said, "Get some rest, Mom." Kai stood and kissed his mother on the cheek.

"Kaplan is coming by tomorrow to read the will."

"We'll be here," Kai assured her. We were out the front door, and the cool night welcomed us, a reprieve from the subdued intensity of the library. "Want to go for a drive?"

"Sure."

Kai drove us up into the mountains and parked. We got out of the car, and he stripped off his tuxedo jacket and bowtie, and threw them into the back seat.

"I wish I could get out of this dress."

"You can." He reached for my zipper.

"I'll be in nothing but a slip."

"Who cares? No one to see you out here."

"I'll be cold." The weather had turned. It was officially autumn.

After he helped me out of the gown, I shrugged into his tuxedo jacket, and we climbed onto the hood and sat next to each other.

We watched the stars winking at us from above. I never saw them in New York due to the city's light pollution. I had settled for so little, but I had thought it was so much. But moments like these were what mattered.

"You're sad."

"Yeah, but not in the way you think."

"Explain."

"I miss her already, but I'm not sure I believe it yet. I can't help but hope she's with my grandfather."

"In a better place and all that?"

"Maybe. I think she's with Tristan and Reece, too, and they're all sitting around a table playing poker, waiting for the rest of us to join them."

"She played poker?"

"Are you kidding? She taught me the game, and she was better at it than anyone. God, I learned so much from both of them—things I never learned from my own parents."

"Tell me what you learned, tell me what you're going to teach our children."

His hand toyed with my hair as he answered, "My grandfather taught me how to play the mandolin, to hold a fishing rod, to recognize the right woman when she came along."

"How did you know I was the right one?" I asked, snuggling close to him, undoing the top few buttons of his shirt and placing my hand against his warm skin.

"I wanted you for more than one night. I started thinking in terms of forever when I met you—and I'd never been one to dream about forever. I didn't think I deserved it. You made me want to stop wandering, made me want to finish something, made me want to love you with everything that I am."

A lone tear, an elegant dewdrop, escaped the corner of my eye. "And your grandmother, what did you learn from her?"

"Everything—," his voice caught in the back of his throat, "everything else."

•••

"Can I get anyone a drink?" Claire asked, ever the polite hostess. We shook our heads, except George, who didn't appear to be listening. I sat on a leather couch in the library, holding Kai's hand. Wyatt was alone in a chair, and Claire perched next to her husband, her spine straight.

Kaplan, the lawyer, picked up the document resting on the desk and cleared his throat. He read Memaw's words, "My liquid assets, including stocks, retirement funds and bank balances are to be divided evenly between my son, George, and my grandsons, Wyatt and Kai. As for my home and all properties, including land—I bequeath to Sage Harper Ferris."

"*What?*" I asked, feeling like I'd gone momentarily dumb. "Can you repeat that?" I stared at the lawyer, uncomprehending. Kai looked like he hadn't even heard the news.

Kaplan reread Memaw's will, and then Claire perused me as if seeing me for the first time.

"This has to be some kind of mistake," Claire said.

"Mom," Wyatt began.

"No, we have to contest this. She obviously wasn't in her right mind." Claire stood, her eyes blazing.

"Memaw was as sane as they come," Kai stated.

Claire turned towards Kai. "Your wife," she spat, "has been in the family for all of five minutes. This is *ridiculous*—how did you do it, Sage?"

"You think I *orchestrated* this?" I gasped.

"Stop it!" Kai pleaded. He stood, ready to defend me.

"Claire," George snapped, coming out of the daze he'd been in for the better part of two days. "That's enough. This was my mother's choice, not yours. Sit. Down."

"How can you be so calm about this?" Claire hissed.

George's eyes were dull when they focused on his wife. "She discussed it with me before she changed her will."

Claire's eyes widened. "What? What are you talking about?"

"About two months ago, shortly after Kai and Sage came home," George said, exhaustion pervading his voice.

With one last baleful glance in my direction, Claire stormed out of the room. George looked after her, his face weary, and said, "I don't have the strength."

"I'll go." Kai said, following his mother.

"Kaplan, I'll walk you out," George said.

"Thanks," the lawyer said. "The rest of the details are spelled out clearly in the will. Call me if you have any questions."

No doubt he was used to triggering emotional landmines. Perhaps this family was normal.

When I was alone with Wyatt, I said, "*I did not—*"

He cut me off. "I know."

"I don't understand. Why did Memaw do it?"

Wyatt smiled. "Honestly I think Memaw thought that if she gave you the land and house, it might give you two a reason to stay."

Setting a hand on my belly, I leaned my head against the back of the couch. I felt a ripple just below the surface of my skin, realizing my child moved for the first time. Even in my state of grief, I was overwhelmed by a surge of joy and a deeper connection with the life I carried inside me.

It reminded me that birth and death were merely front and back covers—the stuff in between nothing more than a novella.

Chapter 23

Kai

My mother and I were outside behind the house, the smell of changing leaves and wood smoke in the air.

Mom crossed her arms over her chest and refused to look at me.

"This isn't about the will at all, is it?" My voice carried across the abyss of resentment. I doubted she'd hear me.

"She's a predator."

"You're still on this? She thought I was a broke musician when we met. She thought I had nothing, and she still wanted me. Besides, she has her own money."

"What are you talking about?"

"Her mother was Penny Harper, the author. She left Sage everything when she died."

"*The* Penny Harper?"

"Yeah. Sage isn't using me. She didn't trap me, Mom. We love each other. Why can't you understand that?"

"That doesn't change how fast you two got married. You still barely know each other."

"You know, it doesn't matter what you think anymore. I'm a man. I wish you could see me as one."

Her face and voice were tight with pain. "You don't know what it's like—to have expectations and then have them—"

"Fall short? That's what you want to say, right? I'm a raging disappointment?" I raked a hand through my hair. "Do you love me?" It came out as an accusation.

Genuine hurt flashed across her face. "Of course I do."

"No," I said quietly, "I don't think you do. If you did, you wouldn't be trying to burn down everything I've tried to build for myself." It was devastating to realize my own mother didn't love me unconditionally.

"And what is it you think you've built? Your father and I have been married over thirty years. You think it's easy? You think love is enough?"

I laughed without amusement. "No, it isn't. But we're right for each other and I can't explain why. We're meant to be together."

"Sure, for now. Until things get too hard for you. And they will get too hard for you, Kai. You ran when Tristan and Reece died. You'll run again, and she'll let you."

My body went cold with anger. "Wow. You've got no illusions about who I am, huh?" I stared at her. "I'm guessing you had no idea I was supposed to be in that plane."

Mom gazed at me, her hawk eyes narrowing. "What are you talking about?"

I knew Alice and Keith hadn't told my parents. They, themselves, wouldn't have even known about it if I hadn't been drinking after the crash. But drunk out of my mind, I hadn't been able to hold the words in my mouth, so I'd spewed them, hoping it would rid me of the blackness. Alice and Keith had carried the truth for two years, letting me tell it when I was ready. If I had never returned, they would've gone on bearing it, but I was back now, and everyone needed to know.

"Reece and I played *rock, paper, scissors* for the first flight, and I won, but I gave him my spot. I thought I was being a good friend. I left when they died because of the guilt." I stared at my mother; she paled with my admission. "It should've been me up there—but I'm glad I lived, do you know why?"

Mom was silent.

"If Reece had been the one to live, he would've died from the guilt. He was softer than us; kinder, gentler—better. I lived through it all, because I *could*. He wouldn't have made it, Mom."

"Alice and Keith…they never said anything."

"Wasn't their secret to share; it wasn't their shame to unburden. Would you have heard them, anyway? Would it have made you understand me better? Curse at me, rant at me, yell at me if you want, but you will leave my wife out of this. If you continue on this way, you'll drive us away, and we'll never come back."

"Are you threatening me?" Her voice was as thin as a reed ready to snap.

"Sage is everything to me, Mom."

I stared at my mother before leaving her alone with her righteousness and my confession. Seeds of bitterness didn't grow into trees overnight, and I doubted I'd be able to fell them in day.

Maybe I should stop trying.

•••

Later that evening, Keith and I were sharing a beer in the kitchen of the Chelser ranch house. Sage was upstairs asleep, and Alice was getting ready for bed. Jules had wanted to stay for the funeral, but I'd told her it was unnecessary, so she had hopped on a plane that morning.

"Memaw left the house and land to Sage?" Keith asked.

I nodded. "Dad knew about the change to the will. Mom shit a brick."

"How did Wyatt react?"

"He was okay with it," I said. "The only one who can't wrap her head around it is Mom. She used it as an excuse to unload all her pent up anger at me. She's pissed I left home, she's pissed I got married really fast. She's just pissed."

"Can you blame her? Take a step back. Maybe she didn't handle her emotions all that well, but can you see her points?"

"Yeah, I can, but enough already. I'm happy. Sage and I are happy. It's like Mom doesn't believe me or something."

"Claire's a complicated woman. It must be hard for her to watch her son live a life she never could've imagined for him."

"But it's *my* life," I gritted. "Mine and Sage's."

"When you have family, it's never really your own. You're tied to other people, son, always will be. No matter where you live or where you go that tether is still there, and it can't be cut no matter how sharp the shears."

"I wish she loved me for me. I finally told her the truth—that I was supposed to be in the plane." I wiped a hand across my face feeling bone-deep tired. "I don't know if that will make a difference to her—I still ran."

"You can't expect to sort out a lifetime of hurt and misunderstandings in a few months, Kai."

"It took two years, but I ran in a very large circle, and where did I end up? Back in the mountains. There isn't enough distance from Monteagle, no matter where I go."

"This is your place, and the sooner you make peace with it, all of it, then maybe you'll begin to heal."

"I'm healed."

"You think you are, until someone pulls on a ratty thread and it all comes undone again. Maybe you should stay. For a little while, at least."

"Stay here?" The idea churned in my mind like clothes in a washing machine.

Keith shrugged. "Memaw gave you guys a house and land for a reason. I'm sure she wanted you to make peace with your soul—and with your family."

I craved a fishing rod in my hand, like an alcoholic yearned for a drink.

"Would Sage consider staying?"

"And live near my mother?" I snorted. "Can I really ask her to do that?"

"No, I mean, would she give you time here—because she loves you?"

"I don't know," I said, meaning it. "It's a lot to ask."

"Would you do it for her?"

"Of course."

"Ask her and find out."

•••

I couldn't stop the feeling of déjà vu as I watched my grandmother being lowered into the ground, and I wondered if my life would be defined by these moments—losing those closest to me. My existence was a series of gray milestones, and I was constantly tripping over them.

It smothered me, the somber faces and black clothes. I turned away, my hand dropping from Sage's. I began to walk and didn't stop until I reached a mausoleum, plopping down on the marble stone steps. Looking out the corner of my eye, I saw Sage's dainty feet in black heels. She perched next to me and plucked a late blooming dandelion from underneath the steps.

"I don't understand funerals. I mean, I do, but they're for the living, not the dead. Closure and all that kind of bullshit, but do people really get closure—ever?" My voice was hushed, mindful of our location.

Sage blew the dandelion, and we watched the seeds travel. "Moments like these aren't about closure."

"What are they about then?"

"Reconciliation."

I sighed. "I can't go to my parents' house after this and sit through another one of these things."

"Don't you think you should be there for your dad? He needs you."

I pulled out a handful of grass, clutching it in my grip. The land was green, alive, in a place where the reminder of death was all around us. "Why didn't you let Jules help you through your mother's death? She's your oldest friend."

"Why do we push away those we love?" she asked instead. "You might never have the relationship with your family that you want, but it wouldn't only be their fault. You're in this, too."

"Can we stay?"

"Stay?"

"In Monteagle. Not forever, but for now? There are things that I…"

"Have to reconcile—I know."

"You're not surprised I'm asking, are you?"

Sage knew me. Like words on a page, she read me.

She smiled and leaned her head against my shoulder. "If you need to stay, we'll stay." She took my hand.

"We'll go back to France," I vowed.

"I know. One day. I love that farmhouse. That turret, that fireplace in the living room." She smiled. "But it looks like our kid will be Southern."

"Wean him on bourbon and fishing," I teased.

"Just like his father."

•••

Tristan chews on a matchstick as he hands me the bottle of bourbon. Even in my dreams, I crave Gentleman Jack. I take a swig.

We are sitting on the edge of the mountain, watching the sun sink into earth. The colors are muted, like a memory that dims or turns gray.

"You say 'I do' out loud, once, but you make a choice, every day—it's active, not passive."

"Thanks for the advice," I say with a grin, but Tristan doesn't grin back.

"I know what I'm talking about."

"You? I'm supposed to take marriage advice from the guy that never saw a girl after he got her into bed?"

"That's why you should listen to me; I never played around on Lucy."

"I didn't think you did."

Tristan finally smiles. "Yeah, right. It's okay. I would've thought that about me, too."

"How did you change?"

"I just did. I'd do anything to see her happy. And she wanted me, bad boy and all."

"The heart wants what it wants, huh?"

Tristan laughs. "Man, the heart doesn't even know what it wants. It latches onto something and won't let go. It knows before the mind."

"The heart can play tricks on you. I think it's the ultimate creator of illusion."

"You don't think this is real?"

"What, talking to you? I know this isn't real."

"I meant you and Sage."

"Oh, that. It's terrifying, so I know it's real," I explain.

"Take this bottle of Jack. It feels real, tastes real, but it's still a dream. How do you know you and Sage aren't a dream in someone else's mind?"

"Because in a dream, I can do this." I throw the bottle of bourbon, and it hits the tree with enough force that it should shatter. It doesn't because the tree moves and catches the bottle in its spindly branches.

"Neat little trick." Tristan smiles.

"Our love is no trick."

"Whatever you say, Kai. Only you know the truth. I'm just a ghost."

Chapter 24

Sage

"I hate you, I hate you, I hate you," I grumbled, as I tied the laces of my tennis shoes.

"Oh come on, you'll have fun, promise," Kai said.

"I like the idea of fishing, but does it have to be so friggin' early?"

"You love me, remember? Do this for me?"

"I do love you." I sighed. "And I'll prove it by holding a fishing rod. On the upside, this is the first morning I haven't wanted to dry heave into the toilet."

I threw on a light jacket, knowing I'd strip it off later after the sun rose, but it would be chilly in the predawn air. The days were still warm, but the nights were cool.

We drove into the mountains and parked on an incline. We hiked up the hill, taking a leisurely pace. When we arrived at the lake, I said, "Okay, the view alone was worth getting up at the crack of dawn." Streaks of sun were bouncing off the water, making me think of silver fish scales.

Kai grinned and handed me a pole. He took me through the motions, but I was clumsy. Never losing his patience, he continued to teach. "No, like this." He adjusted my arm when I cast incorrectly. I watched him and marveled at his skill.

"You'll get better," he vowed, "but it's going to take lots and lots of practice."

"You're going to drag me up here day after day, aren't you?"

"Year after year," he went on.

I shook my head. "Hate to break it to you, sport, but I'm not a fisherwoman."

Kai pretended to be shocked. "Not in front of the kid!"

I laughed, the sound of it ringing through the trees. We fished in silence for a quarter of an hour, and then I spoke. "Should we move into your grandmother's house? Is it too soon?" It had only been a week since Memaw had died—it might always be too soon. If we lived there, would a lingering ghost haunt us? There were so many of them in Monteagle.

"I wanted to talk to you about that. I was thinking about building a house on her property."

"You mean tear hers down? I don't understand."

"No, leave it. Memaw put her money into the land, but her house is too small for a family. We'll use it as a guesthouse, but I want to build us our dream home. A home for our family."

"We might stay forever if you do that." My voice trembled with fear and hope.

"Forever is wherever we want it to be. France, here, New York."

"I hate New York—I never want to go back."

His eyes sought mine. "Could you be happy in Monteagle? Long term?"

"Could you?"

"I'm not sure anymore," he admitted. "Just when I think things won't change on me, they do."

He set his pole down and came to me. Taking mine from my hands, he set it along the bank and hugged me to him. "I can't imagine a life without you, Sage, and I don't even want to try. We'll change, but we'll do it together. That I can promise you."

Pulling back, I shook off the somberness of our conversation. "Now, take pity on me. Can we be done with fishing for today? I'm hungry." It was a few hours past sunrise, and I was ready for food.

Sighing in defeat, Kai packed up our gear and handed me the rods. "Can you take these back to the car? I'll grab everything else."

I started my descent, taking it slow. Though I was showing, I knew I wasn't as large as I felt. Still, I had bruises on my arms and legs because I kept bumping into things—corners of doorways, coffee tables. My mind hadn't caught up with my blundering body, or maybe it was the other way around.

After breakfast, maybe I'd get a nice soak in the tub, wash away the dirt and steep my muscles. Perhaps Kai would like to…

Momentarily lost in thoughts about steaming water and my naked husband, one of my shoes caught the root of a tree, and I tripped. I dropped the poles and tried to put my hands out in front of me, but I went down hard, landing on my stomach.

"Sage!" Kai cried, crouching down to help me. I was dazed, my vision speckled. Gently, he hauled me up, his arms steadying me.

I was wobbly and scared, and I felt stupid.

"Lean into me," he commanded as he guided me back to the car.

My heart galloped in my chest. I rested my hands protectively over my stomach, but something told me my efforts were in vain.

We were driving down the mountain when I felt the cramps start low in my belly. I moaned in pain.

"Kai? I need to go the hospital—and hurry."

•••

We were alone in the hospital room, so no one was there to witness our version of rock bottom. Rock bottom had layers, and every time we peeled back another one, there were more waiting for us. It was deep and gritty–a sharp descent into nightmare.

"My fault," Kai mumbled. His arms were around me, and I felt tremors pulse through him.

"No, it's not like you pushed me. How is this your fault?"

"You wouldn't have been on that mountain if it weren't for me."

I held him, my tears soaking his shirt as I tried to soothe him with my hands and crooning noises.

"I'm so sorry, Sage." He said the words into my hair.

"Not your fault."

"Do you still want me?"

"More than life."

He gripped me. "Don't say that."

"Hold me, Kai, don't let me go."

"Never."

"How do we get through this?" I wondered. My voice sounded very far away, as though it belonged to someone else.

"I—I don't know."

The man I loved didn't have an answer.

"But, we have each other, don't we?" he whispered, the thread of a lifeline in his voice.

I clung to his words, a tiny raft in a vast sea of sorrow.

Chapter 25

Kai

When Sage was released from the hospital, I wasn't sure where I was supposed to take her, so I went to the Chelsers, knowing she needed a mother's care. My own was ill-equipped to handle Sage's anguish—or anyone's, for that matter. Tucking my wife into bed, I rubbed her back until she fell asleep.

Then I left.

Guilt blended with bile, and it threatened to swallow me—it was a familiar feeling.

I parked in an oily lot next to an old beat up truck and went into the shadowy dive. Approaching the bar, I ordered a shot of cheap bourbon and threw it back. It gave me no respite as it burned my insides.

Sitting down on the stool, I ordered another, attempting to drown myself.

I had taken Sage fishing—I had cajoled and pleaded because I wanted to share what I loved.

My fault.

Always my fault.

It was my burden to suffer, and no amount of absolution would make me feel otherwise.

Our baby...

But I still had Sage. She wasn't lost to me, thank fate, but the fist around my heart clenched. Why didn't it just squeeze until there was nothing left? Pulverize it already.

I couldn't swallow more guilt, so I washed it down with another drink.

Later, maybe hours, Lucy strolled into the bar and plopped down on a stool next to me. When I reached for a shot, she knocked it out of my hand. The glass clattered across the bar, spraying the old scarred wood with alcohol.

Her eyes were blue, electric, angry. "Your wife woke up to find you gone. Why aren't you at home, holding her?"

My gaze slipped away, unable to face her, too.

But Lucy would not be denied. She grabbed my chin and made me look at her, made me peer into the mirror.

I did not like the reflection.

"You didn't do this." She searched my face for understanding.

"I'm a fucking tragedy. My two best friends die in a plane crash. My grandmother dies at my wedding celebration. My baby…"

"You'll come through this—you both will." Her voice was hard, unyielding. "You need to be there for her. Drinking in a shitty dive is not being there for her."

I shook my head. "I—"

"Do you want me to split your lip? Tristan and Reece aren't here to talk sense into you, and I know you won't listen to Wyatt, so it's fallen to me. Get. Up."

Somehow, I did as I was told and let Lucy lead me out into the dark.

When had it become night?

"I'm about to break," I whispered.

"Hasn't happened yet," Lucy said, opening the passenger door of her car. "You can come back from this."

"How can you be so cold?" I lashed out. I settled into the seat, and she slammed the door shut behind me. I wanted to hit something.

She walked to her side, got in and started the engine. "How can *you*? You snuck off after Sage fell asleep. How like the Kai-of-old," she taunted.

"I'm a shit—you don't think I know that?"

"Did drinking in a bar help?"

"You know it didn't."

"Then why did you do it? You need to be there for her, and you should let her be there for you."

"I know, God, I know." I rubbed my hand across my eyes. "I hate myself. So much I want to die."

"You don't get to die. Too many of us already have."

It was another reminder that I was unworthy, and that I screwed up every time things got hard. I wondered if my mother was right—I wondered if I'd changed at all.

The sharp anger in Lucy's voice dulled. "This is awful—terrible, but is it any worse than Alice and Keith losing Reece? They *knew* Reece. They watched him grow from boy to man."

I was silent as Lucy drove.

She went on, "Tragedy is tragedy, any way you slice it, but you can let this rip you apart, or you can cling fiercely to everything that matters. There will be more children for you and Sage."

"You sound so sure."

When Lucy dropped me off in the Chelsers' driveway, I didn't wait for her to cut the engine before I was out the door. I stalked into the house and went upstairs. Alice sat by the bed, her gaze accusatory. I didn't pay attention as I crawled in next to Sage and held her while we cried for all we'd lost.

•••

"It's not your fault," Tristan says.

"So people keep telling me." I keep my eyes closed. I feel like someone split me open down the middle, the void within me as deep as the Grand Canyon.

"What's it like?"

"What?"

"Feeling your child kick?"

"Dream Tristan is strangely maudlin and soft-hearted. What happened to the guy that raced motorcycles?"

"I change as you change, your hopes are my hopes. I'm a reflection of you."

"I never got to feel it kick," I murmur. So many dreams lost. "Sage felt it though. She described it like a flutter, but not. All wonder and hope."

"Your teenage self would be embarrassed to be seen with you. You know that, right?"

We have a good laugh, and I feel lighter. The darkness around the corners of my vision ebbs a little. I shake my head. "It's weird; you look at yourself every day in the mirror and see the same face. And, then you start to notice the faint wrinkles around your eyes that were never there before, the laugh lines

*around your mouth don't fade as quickly, your
dreams have become different, but you don't
remember how you got there."*

*"Life is kind of like driving on autopilot,
hmmm?" Tristan comments.*

*"Do we wake up at the end of the road and think,
'Is this as far as I can go?'"*

*"There's not one way, y'know. There are
detours, forks, cattle crossings that make you stop,
take pause."*

"I'm looking around now," I note.

"Do you like who you've become?"

"Very rarely."

*"Sounds about right," Tristan remarks with a
bland smile.*

"I don't think I handle things all that well."

*"You come back, though. Every time. It might
take you a while, but you do. A fucking boomerang."*

"You're not just saying that?"

"You tell me. This is your dream."

Chapter 26

Sage

Sometime the next afternoon, I woke in bed alone. I inhaled, trying to place the smell; it was the scent of comfort, relief—it was chicken soup.

Kai had come home late the previous night—Lucy had seen to it. He'd held me as we fell asleep.

Was he gone already?

I rose, testing my body, feeling sore, used, and battered. Pulling on a pair of slippers and a sweatshirt, I padded downstairs. I was cold.

Alice and Kai were in the kitchen—Alice stirred a large pot of soup, and Kai diced vegetables. I cleared my throat, announcing my presence.

Kai turned, his face ravaged by his own pain, yet he managed to smile for me. Though he had left me for hours the night before, I didn't hold it against him. I'd once blamed Connor for leaving me in my grief, but this didn't feel the same.

"Want some soup?" Alice asked.

"Is it ready?" My voice sounded dry, like the crunching of crisp autumn leaves underfoot.

Alice ladled broth into a bowl and set it on the table. "Chicken soup heals all wounds."

"Even the ones on the inside?" I sank into a chair, not missing the look between Kai and Alice. Kai set down the knife and came to me. Leaning over, he kissed the top of my head and then left the room. I watched him go, wondering how many bowls of soup he'd eaten, and if they had restored him. "Are we going to have a talk?"

"No." Alice pulled out another chair and sat down, and I picked up my spoon. Placing a hand on my arm, she stopped me from taking a bite. "Look at me."

It took a moment, but finally I gazed into Alice's eyes. They were old, battle scarred. They knew things that came from fighting emotional wars she could never win—only temper. Alice knew there was nothing to be said. Some caverns of suffering could not be filled with words.

I was too numb to cry, and I wondered if it would've helped anyway.

•••

Alice left me alone on the couch, wrapped in a blanket. Where was Kai? Probably on the mountain, or maybe at the cemetery. Was he praying, hoping for peace, or had he finally given up?

I wanted to comfort him, but I could barely comfort myself.

I heard the back door open, and then Keith was in the living room. "Put on your shoes."

"Why?"

"Trust me."

I sighed, but did as bid and then followed him to the stables and into a stall. "I can't ride yet."

"I know. This is Mabel," Keith said, patting the brown mare's neck. Picking up a currying comb, he dropped it into my hand. "Brush in circles." He gave me a few whole apples and carrots, and then left me alone.

I stared at the mare. What did horses do when they lost their foals? They went on, because nature designed them that way. It was so much harder to be human.

"What have you lived through, Mabel?" Mabel snorted and shook her head, and looked at me with liquid brown eyes. "I wish you had all the answers and you could tell them to me. Do you have infinite wisdom in all things that matter? Of course you don't—you're just a horse. What the hell do you know?" Pulling out an apple, I offered it in the palm of my hand. It disappeared into Mabel's mouth. The horse nudged me with her head, wanting more, and I obliged. I began rubbing Mabel down, losing myself in time and the repetitive motion. It was soothing, calming, like how a mother would feel patting her infant's back. The attention was for both of them. So, I lavished love on the mare because I didn't have a child to hold in my arms—a child I would never know.

It had been a boy.

Kai's son.

Legacy.

Hope.

My tears came like a bubbling geyser; I looped my arms around Mabel's neck and pressed my face against her. And because Mabel was a horse, all she could give was her solid, sturdy presence.

Somehow, it was enough.

•••

I reached for Kai but found his side of the bed empty and cold—he'd been gone a while. I trudged to the back porch, knowing he would be staring at the night sky. Looking for answers or forgiveness, I didn't know which.

I pressed a kiss to his shoulder and then sat next to him and asked, "You ever feel like you're trying to break through a wall, hoping to find out what's past the grief?"

"Are you on the other side yet?"

"I don't know. It's only been a week. Are you?"

He took my hand and skimmed my knuckles with his thumb, but did not reply.

"Come back to me, Kai."

We were quiet, and a contentment I never thought I'd feel again embraced me. It made me drowsy, and I cuddled into his arms. We were in the thick of autumn. It would be winter soon. Seasons changed, so did people.

"Still want that house?" he asked.

"Yes."

"Forgive me?"

"There's nothing to forgive."

"Still love me?"

"Always."

•••

"Where are you going?" Kai demanded.

I put on a jacket and slipped on my shoes, tugging my hair into a ponytail. "To see your father."

"Sage…"

"Someone has to pull him out of this."

"And you think you're the one for the job?" His eyes were full of concern, unsure.

"I do."

"Haven't you done enough fighting? Do you have the strength to take on his burdens, too?"

"It's been over a month since we lost Memaw, and it's time for him to rejoin us."

Kai hugged me. What could he say? He knew I was right.

"Jules wants to come down."

I shook my head. "No, I can't have another person watching over me." The giraffe Jules had bought as a gift for our child was now mashed underneath our mattress, along with my journal, and everything else I didn't want to contend with.

"Okay," Kai agreed, "but call her and tell her yourself—she doesn't believe me. Call Celia while you're at it. She wants to hear your voice."

"I will," I promised.

I drove to the Ferris' house and used Kai's keys to let myself in. Knowing Claire was not there made it easier, but I still sighed in respite. She'd come to the hospital when I lost the baby, but had stayed in the waiting room. I didn't know if it had been because she hated me, or because she thought her presence would make my pain worse. I knew she would return eventually, but for the time being I could focus on George.

Alice had given me a casserole to bring with me, hoping that might entice George to eat—I brought a bottle of bourbon. I knew what he needed.

"George?" I called out, but he didn't answer. Following a hunch, I went to the library. He sat on the couch, a newspaper that he wasn't reading spread across his lap. He looked at me, his face not registering surprise.

"Are you taking anything to help you sleep?" I asked without preamble.

"Just bourbon." His voice was rusty, like an old, clogged copper pipe. He held up his glass of melting ice cubes and potent liquor. "What are you doing here, Sage?"

"Thought you could use a drinking buddy." I set the casserole down on the table before opening the bottle of bourbon and taking a swig. It was only eleven in the morning, but there was nothing like death to make a person forget the time.

"Not even going to bother with a glass?"

I shot him a look. "Careful, you sound very much like your wife, who already disapproves of me. Besides, there's no one here to witness my crassness except you."

I poured him a double and then settled onto the couch.

"You shouldn't be here."

"Why not?"

"Because." It was a flimsy excuse.

"Because I'm supposed to be sitting at home in the dark mourning my child?"

He flinched. "I'm sorry for your loss."

"I'm sorry for yours."

"Don't."

"Listen, George, we can do this the hard way or the easy way. Hard way is for you to deny me. Easy way is for you to let me sit here, drink until we're hammered, and I'll listen to you talk."

"I don't want to talk."

"That's fine, then I will. I lost my mother, too, remember?"

"And your father. You were a lot younger than me."

"I don't remember my dad," I admitted. "There's no shame in how you're behaving. We all handle loss in different ways."

"You're pretty transparent. There's no guile in you, no manipulation."

"Your wife doesn't agree."

"Claire doesn't know what to think."

"She's irrational."

"Undoubtedly." He paused. "I'm ashamed."

"Of what? Claire? Kai?"

"Myself—for letting Kai go."

"He was here one minute and gone the next—you didn't have a chance to stop him."

"Didn't even leave a note. Can you imagine?" George looked at me; his eyes held wonder, confusion, hope.

"Not one of his best moments."

"Is my son a coward? I used to think he was, but I'm not sure anymore."

"He left, George, but he did come back."

"Claire told me Kai was supposed to be in the plane."

"Yes."

"God, it's been awful for him, hasn't it? I had no idea."

"Some of us are meant to go on, no matter what life throws at us. Kai is no coward. You know, it was his idea to stay and mend the family after your mother died—it was his idea to build a house on your mother's land. I had nothing to do with that."

He took a long swallow of his drink and rubbed a hand over his mouth as though he tasted bitterness. "It's nice having him home. I've missed him."

"He's missed you, too."

"Really?"

I nodded.

He sighed. "I would really like a chance to get to know my son."

"You will," I promised, "but he is not going to be the person you expect him to be."

George looked thoughtful. "I think he may be someone better."

•••

We drank and talked for hours, and I even managed to make George laugh. His face was ruddy with color and bourbon, and half the casserole was eaten right out of the dish by the time Claire returned home.

She popped into the library, her countenance disapproving. "What's this?"

"I came over to cheer George up." I hiccoughed.

Claire looked at her husband as he smiled, his lips curving like the bow of a boat. "It's not even cocktail hour. How long have you been drinking?"

"When did you leave?" George slurred.

"Ten-thirty."

"Then about five minutes after that," George explained, and I couldn't stop a giggle from escaping my mouth. Claire glared at us.

I rolled my eyes, but said nothing. Drinking with my father-in-law seemed to be doing some sort of trick—for both of us.

"Sage?" Kai called out, the front door opening and closing.

"Library," I called back, then grinned at Kai when he came to stand in the doorway next to his mother. "Your dad and I were chewing the fat about life and stuff. Right, George?" I glanced at my father-in-law, whose eyes were closed, and he was on the verge of snoring.

"You outdrank my dad? I'm impressed."

"I'm sleepy," I admitted. "Take me home?"

Claire's watchful gaze followed us, but she said nothing. It was out of character, but I would take any reprieve I could get. Maybe Claire felt bad for all that I had lost. I had no idea.

When we were settled in Kai's car, I said, "Don't take me to Alice and Keith's."

"You said to take you home."

"That's not home. We have a home for the time being—your grandmother's cabin."

"But—"

"I want my own space, and I want to make love to you as loud as I want." I missed our intimacy, our physical connection.

His breath hitched. "The doctor?"

"Cleared me a few days ago."

"How drunk are you?"

"Very."

"Sage…"

"I always want you. Please, Kai, I need you to hold me, so I can feel your heart beating against mine."

We barely made it into the foyer before we fell together onto the floor. It was not making love—it was primal, needy, desperate. And when it was over and he cradled my face in his hands, I felt a deep well open. My breath became shallow and tears seeped out of the corners of my eyes.

"What is it, darlin'?"

"My love for you sometimes overwhelms me."

He pulled me close and rested his lips on my shoulder. "It's nice."

"What?"

"Knowing I'm not alone."

"I'll love you forever."

He sighed. "I'm counting on it."

•••

I was on the front porch of Memaw's cabin, a notebook open on my lap, doodling in the corner of a page. The door opened and closed, and Kai came next to me, holding his mandolin. He pulled up a chair and sat down, his fingers strumming the strings a few times before stopping.

"Do you think death is organized or just completely random?" he asked.

"What do you mean?"

"Like, do you think God, or the universe or whatever just picks people off, or is there a method or something?"

"Are you really asking me if there is an algorithm to death?"

He paused in thought before nodding. "Yeah, I think that's what I'm asking." He played a quick song; it sounded familiar but wasn't. It was probably one he had written.

"I don't know."

Kai laughed though it wasn't a joyful sound. "Neither do I."

Somewhere in the distance, a bird cawed. "Play me something."

"What do you want to hear?"

"I don't know. Transport me. Take me someplace else."

"Climb aboard this magic carpet ride." He dipped his head and closed his eyes. His hands moved over the wooden body of the instrument that defined him. Kai was a mandolin player. He'd been other things, too; wanderer, dreamer, survivor.

Experiences shaped us. Some we clung to, others we threw to the wind. I wondered if we ever had a choice in how the song of our lives played, or if we were notes written in permanent ink, our paths already defined.

Chapter 27

Kai

By the time the trees were completely bare, the plans for our house had been completed. I'd wait until spring to begin building it.

It was one of those rare stretches of life when there seemed to be nothing but possibilities in front of us, and everything was calm.

It felt like hope.

One mild afternoon, Sage and I took a picnic basket to a small clearing on our land. We spread out the blanket and watched the clouds roll by. Sage's eyes were closed, her body warm next to me.

"Do you know that sometimes I watch you sleep?" I asked. Her eyes popped open. I was propped up on an elbow gazing down at her. Her features were soft, but she was stronger than steel. My true match. "Sometimes, I can't believe you're really next to me, so I put my hand on your belly and wait for the rise and fall of your breath."

She smiled, reaching up to stroke my face.

I turned my head and kissed her palm. "Lucy and Wyatt set a date for their wedding, and my brother asked me to be his best man."

"What did you say?"

"I said *yes*." I stared across the clearing, neither seeing the trees nor hearing the birds. "But how can I watch him marry my best friend's wife?"

"Wyatt is your brother," Sage said, "and Tristan is gone."

"I know." In anger, I stood.

"Don't you walk away from me," Sage commanded, scrambling up from the blanket.

I stopped my retreat and spun to face her. "You're right, okay? I know she deserves to be happy, and I know he loves her. I know Dakota should have a father, but I just—can't."

She came to me and tugged on the zipper of my jacket. "Are you mad because Lucy found love again, or because she found love again with your brother?"

"Don't know. I'm trying to sort everything out, and Wyatt is wrapped up in all of that. Sometimes I wish life really was either black or white."

"You don't think I know how that feels? It's what I'm going through with my writing and my mother's death."

"It's not the same."

She shrugged. "Trees bend; you know why? If they didn't, they'd snap."

"Adapt or die," I said into her hair.

She paused. "Do you know the dandelion is both yellow and white?"

I was thrown by the change in conversation. "There aren't two types?"

She shook her head. "The dandelion is yellow before the bees pollinate it. Then it turns white, when it's ready to spread its seeds. There's a time for everything."

"When is it our time? To flourish?"

"When we stop fighting what we can't change. Lucy and Wyatt are going to get married, and you will stand next to your brother. And when the time comes and Lucy tells you she's having Wyatt's baby, you can either be happy you're going to be an uncle, or you can destroy any shot of ending this estrangement with your family. You have to stop looking at Wyatt like he's an outsider. You may never be as close to him as you were to Tristan and Reece, but Wyatt is still here. You really want to push him away?"

"You're not supposed to be this rational."

"Someone has to be," she grinned, "because it's clearly not you."

"Ouch." I took her hand and placed it on my heart.

"Call your brother. Tell him you want to take him out for a drink, and try talking to him. Don't yell, don't throw punches—talk."

"Talk," I repeated.

"He asked you to be his best man. He made the overture; you owe him this."

•••

I sat with my brother in a low-lit dive bar, taking a swig from my pony neck beer. Wyatt's gaze was wary, like he didn't know what to make of me. I didn't blame him. I had been an ass to him most of our lives.

"I'm sorry," I said.

"For what?"

"For a lot, but for starters, not being supportive of you and Lucy."

"I always thought my bachelor party would include a trip to Vegas. Instead, it's taking place in a shitty bar, and my brother and I are having a heart to heart."

"I didn't have a bachelor party. There wasn't time since Sage and I got married a week after I proposed. I never really believed in them anyway."

"And yet you threw Tristan a party."

"Yeah," I sighed the word. "I did."

Tristan's bachelor party would live forever; the parts I could recall, anyway. Lots of alcohol, cigars, and poker. At one point, I bet my argyle socks because I didn't have any money left. I'd thrown those socks into Tristan's casket, an eternal reminder of an inside joke that would last long after both of us turned to dust.

"He was your best friend. And what am I? Just your brother." His tone could've been snide—it wasn't. It was full of understanding. "You don't think I know how this looks? Everyone knew Tristan, everyone loved him—everyone loved Tristan and Lucy together. I'll be the second husband, always second best."

"Is that how you see yourself?" I asked in surprise. My brother always seemed so sure of himself. Solid, but never cocky. Did we have something in common—were we both sinking under the bulk of our own inadequacies?

Wyatt grinned in wry humor. "No, but I know that's what others will think. I don't want to replace anyone; I just want to make her happy."

"A worthy mission," I said. "I'm sorry I never tried to know you, not the way you deserved."

"It's okay, Kai."

"It's not okay," I insisted. "All these years...I don't expect you to forgive me overnight."

"You're my brother," Wyatt said. "You've had your own share of hardships."

Wasn't that the truth?

"Things are going to be different—I want them to be different."

Wyatt tapped his beer bottle against mine, letting years of tension between us clink away as if it had never existed. It was gracious and more than I deserved. Wyatt was a true gentleman. To think I'd spent years of my life taking my brother for granted, never wanting to be close to him because I had Tristan and Reece. Who did Wyatt have? Lucy, and now he'd have me, the way it should've always been.

"Let me buy you a shot," I said, rising. I had a lot to make up for, but it was a new beginning for Wyatt and me. A new beginning for all of us, maybe.

"Bring a few." Wyatt grinned. "It's not a bachelor party if the groom doesn't get hammered."

I laughed. "If there's one thing I'm good at, it's drinking."

"You're good at a lot of things, Kai. That was always your problem."

"You think so? I always thought I wasn't good at anything that mattered." I sighed. "I'll get those shots."

"Make 'em Jack."

•••

I stood in the bedroom doorway, watching Sage turn the page of a book. She was snuggled up in bed, and if I knew her like I thought I did, she'd been there for hours. "I love coming home to you."

Glancing up, she quirked her lips into a smile. "I'm glad. How was your night?"

"Mellow." I plopped onto the bed and kissed her. I'd gotten Wyatt thoroughly plastered before carting him home. I stayed sober. Best man duties. Had to make sure he didn't wind up in an alley somewhere lying in a pile of his own puke. "I have a brother."

"Just now noticing that fact?"

"Yes." My expression sobered. "I can be a real ass."

"It's called being human."

She closed her book, set it aside and pulled me closer to her. I rested my head against her body as she plowed her fingers through my hair, and I sighed in contentment.

"Alice called me with some interesting news."

She toyed with my ear. I couldn't think when she did that. "Yeah?"

"Tristan's parents have reconciled, and they're donating a library to your old high school in his honor."

"Reconciled? Miracles do happen." I lifted my head and looked into her eyes.

"They do. Speaking of miracles—I'm ready."

"Ready?"

"For a baby—give me a baby, Kai."

"You sure?"

She nodded and leaned in to kiss me. I took her into my arms, and it was a long time before I let go.

•••

"You look beautiful," I said.

Lucy turned and smiled, running a hand down her yellow dress. "Shouldn't you be out there making sure Wyatt doesn't pull a disappearing act?"

"What man has ever wanted to leave you, Lucy?"

"Good point." She grinned.

"What does it feel like?" I asked. "Getting married for the second time? Are you just as sure?"

Lucy tilted her head to the side, lost in thought. "Yes, but it's incomparable. Tristan was the eye of the storm, and I'd loved him ever since we were kids. I didn't fall in love with Wyatt until I was an adult, a mother. It's just as strong, just as real, but different." She gazed at me. "I knew I was going to marry Tristan since I was a child."

"What do you mean?"

"I just knew he was going to be the boy I would marry."

"You were eight. How could you know something like that?"

She shrugged. "Just knew."

I sighed. "He'd be glad you're happy."

"Maybe. Last night, I dreamed we talked and he threw things and ranted, but in the end he wished me happiness."

"Do you dream about him a lot?"

"Every now and again."

I wondered if I should tell her I had dreamed about them every night until very recently. Maybe I was finding peace. Maybe Tristan and Reece were finding it, too. Smiling, I held out my hand. "Come on. I think it's time I walk you down the aisle."

254

I wished I could stand in the middle, between Wyatt and Lucy, to let them know I was there for both of them.

"It's okay to be happy, Kai," Lucy said, taking my arm.

"Are you telling me, or yourself?"

"Both."

"Let's go. And try not to trip."

•••

"It was a beautiful wedding," Sage said, sliding out of bed. She cracked open the window, letting in the sound of rain, the brisk autumn air and the moonlight. She shivered in her skin. I missed her for a brief moment until she climbed back in next to me, seeking my warmth.

I pressed a kiss to her collarbone, and her fingers trailed down the length of my spine. "I didn't see most of it."

"You didn't?"

"I was too busy watching you until Dakota started throwing a tantrum."

Sage laughed. "Wyatt handled it nicely."

He'd picked up Dakota, who sat in Evelyn Evanston's lap, before returning to the altar. He had promised to protect and love Lucy, and it only made sense to include her son.

"They're going to have a long, wonderful life together."

Tugging her beneath me, I trapped her with my heat. "Do you want to continue talking about the wedding?"

"Nope."

We melded together, one body, one heart, beating the same tattoo of homage to each other. I lost myself, and when I came back I felt as though we were knotted together—our tragedies and hopes intertwined like tree saplings.

We awoke late the next day, ate breakfast for lunch, and then went back to bed.

"I'm going to be sad when we move out of this cabin," Sage said.

"Why?"

She shrugged. "I don't know. It feels like Memaw's home knows you from when you were a kid, and I wish I did, too."

"You and I will make new memories in a new home—with a skylight so we can see the stars from our bed; with a kitchen where we can dance to Tom Petty, and with four extra bedrooms…" I trailed off.

I didn't say what those rooms would be for, but we both knew—we wouldn't talk about it until there was something to hope for. She snuggled close to me and put her head to my heart; her soft breathing was a lullaby, and it sang me to sleep.

•••

From the front porch of a familiar cabin, I watch the autumn rain come down in twisted sheets. Reece sits on a stool, a beer in his hands.

"You gonna share that?" I ask.

Reece passes it to me. "What's on your mind, Kai?"

"Is it always hard? I mean, always?"

"Harder at some points than others. Life is what you make it."

I find my smile. "Sage wants another baby."

"And you want to make her happy, don't you?"

"It's the only way I have a chance at finding it for myself."

"That's deep," Reece jokes, but then turns thoughtful. "You never think you're good enough, deserving enough, but you are."

"You sure about that?"

"Yep. Things happen; people make mistakes. Happiness can grow in even the darkest of places."

The rain lightens, and I breathe in the smell of fresh greenery. I don't feel relief yet, though the calm of the mountains surround me.

"Stop looking back, Kai. Look forward. You'll find your answers there."

Chapter 28

Sage

I sat on the couch with a blanket spread over my legs, a roaring fire chasing away the afternoon chill. Kai walked into the living room, beaming like a loon.

"You're never going to guess who called me."

"Howard Stern."

Kai grinned. "Nope."

"Well, I'm out of ideas."

"It was Béla Fleck."

"Béla Fleck. As in the famous banjo player you got to come to our reception?"

"How many Béla Flecks are there?" He laughed.

"He called you himself?"

"Yeah. He's in New York giving a few concerts. He asked me to fly up there."

"Why?"

"He loved the song I wrote, and he wants to hear more."

"You're kidding?"

He shook his head. "Even I can't believe it."

"Do you have any other songs?"

"Maybe."

"There's a bit of mystery to you, Kai Ferris," I said with a grin.

"I was going to play them for you."

"Hmmm." I pretended not to believe him. This was hardly a surprising turn. I knew what the mandolin meant to him.

"Should I pursue this?" He sat next to me, his leg bouncing in agitation. He took my hand and studied it. "What if something comes of it? It could take me away from you."

"It wouldn't be forever."

"What happens if you get pregnant?"

"Then we have a baby. Do I really need to explain the birds and the bees to you?"

He laughed.

"It's just a meeting, Kai. See where it leads before you worry about all the reasons why you're scared to do it. We have to stop being scared." My eyes poured into him before unveiling something I was holding close to me. "I've been writing—and not just in journals."

"Ah, someone else is being mysterious."

I grinned. "We have to find the things that make us happy."

"So, writing makes you happy now?"

"Denying it has made me unhappy. See this through, Kai. For you. Let this be all for you."

"You make it easy." He pulled me into his arms.

"It is. Our possibilities are endless—like the stars in the sky."

"Endless, huh?"

I smiled and kissed him. "Like my love for you."

•••

"We're going to be eating leftover hot dogs and hamburgers for two weeks," I said with a laugh, opening another pack of buns and placing them on a plate. Kai fished through the refrigerator and pulled out every condiment known to man.

"What? You don't want hamburgers for breakfast?" he teased.

"I guess I could crumble them up and add them to scramble eggs," I joked. I put the pan of sliced potatoes into the oven and turned on the timer. "Will you set the patio table?" I handed him a stack of napkins and paper plates.

"Sure. I'll get the grill going. And light the bonfire, too. It's going to be a cold night."

"Want a beer while you do manly things?"

He laughed. "Please."

I opened a bottle and handed it to him.

"Thank you, darlin'," he drawled, placing a kiss in the curve of my neck, making me shiver. "Do we have time before—"

The doorbell rang, and we both laughed. "Would you get that?" I asked. "I want to start the mac and cheese."

"How much food are you making?"

"Enough for a going away party."

"I'll only be in New York for a few days." Shaking his head, he went to answer the door and came back holding Dakota, who shrieked in delight when Kai pretended to drop him.

Lucy stuck a bottle of white wine in the refrigerator and then hugged me. "Can I help?"

"Nah, just sit there and keep me company," I said, gesturing to the kitchen chair. Kai grabbed Wyatt a beer and they went outside, taking Dakota with them.

"Wyatt is really happy," Lucy said.

"Well, he just got married. I hope he's happy."

Lucy laughed. "I'm talking about him and Kai. They're finally acting like brothers."

I shook my head as I put the noodles on to boil and checked the potatoes. "Who knew? Are you guys going to go on a honeymoon?"

"I don't know. Is it a honeymoon if you bring your kid?"

"We'll watch him for you."

"That's a nice offer, but I can't ask you to do that."

"Forget about it, we'd be happy to do it. At least for a few days." I winked.

Lucy smiled. "All right, I'll talk it over with Wyatt. Thanks, Sage."

By dusk, everyone had arrived and we were outside enjoying more food than we could possibly eat. The heat of the bonfire stretched around us, pocketing us in warmth while the crisp autumn air nipped at our cheeks.

"Sit down," Alice commanded.

"I can't," I protested. "I'm the hostess." Alice pushed me into a chair and handed me a glass of lemonade. "Don't you dare clean up," I warned her.

"Paper plates, remember? They just go in the trash," Alice said as she picked up a stack and dumped them into the waiting garbage.

I sighed, realizing Alice would have her way. I caught Kai staring at me, the promise of our future written in the smile lines around his eyes. My love for him swelled like a water balloon ready to burst. He wanted to give me everything, but he didn't realize he already had. His heart was more than enough.

I love you, he mouthed across the backyard before turning his attention back to Wyatt and Keith.

"Who's ready for pie?" I asked, standing up. "I've got banana cream, coconut cream, and chocolate cream."

"Bring them all!" Wyatt shouted.

"Yeah, why choose?" Keith demanded.

I laughed and went into the house. I grabbed a knife and pulled out the pies, slicing them and putting slivers onto small paper plates. The sliding door opened, and I looked up into the hesitant face of my mother-in-law.

"Need some help?" Claire asked.

"Sure," I said, wondering if this was Claire's version of an olive branch. It wasn't as though the woman screamed domesticity.

"Is he looking forward to his meeting in New York?"

"Yes. He's still in shock though. Trying not to get carried away."

"Where will it lead?"

"Not sure; it might not lead anywhere. We don't know."

Claire sighed. "I really do want him to be happy. You too, Sage."

"You have a funny way of showing it," I said lightly. I knew I could have been more gracious, but she'd made Kai's homecoming unnecessarily difficult. The way she had treated her son made me furious.

"I know," she said. "It's hard to let go of the vision you have for your children."

I nodded in understanding. My mother had never let go. There hadn't been enough time. If she had lived, I wondered if I would've found my place—to stand proud and eventually embrace my gift, or if I would have continued to push it away. I would never know.

"I'm sorry—about the baby. I never told you," Claire said, jarring me back to the present.

I looked at my mother-in-law, weighing her sincerity. "Thank you."

"My son can have us both; he doesn't have to choose, does he?"

I smiled and touched Claire's arm. "No, he doesn't." She squeezed my hand, and we didn't need any more words.

After distributing dessert, I settled into a chair. Kai came to sit next to me, and I fed him bites of pie, smearing whipped cream on his lips and kissing it off of him. I didn't care that people could see us. I wanted all his sweetness.

"The banana cream is the best," he said.

"No, the chocolate." I smiled. "What do you think? Is this a good sendoff?"

"Decent," he said and then grinned, "but it won't compare to our reunion."

•••

"What are you doing?" I asked from the doorway of the kitchen. Kai was sitting at the table; tools, fishing line, and an assortment of other things were in front of him.

"Did I wake you?" His eyes were tired and his cowlick was in fine form.

"No. What's on your mind?" I took a seat and placed my hand on his thigh. He looked conflicted.

"Am I doing the right thing? Going to New York?"

Definitely conflicted.

"I thought we got past all this," I said.

"Just because we talk about it doesn't mean I stop thinking about it." His fingers fiddled with a fly he was tying. I set my hand on his to still his movements and forced him to look at me. I brushed hair off his forehead and caressed his stubbly jaw. His vulnerability was a layer he didn't show everyone, but he showed it to me. Or maybe he couldn't hide it from me.

God, I loved him.

"What would Tristan and Reece say?"

He smiled slightly. "Tristan would tell me to stop being such a baby. Reece...Reece would want to find out why I feel the way I do."

"Any thoughts on that?" I stood and went to get a glass of water. His eyes tracked up my bare legs before resting on my face. I was in one of his shirts; it was old and threadbare. It was the next best thing to wearing Kai.

He shrugged.

"Everything is going to be okay. You know that right? If this works out and you're away for a time, it will all be fine. Your mother and I are learning to co-exist. You're building a relationship with your brother. And you're not alone. You have me."

264

Kai sighed. "How is it you know exactly what to say to make me feel better?"

"I don't," I teased. "Half the time I don't even know what I'm saying."

"Liar. You're one of the most thoughtful people I know. Why am I so afraid?"

"Because you're human."

"What are you afraid of, Sage?"

I leaned in to kiss his lips. "It's two in the morning. Do we have to have this conversation now? Come back to bed."

"In a bit," he said.

"Okay, Kai." I wondered if his insecurities and doubts would become too much for him, and whether or not his shoulders would start to droop like an old man's. He needed to remember that I was there to share the load. "Just remember one thing."

He looked up from his project to stare at me. "What's that?"

"Remember that I love you."

His mouth formed a crooked smile. "If there's one thing I never forget, it's that." He rose from his chair. "I'm ready for bed now."

Chapter 29

Sage

The sun hadn't yet made an appearance when Kai kissed me on the lips. "I'll be back before you know it," he whispered.

My eyes fluttered open as I rolled over and grabbed his pillow, hugging it to my chest. "Promise?"

"Promise. Go back to sleep. I'll text you when I land."

When I awoke next, it was late morning. I sat up, a wave of nausea moving through my belly. Just when I thought my stomach had settled, I threw up all over the wood floor. I went to the bedroom window and threw it open, closing my eyes in dreamy relief, breathing in a gust of cool mountain air.

This is how it started last time…

I tended to the mess, went into the bathroom and pulled out a box of pregnancy tests I'd bought a few weeks prior. My pulse drummed in my ears as I waited for the answer I already knew.

I was pregnant.

My first feelings were of elation, followed by a moment of sadness for the baby I'd lost. But it was not the time to dwell on the past. There was so much good to live for, and that realization hit me with the force of a tidal wave. I felt exhilaration and hope blast to the far corners of my heart. I was a goblet full of happiness ready to spill over.

My stomach groaned in hunger, and I laughed, placing a hand on my belly and giving it a little pat. I went into the kitchen, turned the iPod dock onto shuffle and got down to making breakfast. While I flipped a pancake, Hall and Oats blared through the speakers. I danced around the kitchen, singing into a spatula. The music was so loud I almost didn't hear my phone ring.

"I was just calling to see how you were doing," Jules said.

"Kai and I can be separated for a few days," I teased. "We won't wither and die."

"Glad to hear it, but I really think you should've come to the city. We could've had a few days of girliness."

"School is in session. You have to teach, remember? Besides, I'd rather have you visit here."

I wanted to share the news with my oldest friend, but Kai deserved to know first. Shoveling food onto my plate, I ate as we talked. I let her babble about Luc, and Jules didn't realize I wasn't my usual chatty self. I was too consumed with thoughts of my own future. We hung up, and I went upstairs to get dressed.

Reaching under the mattress, I pulled out the stuffed giraffe Jules had bought me. After I'd lost the baby, I hadn't been able to look at it, but I couldn't fathom the idea of throwing it away. Now, I couldn't take my eyes off of it. It was a symbol of the life Kai and I would have together. Setting it on my side of the bed, I swiped happy tears from my face and went to visit the plot of land where we would build our home. It was only ten minutes up the path from Memaw's cabin, and when it was completed we'd have a panoramic view of the mountains. I coveted winter with Kai here, nestled on the couch, a roaring fire, snowfall outside our window, and his hand on my belly while we made plans. So many plans…

I returned home early in the afternoon and checked my phone. I had a missed call from Kai, but when I called him back, he didn't answer.

Probably in a meeting.

I changed into overalls and a large, floppy straw hat before going outside. I pulled on gardening gloves, found a spade and lost myself in the smell of dirt and the sounds of nature.

It was late afternoon when my phone buzzed. I was in the middle of digging a hole, but I managed to fish my cell out of the front pocket of my overalls. I pressed talk and put Kai on speaker.

"Hello?"

"Hello, my gorgeous wife."

I laughed and then bit my tongue. I wanted to announce our good fortune, but I held it in. "What are you doing?" I asked.

"I'm having a cocktail at the hotel bar, waiting for Béla Fleck to join me for dinner."

"Shut up," I said. "You live such a glamorous life."

"Are you okay with being arm candy?"

"You know it," I teased.

"What are you doing?"

"Guess."

"Walking around naked."

I chuckled. "You really think I'd do that?"

"A guy can dream, can't he?"

"Guess again."

"I don't know—cleaning?"

"I'd be more inclined to walk around naked."

He laughed. "I know. You're a terrible housekeeper. You spill things."

"That I do," I admitted. "So are you ready to know what I'm doing?"

"Enlighten me."

"I'm gardening."

There was a pause on the other end of the phone. "Can you repeat that? It sounded like you said you were gardening?"

"Yep. I'm wearing overalls and a big straw hat."

"Yeah, I'm going to need physical confirmation of that."

"I'll send you a picture."

"Since when do you garden?"

"Since today."

"What are you planting?"

"Nothing. I'm turning the soil and burying eggshells. Getting it ready for spring."

"I don't even know what to say right now. When did you learn how to keep a garden?"

"I bought a book. *Gardening for Dummies*."

"Really?"

I grinned even though he couldn't see. "No."

"You're adorable."

"Right back at you."

There was a muffled voice in the background and Kai responded to it before saying to me, "Sage? My dinner meeting is about to start. Call you later?"

"You better."

"Love you," he said.

"More than your mandolin?" I asked.

"Maybe," he teased.

I was still chuckling when we hung up. I took a photo of my outfit and sent it to him, hoping it made him laugh. I spent another hour outside until my stomach began to rumble. I cooked dinner, had an uneventful night of watching TV, and went to bed early.

•••

"Whatcha doin'?" Kai asked.

"Attempting to get up," I said, phone in hand.

"I thought it would be relatively easy since I'm not in bed next to you."

"You would think, but I'm *really* comfortable," I said. "When are you coming home? I can't get a good night's sleep without you."

"I have a few more meetings this afternoon, but I think I can change my flight to this evening instead of waiting until tomorrow morning. What do you think?"

Excitement welled inside of me. "I think you should get your butt home."

He laughed.

"How are the meetings going?" I asked.

"Very positive, but I don't want to tell you anything over the phone. Let's wait until tonight to celebrate."

"Celebrate. So you must have good news?" I had some of my own, but I would wait until he was sitting in front me, and I could see his face when I told him about the baby.

"We've got a lot of celebrating to do," he said, his voice turning low. "We're going to be up all night."

A hum of desire pulsed through my veins and settled in my belly. "I look forward to it."

"Love you," he said. "I'll call when I land."

I decided to go for a drive. An hour later, I was in Nashville. I parked outside an expensive, custom-design baby boutique. As I entered, I was welcomed by cream walls, soothing tones, and quiet classical music. I stopped in front of a dark wooden crib and touched the bumblebee themed mobile.

"May I help you find something?" the young sales assistant asked.

"Just looking, thanks."

"Let me know if you need anything," she said, before moving away.

I drifted around the store, flipping through children's books and studying the bright, happy illustrations. I'd never thought about writing a children's book until that moment, but ideas began to come to me—freely and without reserve, like a heart in love. They had been waiting, ensnared in the web of my mind, and now I was ready to pluck them from their resting places. I was excited to return home and begin writing.

On my way out, a set of stencils caught my eye. Dandelions.

It reminded me of a conversation I'd had with Kai. He had asked me when it would be our time to flourish, and I had told him it would be when we stopped fighting what we couldn't change.

We had accepted our losses, and now we were in the springtime of our lives.

I would paint the nursery with yellow dreams.

Chapter 30

Sage

The exhaustion of the first trimester caught up with me while I waited for Kai to return, and I fell asleep on the couch. I didn't awaken until my husband was kissing my forehead. I opened my eyes, staring into Kai's strong face.

"Hi, darlin'," he said in a husky voice that never failed to elicit shivers up and down my spine.

I reached up to stroke his stubbly jaw. "What time is it?" He sat down next to me, and I hauled myself up, leaning into him. Sleep addled my mind and body. I wanted nothing more than to close my eyes and fall back asleep in Kai's arms.

"A little after eight."

"Eight? Oh, man! I had plans to make you a special welcome home dinner."

"That's okay."

"No, it's not! I went to the store, and I bought gourmet cheese and a rabbit."

"Rabbit? You know how to cook rabbit?"

"Celia gave me a recipe. I was going to try it out tonight."

Kai frowned. "Don't worry about it. We'll order Chinese or something."

I buried my face in my hands and started to cry. "There's nothing special about Chinese!"

Kai pulled me against his chest and stroked my hair while I wept against him. "Hey," he said. "Why are you crying? You love Chinese."

I wiped my nose and sniffed. "I was going to make you a home cooked meal and then tell you I was pregnant. You can't tell your husband you're pregnant over Chinese food!"

"Pregnant?" he whispered. "You're pregnant?"

I nodded and turned watery eyes to his. "I wanted to tell you in a special way, Kai. Not like this."

He laughed softly and kissed my tearstained cheeks before settling on my lips. "Best welcome home gift I could've ever asked for."

I clutched his shirt in my hands and sobbed all over him.

"Do you want me to order you beef Lo Mein?" he asked, completely unperturbed by my show of irrational emotion.

"That would be really nice," I blubbered.

He grinned and handed me the box of tissues that were on the coffee table. He took out his cell from his jeans pocket and ordered our takeout.

"Come here," he said, after he hung up. He leaned back against the couch. I draped myself across him while he stroked my hair, his lips caressing my forehead. "I was just wondering if I could be any happier, and then you tell me we're having a baby."

I nuzzled against him, and we lounged in companionable silence. I listened to the drumming of Kai's heart, imagining the tiny heartbeat that would soon live inside me.

"What happened in New York?" I asked, wanting to continue the joy.

"Béla Fleck wants to lay down tracks in the spring. He's asked me to be a guest artist on his new album."

"Oh. Oh, *wow.*"

"You know what that means?"

"What?"

"I get to write songs and practice them this winter. It means I get to stay home with you." His hand touched my stomach. "Both of you."

I breathed a sigh of utter contentment. "Life is rarely perfect, but this moment, here with you…"

"I know."

The doorbell rang. Kai rose to answer it and then came back with a bag of Chinese food. We pulled the coffee table close to the couch and didn't bother with plates. We laughed and talked as we devoured egg rolls and hot and sour soup. He fed me a steamed wanton, and I ate the entire container of beef Lo Mein.

After we finished, we headed upstairs to bed. We didn't bother cleaning up, knowing it could wait.

•••

"I'm not ready to tell anyone," I said. We'd dozed for a few hours and then awakened, sleepily turning to one another again. I was cradled in his arms, tracing zigzags across his chest.

"Why not?" he asked.

"I just—want to make sure."

"Make sure?"

"Make sure nothing goes wrong this time."

His arms tightened around me, and I hoisted myself up to stare in the direction of his eyes. I brushed my lips across his chin.

"We're having dinner with my family tomorrow. They'll know something when you ask for club soda instead of bourbon."

I shrugged. "Let them guess. It's bad luck to tell anyone before the third month anyway."

"You don't really believe that, do you?" he asked.

"We told people before the third month last time. Look how that turned out."

He threaded his hands through my tangled hair. His thumbs gently rubbed behind my ears before he scratched my scalp with his strong fingers. I curled into him like a cat.

"I was so happy," I whispered. "I *am* so happy, but what if—"

"No."

"But—"

"No, Sage," he said more forcefully. "No more fear. Do you want the baby to feel that? Feel that kind of fear?"

I was quiet for a moment before I asked, "What happened to us? I thought you were the one that was afraid, and I was the one that had to talk *you* down?"

He kissed my lips, his mouth warm and beautiful, and full of comfort. "Are we going to plan for the worst or hope for the best?"

"We've already experienced the worst, haven't we?" I placed my head against his heart; it pulsed in my ear, solid and steady with hope.

"We've got nothing but happiness. And anything that comes our way, we can deal with—even your fear."

"You sure about that?"

"Yeah, I am. You taught me that."

"Show me what I've taught you," I commanded.

"I don't remember." His hand stroked the knobs of my spine and I said, "There's a good chance this might all just be my hormones going insane."

He laughed, and I felt the rumble under my hand. "I thought about that, but even if it is, I'll still find a way to reassure you."

I breathed him in and closed my eyes, warm relief rushing through my limbs. "It will be winter soon."

"Can we build a snowman? We haven't done that together."

"There's a lot we haven't done together yet. Snow angels, for instance," I said. "There's nothing like lying in the snow, closing your eyes and catching snowflakes on your eyelashes and tongue."

"Is that something you and your mother used to do?"

"One of the many things. I still can't believe she's not here to make snow angels with us."

I rolled onto my side, and Kai pressed himself against my back. His hands splayed across my belly, reminding me that I sheltered the center of our world in my body, reminding me to be grateful for the joy.

Chapter 31

Sage

I clambered out of the car and slammed the passenger door shut. I stared at my in-laws' large and imposing house, but for some reason I no longer found it intimidating.

There was a nip to the air, and I anticipated the first snow of the season soon. Kai came around to grasp my hand. He brought it to his lips and smiled, the corners of his eyes crinkling. I shivered and not just from the cold.

"We agreed, remember? Not to tell anyone until the third month," I reminded him.

"I know," Kai said.

"Wipe that grin off your face," I commanded. "You look way too happy."

"I'm about to tell my family that I'm going to be a guest musician on Béla Fleck's newest album. I could be smiling for that reason."

"You could be, but you're not," I teased. "You look like an actor from a chewing gum commercial. Tone it down."

"Yes, ma'am."

We walked into the house, the smell of dinner wafting from the kitchen.

Meat.

I hoped it was lamb. We headed to the library, knowing the family was partaking in cocktail hour.

"About time y'all arrived," George grumbled, standing up from the couch and setting down his bourbon. He hugged me before turning to his son and shaking his hand.

Wyatt slapped Kai on the back, and Lucy embraced me quickly. I turned to Claire, wondering what to expect from her. At Kai's going away BBQ we had seemed to come to an understanding.

She smiled at me, looking as nervous as I felt. My mother-in-law was beautiful when she smiled. Without thought, I enfolded her in my arms, refusing to let distance continue to rule our relationship. I heard her sigh of relief in my ear, and I pulled back.

"I'm glad you're home," she said to Kai.

He kissed her cheek and squeezed her hand. "It's good to be back."

Without asking, George poured two bourbons and handed them to us. "To homecomings," George said, holding up his glass. We clinked glasses and smiled, and Kai took a healthy sip. I faked a swallow, but caught Lucy scrutinizing me with a narrowed gaze, and I turned away.

"Dinner is ready," Claire said. "Let's go into the dining room."

We settled around the table and I asked, "Where's Dakota?"

"Spending the night with Tristan's parents," Lucy said. "We'll pick him up in the morning. We promised him a trip to the zoo."

I looked at Kai. "Why haven't you taken me to the zoo?"

He grinned. "You want to go to the zoo? We'll go to the zoo."

"You're welcome to come with us," Wyatt said, his gaze darting between his brother and me.

"Sounds fun," Kai said without pause. I glanced at Lucy, and we smiled in mutual understanding. Fences were mending.

As we were served our soup, a split pea and ham, George piped up, "I want to hear about your meetings in New York."

Kai leaned back in his chair, his foot touching mine underneath the table. He looked peaceful and happy as he explained what would occur in the spring.

"This calls for champagne," Claire said.

Kai groaned. "No champagne, Mom. That stuff is terrible."

"Bourbon," Wyatt and George said at the same time.

Kai laughed and shot me a look. "Nah, I'm good. Let's just enjoy the food."

I breathed a sigh of relief. Kai was trying to spare me from having to refuse liquor. I tried the soup, pepper and ham gliding over my tongue. Everything tasted better. I was almost finished when my stomach rolled. Apparently my morning sickness didn't know the time of day. I set my spoon in the bowl and took a deep breath, pressing a hand to my lips.

"Sage?" Claire asked. "Are you feeling all right?"

"Sage?" Kai whispered.

I shoved back from the table and ran from the room. I found the nearest bathroom and threw up the creamy, delectable soup. I gripped the edge of the sink and groaned. I was washing out my mouth when there was a knock.

"Sage? It's me."

I opened the door and let Kai inside. There was a slight smile on his lips. "I thought morning sickness only happened in the morning."

"Not this time, I guess." I frowned. "What did you tell them?"

"Nothing."

"*Nothing*?"

"You won't let me."

"I just threw up in the middle of dinner. I can't lie my way out of this." I glared at him. "Stop looking smug."

He took my hand and led me back to the dining room. Four faces stared at us, waiting for an explanation. I sighed. "I'm pregnant."

Lucy cracked a smile and shot a look at Wyatt. "Told you! Wyatt thought it was the flu."

"She was pale and shaky," Wyatt defended.

"Pregnant?" Claire stood and came to us, her eyes never leaving my face.

I nodded.

She reached out to grasp our hands, her voice quivering when she said, "This *definitely* calls for champagne."

"Absolutely," George said. He left the dining room and returned a few moments later with a chilled bottle.

"Want me to open that?" Lucy asked. George thrust the bottle at her. "I was a waitress once upon a time," she explained to me.

I raised an eyebrow. Claire set down flutes, even one in front of me. "Just to cheers," she said, patting me on the shoulder. Lucy moved around the table serving the bubbly liquid. We raised our glasses, and Kai stared at me, his grin wide.

He gripped my hand and said, "To a perfect moment."

•••

"If you want ice cream," Lucy said to Dakota, "then you have to get down off of Uncle Kai's shoulders."

Kai winked at me, but said to Dakota, "You can get back up there when you're done."

"Promise?" Dakota asked.

"Promise." Kai lifted Dakota to the ground, and the little boy latched onto Wyatt's hand. Lucy took her son's other hand, and they approached the snack stand that served ice cream, pretzels, and cotton candy. Half the fun of the zoo was the food.

"Dakota loves his Uncle Kai," I said, kissing Kai's cheek.

He wrapped an arm around my shoulder and kept me close to him. "It's because I buy his affections."

"You're not the one getting him his ice cream."

"No, but I did promise to take him to a baseball game and buy him a hot dog."

He tightened the plaid scarf around my neck. It was chilly and we wore gloves, but it wasn't quite cold enough for hats yet.

"What kind of ice cream did you get?" I asked Dakota when he came running back to us, Wyatt and Lucy trailing behind him.

"Chocolate."

"Is chocolate your favorite?" He nodded. "Mine, too."

He held out his cone and grinned. "Wanna share?"

I crouched down and took a small lick. "Hmmm, delicious. Thank you. Thank you for sharing."

"I like to share." He looked at his mother.

"Did you teach him that?" I asked Lucy.

She shook her head and gestured with her chin to Wyatt. Wyatt ruffled his adopted son's hair. "You ready to see the monkeys, bud?"

"Yeah!" Dakota shrieked. His mouth was stained with chocolate, but like all prepared mothers Lucy held a stack of napkins and wiped Dakota's face. He squirmed, trying to get away, smearing the chocolate even more in the process.

"Almost done," she said. She threw the soiled napkins into the trash and grinned. "Let's go."

I watched the three of them trek towards the primate building. They were a family.

"God, he looks just like Tristan," Kai said.

I squeezed Kai's hand gently as we walked.

"If I bought you an ice cream, would you share it with me?" Kai asked.

I looked up at him and smiled. "Not a chance."

He laughed. "It's because I'm not as cute as Dakota, right?"

"Definitely."

"This is nice," he said.

"It is," I agreed.

"I've become a family man."

"So you have."

"I know they want to see the monkeys, but can we sneak away to see the penguins?"

"I'm good with that. Penguins are cute. They mate for life, you know."

His eyes found mine. They were vast, a pool of flinty blue. He swallowed, emotion catching in the back of his throat. "Yeah, I know."

•••

The soft sounds of Kai's mandolin teased me awake. Before I even opened my eyes, I knew it was the middle of the night. It was happening with greater occurrence—Kai and I would fall asleep together, but inevitably, he'd stir, slip out of bed and spend a few hours writing music. Come dawn, he'd collapse next to me, sinking into a deep, rhythmic sleep.

I got out of bed and went downstairs. Kai sat on the couch, his mandolin across his lap. A pad of paper rested on the coffee table, and he scribbled something before looking up. The fire cast him in demonic shadows and hid the tiredness in his eyes.

"Did I wake you?" he asked, setting the instrument aside. I sat down next to him and curled into his side.

"Not really. I was coming out of a dream."

"What did you dream about?"

"Dragonflies."

"Dragonflies?"

I nodded. "I was on the bank of the lake, the one behind the farmhouse. The dragonflies were all different colors, and I felt the beat of their wings against my cheeks. A fish shot out of the water, parting it like a seam. It looked like a trout, but it was gold. Its scales caught the sun and shot prisms of light across the lake. I thought it was beautiful. Then it suddenly opened its mouth and devoured the dragonflies—and me, in one bite."

"Where was I?" he asked.

I shook my head. "I didn't even think of you. Not in the dream."

"Your heart is racing," he said, his hand at my neck.

"Play me a song." I pulled away from him. His brown hair had grown past his chin. It fell into his eyes, and he brushed it back. The scruff along his jaw made me sigh in longing. But none of that compared to the look on his face when he picked up his mandolin and played me a song from the depths of his heart.

There weren't lyrics.

The song didn't need any.

When he stopped, I could barely make out his shape through my tears. "How do you do that to me?" I whispered.

He placed his mandolin in its case. I pulled him to me, my back hitting cushions, his body looming over mine. Kai traced the arches of my brows, the curve of my mouth, the apples of my cheeks with his thumbs.

"We are so lucky," I said into his lips.

"You and me?" he asked, brushing away emotion that had escaped the corners of my eyes.

I smiled. "Yes, but I meant the baby and me. We're lucky to have you, Kai Ferris. We're lucky we get to love you."

Chapter 32

Sage

The Ferris library was overrun with family. George and Claire had invited the Chelsers to spend Christmas with us. The tree had been trimmed for weeks, long before the first snowfall. At the moment, we were waiting for a blizzard, but none of us cared. We were inside, warm and happy.

Alice handed me another glass of her homemade Eggnog and I took a sip, enjoying the sugary creaminess. I sighed. Though it was good, it would've been better with rum.

"It's too bad the Germains couldn't come for Christmas," Keith said, his arm around his wife. "I would've liked to have met them."

"Celia said Christmas is their busiest time of year. And Jules wanted to spend the holiday with Luc. Can't say I blame her."

"You guys ready to open presents?" Wyatt asked.

"But Christmas isn't until tomorrow morning," I said.

"We're a present-on-Christmas-Eve kind of family," Kai explained. "What was Christmas like with your Mom?"

I laughed with fond remembrance. "No real celebration. Chinese food and a movie. Then we'd hit Max Brenner and have hot chocolate and fondue. It was great. The city was deserted and quiet. Almost magical."

"Did you have a Christmas tree?" Wyatt asked.

"We had a shrub of sorts."

"You don't miss New York at all, do you?" George asked.

"Not even for a second."

"Okay, presents," Claire said. Dakota sat in her lap, and she brushed his hair off his face.

I stood, but everyone waved me back down. "What's going on?"

"You'll see," Kai said.

I peered at him. "What do you know?"

He smiled. "Nothing."

"Here," Lucy said, setting a green wrapped box on my lap.

"This is from Jules and Luc," I said, reading the note.

"They're sending gifts as a unit? That's serious," Kai said.

I unwrapped the present and held up a pair of baby tennis shoes. "These are so cute I want to punch someone," I said.

Everyone laughed and then Wyatt handed me a shiny red box. "This is from us."

"And me!" Dakota said.

I looked at him and grinned. "Will you help me?"

He slipped off of Claire's lap and bounded over to me. He ripped off the wrapping paper, and I pulled out a knitted green baby blanket. I was starting to see a theme for the gifts. "This is beautiful," I said, running my hand across it. "Thank you."

"Momma made it," Dakota explained.

I looked at Lucy. "Really?"

She nodded. "I knit now."

"What did you do, Wyatt?" I demanded.

"It was my idea," he said with a grin.

"Ah, the idea man," I said. "Team effort, I like it." Kai took the blanket from me and set it aside. I glanced at him. "Did you plan this?"

"Plan what?"

"Did you tell everyone to get us baby gifts?"

"Maybe." He smiled.

I leaned against him. "This is Christmas, not a baby shower."

"They all agreed with me," he said. "We wanted to celebrate."

"Ready for the next gift?" Keith asked.

I nodded.

Alice handed me an envelope, and I took out a photo. "What—?"

"Keith made you a crib," she said.

"Made?" I squeaked. "You *made* this?"

"Totally upstaging our gift," Wyatt said with a smug grin.

Keith beamed. "It's at the ranch," he explained, his bright blue eyes searching mine. "I can bring it over to the cabin whenever you're ready for it."

I shook my head, tears falling down my cheeks like snowflakes from the sky. I was up off the couch, lunging for Keith and Alice's arms. They held me while I cried, even after Kai came over and joined in the hug.

I pulled back and smiled. "Thank you," I said, my voice hoarse. I turned to George and Claire who were holding hands and smiling.

"Please tell me your gift won't make me cry again. Please tell me your gift sucks."

George laughed and then gestured to the mantle. My eyes traveled over the ornate stockings, reading each of the names, every member of the family until I came to the last two. One had my name sewn in thick green thread—the other was unmarked, for the child I carried.

"Son of a…" I whispered, overwhelmed with love.

Alice handed me a tissue, and I dabbed at my cheeks.

"Also, Celia and Armand are flying in from France for New Year's. That's their gift."

"You know what would make this night even more perfect?" I asked.

"What?" Kai stroked my cheek without a care that we weren't alone.

I grinned. "Alice's apple tarts."

"Finally!" George said.

•••

"Are you sure you can't stay longer?" I asked, pulling back from Celia's embrace. "It feels like you just got here."

She shook her head with regret. "Believe me, I wish I could, but we left Luc in charge of the bed and breakfast. Who knows what state of disarray it will be in when we get back?"

Kai unloaded the Germains' suitcases from the car and set them on the curb. He shook Armand's hand and then hugged Celia goodbye.

"Love you," Armand whispered in my ear as we embraced. "We'll see you soon."

Kai and I got back into the car and watched as Celia and Armand ambled inside with their luggage.

Sadness invaded my heart as I watched my surrogate parents leave. When we drove towards downtown Nashville, Kai reached over and touched my knee in silent understanding.

"I miss France," I said.

"You do?"

I nodded. "I like it here, of course I do. It's beautiful, and we have family here, but we have family there too. *Tours* is home to me, I think. It's where we fell in love. You bought us a farmhouse. I breathe differently there, I *feel* different there. I don't know how to describe it."

"I do. It's how I feel when I'm in the mountains." Kai paused and then said, "I think we should move back to France."

"What?"

"After I'm done recording in New York, we should move back to France."

"You just admitted to feeling at peace in the mountains. I can't you ask you to give that up. What about the house you want to build us? What do we do?"

"We do whatever we want," he said. "We won't start building the house until the spring anyway. Wyatt can oversee things for me. It will be done by next fall. We can come back to Monteagle, Sage— whenever we want. Every summer or winter. I don't care."

I fisted my hands in my lap, wondering how I had managed to find a man who wanted me as the center of his world, who let our lives revolve around my happiness.

Kai was selfless.

"I used to think it was mountains. Now, it's about making you happy because it makes me happy. I don't need much else."

"What about your parents and your brother? I don't want them to think I'm choosing the Germains. That I'm making *you* choose the Germains."

"Dad is semi-retired anyway. Mom doesn't work. The Germains run two businesses. My family can travel. The door is always open to them. But we can live in two places. We have choices."

"Choices."

"You don't have to worry. About anything."

"No, I guess I don't. I didn't realize…"

"Realize what? That I'd give you everything you ever wanted?" he teased.

"You gave me yourself, Kai. No better gift than that."

"You should be happy today. Today is the day we find out the sex of our baby."

"I am happy."

He parked the car in the lot of Nashville OBGYN Associates and cut the engine. "We should make a bet. I think it's a boy."

I smirked. "What do you want to bet?"

"A kiss."

"So either way we both win?"

He smiled. "I've already won."

Chapter 33

Sage

I rolled over and kissed Kai's shoulder. He scooted closer, throwing a leg over mine and made a startled noise when I put my cold foot in the crook of his knee.

"Ahhhhh!" he gasped. "What are you doing to me!"

I wheezed with laughter. "My feet are cold and you promised to take care of me forever, remember?"

"Yeah, but *come on!* Warn a guy first, huh?" He crawled out of bed, opened a dresser drawer and pulled out a pair of his wool socks. He came back, removed the comforter, and searched for my feet. He tucked me back into bed before slipping in next to me. He wormed his way under my t-shirt and rested a hand on the elegant swell of my stomach.

"You feeling okay?" he asked.

"Hmmm. Better now. Warmer." My eyes closed, the feeling of Kai next to me making me drowsy.

"Should we talk about names?" he asked.

"Do we want to honor those we've lost?"

"There are so many of them," he said.

"How do we decide?"

He was quiet for a long time, but I knew he hadn't fallen asleep. Then he spoke, "Maybe we should name her in her own right then."

"Are you sad we're having a girl?" I asked. I knew what it meant for a man to yearn for a son. Or at least I could imagine it. I was a woman; I carried and brought forth life, I would know my child before the world did. It wasn't the same for Kai. He was a man's man—I couldn't wait to see him cradle our daughter in his hands; hands that gutted fish, hands that stroked a stringed instrument and played the most beautiful songs that had ever been created, hands that made me cry out in longing.

"Sad?" He shook his head. "She'll be like you."

"You think?"

"Yeah, except I'm going to teaching her how to fish when she's young," he warned as he kissed my belly.

I'd felt her kick a few days ago, but she was quiet now. Maybe dreaming of eddies and rivers. Maybe dreaming of mornings with her father when it would just be the two of them. Even if she was like me, I had no doubt she would be a daddy's girl. I had never known my own father, and with that thought I wondered how he would've shaped my life.

My chest rose as I breathed for myself, for my daughter—Kai's daughter.

"A tiny you," he whispered as he drifted off to sleep.

•••

The snow fell steadily, and Kai continued to write music. He wouldn't play for anyone except me and the baby. Each night, I received a private show in front of the fire. He was stunning in his talent. The baby swam circles in my belly while we listened to Kai's musical poetry.

Happiness was a greater inspiration than tragedy.

One late winter evening, Kai set down his mandolin and said, "Damn, you're beautiful."

I snorted with laughter. I rested on the couch, feeling bloated and fat. "I think you may be a bit biased," I teased and then sang, "'I know an old lady who swallowed a horse…'"

Kai laughed. His skin was streaked gold in firelight. I wanted to nibble him like a decadent caramel.

"I know that look," he said, leaning in to me.

"Not my fault," I joked. "Pregnancy hormones make me randy."

"Who's Randy?"

"You dork!" We laughed until we could hardly breathe.

"You were like this before the baby, don't lie. You can't get enough of me." He stood and pulled me up like the twenty extra pounds I had gained were nothing.

"Well, that's true." We headed for the stairs.

"I can't get enough of you, either," he pointed out.

I removed my shirt, pushed down my sweats and stepped out of them, leaving a trail of clothing to the bedroom. His hands reached around to cup my roundness. I wanted him to seep into me like watercolors on a canvas. His fingers traced the seams of my stretch marks. They existed no matter how much he attended to them, no matter what lotion he rubbed onto my body. I didn't like them, but Kai kissed each one in reverence.

"Some of us wear our battles on our skin, others on our hearts," he said.

I touched his brand, a T&R for the friends he had lost. "Some of us have both." I held out my arms to him and he hugged me tight, despite my belly between us.

"It doesn't matter," he said into my neck, "because you're my salve."

•••

"I swear to God, this baby is part fish!" I complained. "You're the fish whisperer, do something!"

Kai grinned, like I'd given him a compliment, his teeth white against his handsome new beard.

"*Your* child is making me miserable!" My feet hurt, my clothes chafed my skin, and I was annoyed—all the time. Usually at my husband. The moments when rationality did make an appearance, I remembered how much I loved him, how much I loved our life together, how much I already loved his child.

I picked up my mug of ginger tea. The fresh flowers Kai had brought home from the grocery store were losing their potency. Maybe I was sick of winter, sick of being stuck inside. The weather was about to break, I could feel it, but it hadn't come yet. Soon, I hoped.

"I have a surprise for you."

"Me? Or the baby?"

Kai didn't reply as he got up and went to the front closet. He came back with a large cardboard shoebox. I opened it and withdrew a pair of brown UGGS.

"Try them on," he urged.

I managed to pull on the boots, sinking my feet into soft wool. "Oh. My. God." I sighed. "These are the most comfortable things I've ever put on my feet."

He laughed. "Glad to hear that."

"It makes winter almost worth it."

"I can't remember a winter this brutal or this long," Kai said.

I gazed out the window; I was bombarded with beauty. It was all around me. Not just in my view of snow-capped peaks, but also in the man I had married, in the child I carried. There were so many blessings; I wondered how I'd become so fortunate.

"She still giving you trouble?" he asked.

I winced, trying to dislodge her foot from underneath my ribs. My insides felt like they were black and blue.

Kai pulled up my shirt and muttered nonsense syllables against my belly. The baby shifted, and he placed a cheek against my body. We were skin to skin.

Skin.

Nothing more than a thin veneer that held our child safe and warm.

•••

I buried my head in my hands and sobbed uncontrollably. The more I thought about it, the harder I cried.

"Sage? Darlin'? What's the matter?" Kai asked as he shut the front door. He carried a hot pepper sandwich on a baguette, and the smell made me forget my sorrow.

"Is that my sandwich?" I reached for a tissue and blew my nose before crumbling it up in my fist. Kai sat down next to me and handed it over. I took a bite and moaned in pleasure. Nothing, I mean, nothing compared to satisfying a pregnancy food craving. I finished the sandwich, sipped on a ginger ale, and glanced at my husband.

He peered at me like I was an alien. "You okay?"

I put my hand on his leg, trying to reassure him that I wasn't going to throw a vase at his head. I'd only done that once, a few weeks earlier. It hadn't even hit him. He wasn't one to hold grudges.

"There was a really sad commercial on television," I explained.

Bless his heart, he didn't even flinch. There was crazy, and then there was *pregnancy* crazy.

"I love you," he said with a charming grin. I stroked his beard and leaned into his body. His arm came around me, and I sighed.

"How much do you love me?"

"You want ice cream, don't you?"

I nodded into his chest. "With extra sprinkles. *Please?*"

He brushed his lips across my forehead, then trailed down my nose and settled on my mouth. Before he could pull away, I reached for his belt and kissed him back, smelling of spicy peppers and desire.

"God, you're perfect," he said.

I cried again, only this time it wasn't in sadness.

Chapter 34

Sage

Spring came, and it was wet with gloomy skies. A bout of massive hailstorms littered the countryside, laying waste to all that tried to bloom. But the mountains were green, and my body was round and ripe.

"I look big, don't I? I mean, really big."

Kai bit his lip, like he was debating on smiling. "Why do women do that?"

"Do what?"

"Ask questions they already know the answers to."

I glared at him. "You could be a little more sensitive. I know I'm almost six months pregnant, but come on…people think I'm carrying *twins*. I'm huge!"

"That was one person, and she was a twenty-year-old cashier at the grocery store. She smacked her bubble gum for Christ's sake. Who cares what she thought?"

"I don't care what she thought," I yelled. "I care that she said it out loud! Whatever happened to having a filter and not saying *every single thing* that comes to your mind?"

He rubbed a finger across his mouth. I knew he was smiling, the bastard. "It's a generational thing."

I arched an eyebrow. "Generational, huh? Okay, Grandpa."

Kai sighed in mock defeat. "I miss my wife. She used to be so nice…"

I gnashed my teeth at him. "You're lucky you're cute, Ferris. That's the only way I'd allow you to get away with teasing me."

"Can I hug you? Or do you have a weapon I need to know about?"

Before I could answer, he came to me and I collapsed my bulk against him. He held me for a moment and said, "I think I have something that will cheer you up. Put on your shoes."

"Why?" I asked. We walked to the front door, and I used his arm to steady myself while I slipped on the UGGS he had bought me. He grabbed my light jacket and helped me shrug into it.

We stepped outside, and I breathed in the fresh air. It was in the mid sixties, but the sky was clear. Perhaps it wouldn't storm today. "Where are we going?" I asked as Kai took my hand and led me up the path.

He didn't reply, and ten minutes later he stopped when we came to a cement spot surrounded by a small clearing with a panoramic view of the mountainside. "It's not much to look at yet," he said. "It's just the foundation, but it's solid enough to build the home of our dreams."

I gripped his hand, letting my tears fall in the silent morning.

•••

"You have your wallet?" I asked Kai.
"Yep."
"Got your ticket?"
He nodded.

"Lyrics?"

He pulled them out of his shirt pocket. They were hardly legible, and the papers were wrinkled.

"You ready?"

He grinned and kissed me. Dropping to his knees, he stroked my belly and kissed it. "I'll see you soon," he said to my stomach.

"I'm up here, buddy," I said with a smile, my fingers toying with his beard.

He kissed me again, slower, almost endlessly. I sank into him. "Love you," I whispered, pulling back.

Kai tugged on a strand of my hair. "Love you, too. I'll call when I land." He picked up his small travel bag and mandolin case. I opened the front door and stood on the porch, watching him depart.

I traipsed back into the house and settled myself on the couch.

A few hours later, my buzzing phone jarred me awake. It made a loud rattle across the coffee table.

"Just wanted to tell you that I landed, and I'm about to get into a cab and head to the hotel," Kai said.

"That's nice," I mumbled.

"You were asleep, weren't you?"

"No…"

He laughed. "Liar. Go back to bed you little incubator. I'll talk to you later."

I made myself a sandwich and went upstairs to the nursery. Keith had come over a few weeks ago and dropped off the crib. It was pushed against the far green wall. Kai hadn't let me climb the ladder to stencil the dandelions, so he'd asked Alice to do it. They dotted the trim in pale yellow. I sat in the comfortable rocking chair and ate my meal, content that our daughter would grow up in a room full of dreams.

After taking some time in the nursery, I headed out to the front porch, wanting to catch the last of the afternoon sun, and maybe the sunset. George's car pulled into the driveway, and even though he hadn't called, I wasn't surprised by his appearance.

"Hi," he greeted, trudging up the porch steps.

I stood and hugged him. "Hi."

"I'm on my way to the country club, but thought I'd swing by and check in on you."

"Can I get you something to drink? I have some freshly brewed iced tea in the fridge."

He smiled. "Thanks."

We walked inside and into the kitchen. "Ice?"

"Please."

I dropped some cubes into a glass, added a slice of lemon and the tea.

He took a sip. "Peach?"

I nodded.

"It's good."

"Thanks."

"Sorry I didn't call first."

"It's okay. I kind of like you showing up unannounced. It has a very intrusive family feel," I teased.

He laughed. "There's a purpose to my visit, not just to surprise you. I was wondering if you'd like to spend a few days with us? You know, while Kai is gone?"

I opened my mouth to refuse, not wanting to be a burden, but I found myself saying, "That sounds really nice."

He looked pleased. "Really?"

"Yeah, it can get kind of lonely up here. Thanks for the offer, George. It was very thoughtful of you."

"It was Claire's idea," he admitted.

"Was it? Well, that's a bit of a surprise."

He nodded. "For you and me both. I can swing by and pick you up on my way home from the club. Give you a chance to pack a few days worth of clothes."

"Perfect."

•••

"You're never going to guess where I am," I said to Kai over the phone.

"I love guessing games. What are you wearing?"

"Don't make this dirty," I teased. "I'm in your parents' house—in your childhood bed."

"I don't understand."

"Your father invited me to stay over for a few days, but it was your mother's idea."

"I'll be damned."

"I think she's finally coming around to the idea of me."

"You're my wife and the mother of my child. It's about time."

I laughed. "Hey, she's trying to make peace. Anger is exhausting."

"Damn straight."

A patch of silence fell between us, and then I asked, "How's New York?"

"Loud, dirty and expensive. I don't know how you ever lived here. On the upside, though, Jules is driving down tomorrow and we're having lunch. I'll show her the studio."

"Not fair."

He sighed. "It's not too late you know, for you to join me up here."

"I—can't." I hadn't been back since my mother had died. I'd never seen her headstone. I wasn't ready.

We were silent again before he said, "Listen, I should get some sleep. I've got an early morning. And the sooner I go, the sooner this is done, and I can get back to my girls."

I patted my stomach. "We'll be waiting."

I attempted to fall asleep, but I was restless. I got out of bed and quietly crept downstairs to the kitchen. I was rummaging through the freezer for the carton of vanilla bean ice cream when the kitchen light turned on.

"Gotcha," George said with a grin.

I smiled back. "Sorry, did I wake you?"

He shook his head. "Nah, just had a hankering for something sweet."

"Me too."

"You were going to take that last piece of strawberry rhubarb pie, weren't you?"

"Maybe."

"I'll fight you for it."

"I'm carrying your granddaughter."

He laughed. "Trump card. You win."

"Let's share it."

"Better idea. That way Claire can't yell at me about my cholesterol."

"She loves you. Wants you to be around for a while." I opened the drawer and pulled out two spoons and the ice cream scooper. The last piece of pie was on the cake stand underneath a glass lid. George went to the cupboard and withdrew a plate. I placed two huge scoops on top of the pie and stuck the tub back in the freezer. We settled at the informal kitchen table, but before I took a bite I snapped a photo on my cell phone and sent it to Kai saying, "Wish you were here".

"Trying to make him jealous?" George teased.

"Alice will bake him a welcome home cobbler. He's got nothing to be jealous about."

"Hmm. Hopefully it'll be peach. Alice makes a damn good peach cobbler." He licked his spoon before diving back into the ice cream. "So why are you awake?"

"Late night call with Kai," I explained. "Plus I'm pregnant. I'm asleep and awake at the oddest hours."

He chuckled.

"Why are *you* awake?" I demanded.

"Age. Can't sleep through the night."

I snorted with humor. "I don't buy that excuse."

"No?" He looked thoughtful. He pushed the plate towards me and set his spoon down. "I've been doing a lot of thinking."

"About what?"

"Retiring."

"You're semi-retired already," I pointed out.

"I know, but I don't think I want to work anymore. At all. I want to play more golf, have more time with my family. Be able to travel."

"Have you told Claire?"

"Yeah, she knows I'm thinking about it. I'd been thinking about it before Kai came home and now..."

"Now there are more important things than work?"

"Exactly."

We smiled at one another until Claire's voice interrupted our moment. "What's going on in here?" she demanded. She wore a silk white robe and house slippers.

"Busted," I stage whispered.

"We're sharing dessert," George said with a boyish smile. I saw Claire's lips twitch in amusement, but she feigned anger. She stalked to the cupboard and pulled out a bag of marshmallows and a tin of gourmet hot chocolate.

"If you're going to do this, you're going to do this right," she commanded. "George, get me the mugs."

•••

"You're so going to think I'm the bestest best friend that has ever lived," Jules said over the phone.

I laughed as I threw my dirty clothes into the washer. George had dropped me off at the cabin earlier in the day. I'd enjoyed my time with my in-laws, but I was ready for Kai to come home. It had only been four days, but it was still too long to be apart.

"Oh, really? Why is that?" I asked.

"I'm coming to France this summer. After you move back."

"For how long?"

"The entire summer. Before the baby's born. After the baby's born. And if I can get things in order…"

"Order?"

"I'll be a permanent resident. I'm shackin' up with Luc."

I nearly dropped my phone. "*Shut. Up.*"

"Told you. I'm awesome."

"You better not be lying to me. I will kill you."

"Not a lie. I better start practicing my French now."

"Yeah, and kissing doesn't count." My phone beeped, and I looked at the screen. "Jules, I gotta go. It's Kai on the other line."

"Okay, call me later."

I switched over to call waiting and said, "Hello?"

"It's me."

"Hi, Me."

He laughed. "I'm coming home early."

"Really? You're not teasing me, right?"

"Not teasing. Did Jules tell you her news?"

"How did you know about it before I did?"

"I had lunch with her, remember?"

"You both are sneaky sneaks." I was beaming. "So when are you coming home? Tomorrow? The day after?"

"Tonight."

"Tonight? Too good to be true," I said.

"Try and stay awake."

"I make no promises."

"See you soon, darlin'."

We hung up, and I finished loading the washer. I heard a rumble of thunder in the distance. Spring storms seemed to come out of nowhere. I went out onto the porch and watched the rain. It came down hard and fast in sheets, but it abated quickly, like it had an explosive temper.

Even after the rain had stopped, dark clouds continued to loom, and I knew there was a good chance the squall hadn't yet run its course.

Chapter 35

Kai

I paid for my cup of coffee from the airport Starbucks, took my change and shoved it into my pocket. I had some time before my flight boarded, so I wandered into a gift store that had everything from snacks to magazines. As I scanned the tacky shot glasses and t-shirts, my eyes landed on the wall of books. One name, in big black letters, stood out from all the rest.

Penny Harper.

I picked up the book, flipped it over, and quickly read the blurb. My mouth quirked into a smile as I gently placed the book Sage's mother had written back in its spot.

"It's a good read. If you were on the fence about buying it," a man said. He looked like he had popped out of a GQ ad. He was tall, blond haired, and blue-eyed and wore an expensive suit; the silver Rolex at his wrist caught the light.

"Thanks," I replied. "I'll think about it."

"I'm a fan of Penny Harper," he went on. "Read all her stuff, but that is her best work. By far."

"Doesn't seem like your genre."

"Not usually," the man agreed.

"Why did you read it, then?"

A sad smile flitted across his face. "I was trying to impress a girl. She wouldn't let me take her out on a date until I'd read it. Anyway... Gotta catch my plane."

I decided against buying Penny's book. After all, I could just borrow a copy from Sage. I left the store and headed to my gate. I sat down, tapping my hand against my leg, my thoughts turning from Penny Harper to her daughter.

Would I ever see Sage's name on a book? Would it become a *New York Times* bestseller and grace the shelves of bookstores around the world? Sage had a gift, one she had only started to embrace, but I would be there when she accepted it.

I couldn't wait to get home to her.

•••

"Told ya," Tristan says.

"Told me what?" I demand.

"Told ya you'd find your way," he grins.

Reece laughs. "Took you long enough to listen."

"I'm a stubborn ass," I say.

"We know," Tristan and Reece say at the same time.

I sigh. "It looks different here." I glance around. The lake isn't silver, but golden and it looks like it's covered in ice.

"Think we can walk across it?" Reece asks.

"Maybe, try it out," Tristan urges.

"Okay." Reece steps onto the lake. When its clear he won't fall through, he looks at us and grins. After he reaches the middle, he drops to his knees. "You guys have to see this!"

"What is it?" Tristan asks, even as we go to join him.

Reece doesn't reply, he just points. Tristan and I crouch. I touch the surface of the golden ice, but it's not cold and I wonder if it's ice at all. Underneath, the water ripples and I can barely make out the floating shape. But soon, I can see what it is. There is a goldfish, bright as the sun, swimming in circles.

I stare at it for what seems like an eternity, and finally, before my eyes, the goldfish breaks through the ice.

It begins to transform; fins turn to arms, its tail turns to legs. Scales melt into glowing, golden skin. It has become a woman—a beautiful, naked woman with chestnut colored hair and gray eyes that carry many secrets.

I don't know where my friends have gone. I am alone with the goldfish woman. She smiles and holds out her arms to me. Unable to stop myself, I go to her. She wraps me in a tight embrace.

I see nothing but golden light.

Chapter 36

Sage

I awakened in the middle of the night to the sound of thunder and a banshee wind whipping tree limbs against the glass windows of the cabin. Somehow, I managed to tumble back into dreamland before I could think about moving upstairs.

I woke just as the sun was climbing over the mountains. I sat up, stretched my neck, and rubbed the crick in my lower back. I checked my phone; I had received a text from Kai at 1:00 AM saying he'd landed.

I called his cell, but it went straight to voicemail. I frowned. He'd gotten in late. Maybe he had decided to rent a hotel room by the airport to catch a few hours of sleep before driving home in the morning.

I was in the middle of making breakfast when I heard a car pull up in the gravel driveway.

Kai.

I turned off the burner, dumped my scrambled eggs onto a plate, and went to open the door, excitement blooming inside me.

"Mrs. Ferris?"

I stared in confusion at a young police officer, and my smile slipped from my face. I nodded slightly.

"I'm sorry to bother you this early, but we found your husband's car off of…"

My vision went blurry, and I dug my nails into the palm of my hand to keep from fainting.

Words had lost all meaning in the wake of true destruction.

I collapsed like a matchstick dollhouse, broken, defeated in the new day's light.

•••

"She hasn't moved in hours," whispered a voice. It might've been Alice, or maybe Lucy. It all sounded the same. Nothing penetrated the grayness of grief.

Kai is dead. Kai is dead. Kai is dead.

The chant played over and over in my mind, a wail on repeat. My lungs felt like iron spikes had punctured them.

My tears had long since dried, and my cheek was stuck to the wood floor.

"Sage?"

I opened my eyes and stared into the concerned face of my best friend. Jules lay next to me, her body mirroring mine. I watched her mouth speak; yet I didn't hear words. I blinked.

"Sage?" Jules said again. "Would you like to move to the couch?"

"Maybe we should call Keith. He can come over and lift her," Alice suggested from somewhere above me.

"He's with George, Claire, and Wyatt," Lucy replied.

"Sage will get up when she's ready," Jules said.

Ready? How will I ever be ready?

Standing up would mean that Kai was really gone. It would mean he had lost control of his car in the middle of a storm, and that he had hit a tree and died in his beloved mountains.

It would mean we would never have a life together.

On the floor, which was encrusted with my dried, salty tears, I could pretend for one more moment that Kai was coming back.

Sometime later I fell asleep, but woke again not long after—screaming. Jules' arms surrounded me while sobs wracked my body. When they subsided, I croaked out, "Water." I touched my head. It throbbed in pain. Someone gave me a glass.

Lucy.

Alice went into the kitchen, and when she returned she set a sandwich in front me, but I didn't touch it. I drank more water.

I didn't know how long I sat on the floor, but eventually I stood. Alice and Lucy helped me to the couch. I felt like someone had pulled a plug in my heart, and all my joy had drained out of me.

"Sage, you have to eat something," Jules coaxed.

I dutifully shoved food into my mouth, but almost choked on it. I dozed off again.

I dreamed of Kai. I traced the smile lines at the corners of his eyes, and he held me against his chest. We swayed to the song he had played for me when we first met.

When I awoke, my cheeks were wet again. I'd been crying in my sleep.

I looked out the window. The sky was inky purple; it would be dawn soon.

•••

It was night.

I touched his side of the bed, curled my fist around smooth sheets and then flattened my palm. Staring at the ceiling, I debated looking at the clock. Time no longer mattered. With each pulse of my heart, I was unable to forget.

Not even in sleep.

Not even in the dark.

I felt like a starfish with one of its limbs ripped off. Would I be able to grow it back?

I sat up and shoved hair out of my face. I padded downstairs and went into the kitchen.

Kai's flies and the contents of his tackle box were spilled across the kitchen table like child's toys on the living room floor. His fishing pole rested in the corner by the back door, like it was waiting for him to come home.

I picked it up. It felt wrong in my hands, so I set it down.

I filled a glass of water and took it to the couch. I sat in the blackness and the silence until the sun soared over the mountains. It had been cloudy for days, yet bright beams managed to paint through the gray.

For others, it would be a beautiful day, a welcome change from the gloomy weather. For me, it would be the day of my husband's funeral.

•••

"Have you eaten today?" Alice asked.

I clasped a pearl earring to my lobe and shook my head.

"Can I make you something?"

I swiped my hair back into a bun as I met Alice's eyes in the mirror.

She needed to be needed. She was a mother without a child. I was a child without a mother. And a wife without a husband.

"Toast would be nice."

"How about something more substantial?" She looked at my swollen belly.

"Toast."

Resigned, she nodded. Before she left the room, she pulled me into her arms. I felt like a moldy old tower with most of its bricks missing. I was teetering, ready to fall. Alice left me, and I could hear muffled conversation downstairs.

I stared at my reflection. My eyes didn't look haunted—they looked empty. I lifted my chin, but my lip quivered. I bit it hard, giving myself pain to distract me from my emotions. I gripped the edge of the dresser, my knuckles white.

"You will not fall apart, you will not fall apart," I whispered.

I took the stairs slowly, my heels clacking on wood. The swell of conversation dimmed. I found Celia's eyes first. Armand stood next to her.

Jules was tucked away in the crook of Luc's arm, her face pale and her eyes watery. It hurt my heart—seeing them together. Knowing they were happy. Knowing they'd found each other.

Knowing what I'd lost.

Keith stood tall and somber. He'd removed his cowboy hat, showing neatly combed hair liberally streaked with gray. His black cowboy boots were shined with polish, and I focused on them. Alice came out of the kitchen with a plate. She handed it to me. I picked up a piece of toast and stuck it into my mouth, forcing myself to chew. My stomach rebelled, and I thrust the plate at her before I ran for the front door. I barely made it outside before I threw up in the green bushes.

I coughed and choked, and I spent a moment bent over at the waist. I heard footsteps on the porch and rose. Celia held out a glass of water. I walked to her and took it. I swished it around my mouth and spit it out.

"You ready?"

"Loaded question, isn't it?" My voice was a croak. I set the glass down on the porch. She came to my side, then took my hand and squeezed it.

I closed my eyes as we drove towards the cemetery, towards the moment when I would have to bury Kai.

•••

Wyatt stood by his brother's grave, his eyes downcast. I could see the tears on his cheeks. Lucy stood next to him. Her red hair was a bright flag of color in a sea of black.

I went to Claire. I took her hand, and she clasped onto mine. We had become family by marriage; now we were a family in sorrow.

Where is George?

White, elegant roses covered the casket that housed my husband. I felt my legs about to give way. I didn't want to take Claire down with me. I tried to drop her hand, but she held on.

"Breathe," she whispered in my ear. "Just breathe."

I sucked in air and choked on a sob as they lowered Kai into the ground. It started to rain and someone opened an umbrella to shield me.

I lived my life under an umbrella of death.

Mud stained the living grass, and still they shoveled the wet earth onto him. They were smothering him. Kai was drowning in dirt and rainwater—drowning in spring.

I wished to place my body on top of his, feel his lips on mine.

I didn't want him to be alone.

I pushed the umbrella out of the way and turned my face to the storm. The sky cried with me.

I was not broken—I was annihilated.

I wanted to collapse and never get up again.

But I had to.

For the baby.

Kai's baby.

•••

I lay on Kai's childhood bed, dozing as the sun set. I felt a body sink down next to me and for one moment I believed it was Kai. But there was no smell of mountains, no scent of sunshine.

Kai was gone.

"Are you awake?" Wyatt asked.

I rolled over and looked into Wyatt's golden brown eyes. The Ferris brothers did not physically resemble one another. I was eternally grateful for that fact.

"Did I dream it?"

Wyatt paused before shaking his head *no*.

"It's not fair," I whispered.

"I know."

I turned my head away. "George didn't go to the funeral, did he?"

"No. He couldn't face it. I think—I think this might kill him, Sage." We lapsed into silence before he said, "Are you still planning to return to France?"

"Yes." I sat up and rubbed a hand across my face.

"I wish you'd stay," he murmured before rising.

I took a deep, shaky breath. "To stay would kill *me*."

•••

I awoke before the rest of the house. Grabbing my belongings, I went out onto the front porch to call a cab. It arrived fifteen minutes later, and I climbed into it, sliding across the ripped black leather seat. I gave the driver the address to Memaw's cabin and then directed him when he almost lost his way.

The house was quiet.

I journeyed upstairs and paused outside the bedroom I had shared with the love of my life. I made myself cross the threshold and swallowed the lump of emotion in my throat.

I changed out of my funeral dress and threw on a pair of jeans and one of Kai's t-shirts.

It smelled like him.

I went to my side of the bed, lifted up the mattress, and pulled out a stack of papers. If it hadn't been for Kai, I never would've found the strength to write. He'd become my foundation, my support beams, my lean-to out of the rain. He'd been the reason I claimed my gift.

He'd been my inspiration.

I set the manuscript down on the bed, and slipped on my shoes. I walked the familiar path to the foundation of our unfinished home.

I wanted to burn it to the ground, but it was cement.

Something caught my attention out of the corner of my eye. Crouching down, I plucked a dandelion from its resting place. I made a wish, took a deep breath and blew. The seeds swirled around me before being carried away by the spring breeze.

Who knew where they'd fall or if they'd take root?

The wind changed, and a seed I thought long gone floated back and caressed my cheek.

I closed my eyes.

I felt Kai at my back, solid and sturdy as his arms came around me, settling low on my round belly, sheltering us.

The baby kicked.

Kai's lips grazed my hair, and I smelled the sunshine on his skin. My hands covered his, and I sighed, lost in a moment of contentment.

There's powerful magic in a dandelion wish.

To dream is beautiful.

To love is a blessing.

To hope is human.